Friends

for

Life

Liz Murphy

Independently Published 2024

ISBN-9798875598012

For my two gorgeous daughters Rachel and Eleanor
and my darling Steve.
Love you all always

About the author

Originally from Scotland, Liz Murphy moved to London in the mid 1980s as a features writer on Woman's Own. She went on to work on some of the biggest weekly and monthly magazines in the country including Good Housekeeping, House Beautiful, TVTimes and Sky magazine, where she held senior editorial positions. Liz is also a qualified mat and reformer Pilates teacher.

The sudden death of her husband, Steve, prompted her to reassess her priorities, following which she left magazines and now focuses her time on teaching Pilates, playing tennis, singing in a choir, being a school governor and writing for pleasure. She has two grown-up daughters.

Friends for Life is her first novel.

Acknowledgements

This is by far the biggest writing project I've ever undertaken and I owe a great deal of thanks to many people for their help and encouragement along the way.

To my youngest daughter Eleanor for your suggestions on several plot points, being my first and most honest reader, and for listening patiently to my daily commentary on the progress of the book. Your contribution was incredibly valuable – but for clarity, I did see all those eyerolls!

To my eldest daughter Rachel for being an insightful editor, and for always giving me a different perspective not just on the book, but on life itself.

I'm so grateful to the support I've received from both of you these past difficult years as we all three find our place in this differently shaped family.

I also owe a huge thanks to my niece, the uber talented and extremely generous Shari Low. Your honesty, encouragement and belief kept me going through dozens of rewrites and have meant so much to me.

Finally, to my friends who supported me when times were tough and who continue to help me shape my own new future. I am lucky to have you all. Special thanks to Lindsay Nicholson, who's been a great friend, a mentor and an inspiration, and to my bereavement buddy Jean - we've known each other only a short time, but you have helped me beyond measure.

Table of Contents

PROLOGUE

Three deaths...three grieving women

Kate

September 2022

His hand was frozen. Jason's hands were never cold. Quite the opposite, they were always toasty warm. 'My furnace,' she used to call him in bed, when he'd happily heat up her chilly feet with his. 'Do you have blood circulation?' he'd ask, laughing. 'Or does blood just pool in your feet and freeze?' Now it was his hands that were cold.

It's not helping, she thought, that you're lying on this concrete patio. He lay where he'd fallen, less than two hours ago. He'd been carrying out cutlery for them to have dinner at the outside table when he suddenly dropped the knives and forks and fell to the ground, like a tree chopped off at the base.

She'd done CPR, the paramedics had been there pretty quickly for London, but nothing helped.

'Sometimes the heart attack is just so catastrophic that there's absolutely nothing we can do, even if we're on the spot,' explained the kind paramedic. 'It's just incredibly bad luck.'

He'd lain a blanket over Jason while a bewildered Kate knelt beside him, holding one of his hands. As the minutes went by his hands grew colder and Kate tucked them under the blanket to get warm. A natural reaction. But Jason's hands would never be warm again. As the realisation grew, her tears fell.

Rose

September 2022

The loud bang at the door came after bedtime. Rose had been asleep, but now she was bold upright. She looked for Richard beside her. He wasn't there.

There was more knocking. She leapt out of bed, ran downstairs in her pyjamas. Heard her mother's voice, confused, calling, 'Who is it Rose? What do they want?'

She opened the door. Two police officers were standing on her doorstep. Then in her hallway. They told her about the terrible car accident, explained they feared her husband had been involved, killed. Then the scream, piercing as she crumpled to the hallway floor.

They loaded her into their car and drove her to the mortuary. 'Are you sure you want to do this now?' asked the police officer in the waiting room. 'You could wait for a relative or a friend to be here with you.'

'No,' she insisted, quietly. 'I need to know now.'

They opened a curtain in the wall and through the window she could see into a room where a person lay, three quarters covered by a sheet, just a head emerging from the snowy whiteness. The face bore a small cut on the forehead, but apart from that it was perfect. Handsome, as always. The face she'd fallen madly in love with all those years before. The face she'd never stopped loving. The officers had been right.

That was the last time she saw her Richard.

Pascalle

May 2018

The hospital room was quiet now. Half an hour ago it had been full, or so Pascalle felt. Their two daughters, a son in law, Trevor's sister and brother, and herself. All scattered around the bed waiting for that moment, the final breath, the end. It had come soon enough.

In front of their eyes, Trevor slipped quietly from life to death. No drama. No final gasp. No sitting up and grabbing of hands. Just a breath and then none. Alive and then dead.

The doctor confirmed what they already knew. The nurses smartened his bed, and then the family all kissed Trevor one final time and left. Only Pascalle remained, cherishing these last moments alone with the love of her life. The quiet man who'd captured her wild French heart and kept it beating fast all these years.

Pascalle took his hand in hers one last time, squeezed it gently and whispered, 'Au revoir mon amour. Je t'adore toujours.'

She pushed herself upright, dipped to kiss his lips, smiled down at his lovely familiar face, turned and walked out of the room. 'À bientôt.'

ONE

November

Kate Latimer was standing in the curtain department of John Lewis staring at a fabric sample hanging at the end of a long row. The fabric was in a vibrant blue, teal and grey Ikat pattern.

'This could be the one,' she declared to her daughter Lila who'd passed up on Saturday morning brunch with her flatmates to come on the shopping trip with her.

'Didn't you say that about the cream pair dotted with sweet purple flowers, the William Morris Strawberry Thief design and those silver-grey ones that looked like they had clouds floating all over them?' asked Lila.

'Yes I did, but when I got them home they just didn't look right,' Kate responded. 'I think these will be different.'

'Mum, what exactly are you looking for?' asked Lila, exasperation in her voice. 'Do you even know?'

Kate couldn't really blame her daughter for becoming frustrated with her. She could see that Lila was doing her best to support her, but it was obvious that her patience was wearing thin over the whole bedroom curtain dilemma. And she had asked a good question. What *was* Kate looking for? She was 58 years old, had successfully raised two children into responsible adulthood, held down a full-time job as a magazine journalist and still managed to be a reasonably sane and rational person. So why was it that ever since her husband died, she couldn't do a simple thing like choose a pair of curtains for her bedroom? If she knew the answer to that she wouldn't be on her fourth visit to the store. Her bedroom windows wouldn't be standing bare at this moment in time.

Suddenly Kate felt a rush of frustration of her own and snapped: 'I want your dad back Lila, that's what I really want.'

As soon as the words were out Kate wanted to snatch them back. One look at Lila's stricken face told her that she'd gone too far.

'Oh, my darling, I'm so sorry,' she said, gently pulling her daughter into her arms. 'I shouldn't have said that. I know you're only trying to help. The trouble is, I don't know what I want. Your dad's tastes were totally different to mine, but now he's not here to say "No" to everything I pick, I can't seem to make a decision.' Kate sagged. 'Let's go and have a cup of tea. And to show you how sorry I am, I'll treat you to a huge slice of cake.'

Lila smiled. 'If it's a big enough slice, then I just might forgive you.'

As both women wandered over to the cafe, Kate thought about how amazing her children had been once they'd got over the initial shock of Jason's death. She'd never forget the devastation in their voices when she'd phoned each of them in turn to tell them the terrible news that their dad had literally dropped dead on the garden patio.

'Oh my God Mum, what are we going to do without Dad?' her son Luke had asked, bewilderment in his voice. 'How can we be a family without him?'

Lila had been completely disbelieving. 'What? You can't mean it. Dad? *My* dad?' And she'd sobbed quietly down the phone. Then she'd suddenly stopped. 'Oh Mum, you're all alone there, aren't you? I'm coming round.'

She'd arrived within minutes - the flat she shared with friends was less than a mile away - and had rushed into her mother's arms saying 'I'm here, I'm staying. What do you want me to do first?'

Luke had arrived shortly after. He lived on the other side of London with his wife Cyn and got there so quickly Kate knew he must have driven like a maniac. He'd fallen into Kate's arms sobbing uncontrollably, all the while saying, 'I can't believe it Mum. Dad can't be dead. What are we going to do without him?'

'I know, son,' said Kate. 'I know. But we three are still here and we can help each other to get through this.'

That night Lila had been amazing. She'd drawn up a rota so that at least one of them would be with Kate during the days and nights leading up to the funeral. Every time Kate had a wobble, a moment of wondering how on earth she'd survive this, one of them was with her. They'd gone with her to the register office to register their dad's death and helped her make all the funeral arrangements.

'You don't have to do any of this,' she'd told them. 'Don't get me wrong, it means a lot to me that you are, but you also need time to grieve for your dad, in your own way.'

'We want to help, Mum,' Lila had been firm. 'If we do it together, it'll be easier for you.'

Luke had nodded in agreement with his younger sister, but Kate could see in his eyes that he was finding it hard. At 28 and 24, Luke and Lila may be adults but they would always be her children. One day she'd noticed that Luke was particularly down and suggested he go home.

'If you want to spend some time with Cyn, away from all of this, then go. I'll be fine on my own. That's how things are going to be from now on, so the sooner I get used to it the better.'

Luke looked at her, tears brimming in his eyes. 'Mum, it's not that I don't want to support you, it's that I just can't believe he's gone. We were at a football match two days before he died and we'd had a great time. He was his usual self, shouting abuse at the referee, buying pints for all my mates in the pub, laughing and joking. How can it be that someone so full of life isn't with us any longer?'

'I keep asking myself the same question,' she'd replied, shaking her head.

'Don't worry Mum, I'll stay. I don't want you to be on your own, and anyway being here where I can see all his things, makes me feel close to Dad. As if he might walk through the door any minute, and we can get back to being us again. The Latimers. A family.'

A lump formed in Kate's throat. She desperately wanted to make her son's pain stop, but she also knew that their family life hadn't been quite the rosy picture he remembered. Jason hadn't been the man Luke thought he was, and maybe someday he'd find out the truth. But it wasn't going to be today, so she put her arms around her son's shoulders, held him tight and let him cry.

The following week, at the funeral, one of the worst days of Kate's life, she'd been grateful to have both her children beside her. All three had paused together at the door of the crematorium, ahead of the 100 mourners ready to walk in behind them, with Lila holding one of Kate's hands and Luke clasping the other, feeling sad beyond words at what lay ahead of them. But Kate was also proud of her two grown up children.

'Are we ready?' she'd asked them both. When they nodded, she'd squeezed their hands and said, 'Let's go, and be strong for each other.' Then they'd walked tall down the aisle towards the coffin that held her husband and their dad.

Now here was Lila helping her again, tucking into an enormous slice of carrot cake and listening to Kate prattle on about how she and Jason had disagreed on most things to do with the house, so everything they had was a result of compromise, and Kate had hated most of it for years.

'Do you remember when we bought the sofa for the living room?'

'I remember you two having an almighty row over it,' Lila replied.

'Exactly. That sofa took us to the brink of divorce and all because I wanted a corner unit big enough so that we could all snuggle up on it together and your dad thought it was a ridiculous idea. He made his very firm views known in the shop and totally embarrassed me. We left empty-handed and I was so furious with him when we got home that it was one of the few times I couldn't contain my anger.'

'Yes there *was* a lot of shouting,' Lila recalled, rolling her eyes. 'I never did understand what all the arguing was about. But you did get the sofa in the end.'

'Well, we went back a couple of weeks later and got *a* sofa, but it wasn't the one I wanted. Dad vetoed all my choices, so I had to settle for one that was the shape I wanted in colours and fabric that he liked, but I think it's ugly and to this day I can't look at it without remembering that horrible row. So, while all this angst over a pair of curtains might seem silly, it's important to me because they'll be something I'll have chosen because I love them.

'It's tough enough not having your dad there without having to look at that droopy old pair of yellow curtains every time I open my eyes. Heartless as this may sound, for the first time in my life I can have anything I want, and I have the money to buy it, but somehow that's made the decisions harder. All I know is that I want to be surrounded by things I love, that lift my heart and don't remind me of unhappy times, and I'll know what I want when I see it.'

'Look I get it about the curtains, Mum,' Lila nodded. 'I get that you want change, to move on, I really do. And I agree that the old ones are pretty ugly, I just wish you'd decide.'

'Me too,' said Kate. 'I am leaning towards the Ikat.'

'Are you sure Mum? Really sure? Even though the Ikat is mainly blue which was Dad's favourite colour so most of the walls are in shades of pale blue?'

Kate laughed out loud. 'Good point,' she managed between peals of laughter. 'Thank you for raising that. You really are a cheeky madam sometimes, Lila, but I appreciate your honesty, and I am prepared to put up with the blue because the Ikat also contains a rather racy teal.'

'Right,' said Lila decisively, gathering up her coat and bag. 'Let's go and buy them and at least get them home before you change your mind.'

Kate, still laughing, threaded her arm through her daughter's as they headed over once again to the curtain department. She felt good about her decision. If only she felt as good about everything else in her life.

TWO

November

'Welcome everyone. Thank you for coming again. I hope you're finding the experience useful.'

Rose Bud wondered if anyone had ever said, out loud, in front of everyone, 'No, it's shit. A terrible way to spend four Sunday afternoons of my life. I wish I'd never started this.'

She looked around the church hall at her fellow bereaved persons who were sitting in a circle smiling at the woman who was leading this bereavement group and who'd asked the question. She in turn was smiling back at them. They all nodded, someone murmured, 'Yes, last week was very useful.'

This was the second week of Rose's fourth bereavement group. Does that make me a groupie? she'd wondered. It certainly made her feel unsuccessful. She'd gone to each one full of hope that she might be able to express how devastated she felt, and voice the suspicions that kept swirling around inside her head, keeping her awake every night since her husband Richard had been killed in a car crash. She might even be able to ask out loud the questions about why he'd been on a road miles from where he was supposed to be, and why did her elderly mother's finances – finances that Richard was supposed to be looking after – not seem to add up. All of this churned away inside of her, day after day, yet when a space was left for her to speak, she couldn't seem to put her fears into words.

She'd even tried a private bereavement counsellor, thinking that perhaps without an audience she'd feel more able to open up. The counsellor had been nice, very professional, left plenty of space for her to speak, but even there, no words emerged. Instead, there were a lot of silences. Expensive silences.

Every day her feelings of desperation grew, so here she was trying again with another group. Maybe this will be the one, she thought hopefully as she took her seat in the obligatory circle. Welcome over, she looked round the circle and realised that some of the people were crying.

'Oh God,' Rose thought, 'why do people have to do that in public?'

Crying in public wasn't in Rose's vocabulary. In fact, even in private crying was to be avoided. When she'd fallen over as a child and grazed her knee, she would bite back the tears. Then when her father Vernon had died four years before she'd only allowed herself one massive session of sobbing before deciding she needed to be strong for her mum, Violet, who had dementia and was struggling to take in the death of her husband.

Somehow Richard had seen through her stoicism and must have realised how desperately Rose needed help because he'd surprised her by suggesting that his mother-in-law rent out her little three-bedroom terrace and come to live with them. Rose was an only child with few close relatives, and she and Richard hadn't been lucky enough to have children, so she'd been really pleased that he was stepping in like this. How many sons in law would be happy with that arrangement, never mind suggest it?

However, she was a little surprised when he'd offered to deal with all the paperwork involved in renting the house and take on the management of Violet's financial affairs. Like her, he was a trained and practising accountant, but it wasn't like him to volunteer to take on work.

'It'll take a load off you, Rose,' he'd persuaded. 'Then you only have your mum to think about.'

'And my business,' Rose had countered. 'When you run a one-woman accountancy firm you have to put in the hours otherwise clients' accounts don't get done and I don't get paid.'

Richard had shrunk back as though stung by her comment. 'Is that a dig at me?' he'd asked. 'Are you still cross with me for leaving your business and getting a job with a firm in the city? If you are, I did it for both of us. With the money I earn now you don't have to work.'

'That wasn't a dig and I'm not looking to get into that argument again,' said Rose. 'It was just that you blindsided me when you went off and got the job without even consulting me and yes I was hurt at the time. I'd thought we were partners in everything, life and business. It's taken me 30 years to build up my own practice and I can't just walk away from it, even if it is to spend time with my mother.'

'Maybe you could slim it down then,' Richard suggested. 'Why don't you keep your oldest and most dear clients and then you can still have your business, some financial independence, but also time for your mum. She's getting more forgetful and confused - she almost set the house on fire last week when she forgot she'd put the grill on. I think she really needs you around right now.'

Then he'd smiled the megawatt smile that even after three decades of marriage still made her knees melt and Rose knew that she was beaten. She also had to concede that he was talking sense, which made her chuckle because Richard was more known for his charm than his good judgement.

'You won't regret it,' Richard whispered as he took her into his arms and held her tight.

'Won't I?' she'd thought.

Well, that was all water under the bridge now, because Richard was dead and Rose was alone, dealing with everything. Crying definitely couldn't be on the agenda.

Rose felt herself being drawn back into the room and realised that the group leader was looking straight at her, asking her a question. 'Rose, what have you found to be the worst thing you're now having to deal with?' Rose fought the desire to spit out, 'That's a really stupid question! The very worst thing is that my husband's very dead.'

Instead, she took a deep breath, gathered some thoughts and opened her mouth to speak. Nothing came out.

'Take your time, Rose,' encouraged the leader. 'There's no hurry.'

She tried again. Nothing. Rose knew she looked like a goldfish out of water. Panic rose inside of her, she felt her face flush and her ears start to ring. Please let some words come out.

She tried a third time. When it came, her voice was croaky and quiet, but it was steady.

'No longer hearing his voice,' she said. 'That's one thing. There's more.'

The leader smiled at her gently. 'Go on Rose. Please, go on.'

'Not having him put his arms around me or take my hand in his,' Rose continued. 'Not having him to talk to, cook with, go on holiday with, sit in the garden with, read a book beside.'

She stopped, felt the tears swim into her eyes and tried desperately not to let them fall. 'He was half of me,' she managed. 'My other half. My soulmate. How can I possibly live without him?'

*

When Rose got home after the group she was completely wrung out. It was still early evening, but she needed a lie down. She walked into the kitchen to get herself a glass of water, turned on the light and jumped when she saw her mother sitting at the table.

'Goodness Mum, what a fright you gave me. Why are you sitting there in the dark?'

Violet was staring straight at Rose, silent and with a suspicious look on her face.

'Mum, are you okay? Was I longer than I said I'd be? Sorry if you felt lonely.'

Without breaking eye contact, Violet said: 'I don't know who you are, but you'd better get out of my house before my husband comes home. If he catches you here, he'll call the police.'

Rose's heart sank. 'Mum, it's me, Rose. Your daughter. Remember?'

'Rose isn't here just now, she's at her house, with her husband Richard. He's such a lovely man, lovely manners, always teasing me.' She stopped short, her expression hardening. 'They'll both get the police onto you if you don't leave at once.'

Rose closed her eyes and let out a long sigh. Several times in the last month her mum hadn't recognised her, and the episodes were getting more frequent. If she kept on reminding Violet who she was eventually she might get through, but after the afternoon she'd had, she didn't have the emotional energy to try.

'Mum, if it's okay with you, I'll go to my room to lie down for a little while,' she said wearily.

'Is it bedtime already?' Violet asked, her expression and voice lightening.

'No Mum, not bedtime yet. I just feel a little tired and I'd like to rest for a couple of hours. Why don't you take one of the papers and sit in your chair by the kitchen window and have a read of it. I'll put on the radio so you'll have a bit of company. I won't be long. I'll be back down before you know it.'

Rose indicated a chair by the window and Violet nodded in recognition. 'Yes, I like sitting there.'

She helped her mother settle knowing she'd be happy there for a while, and as she left the kitchen she smiled at her mother's contented face as she scanned the newspaper. She looks as though she doesn't have a care in the world, thought Rose. Lucky woman.

Rose dragged herself upstairs and just as she was walking into her bedroom, her eye was caught by a framed photograph sitting on the landing table. In it a young Rose and Richard were standing on soft white sands, arms wrapped around each other, broad smiles on their tanned faces. It had been taken on their honeymoon. Rose picked up the photograph and looked into the two hopeful faces.

The start of our life together. God, we were so happy then. Or at least I was. Were you Richard? Were you ever really as happy with me as I was with you? The words I'm not so sure, flashed unbidden into Rose's mind. 'No,' she said out loud. 'No, I can't think like that. Richard loved me. I *know* he did.' But a whisper of 'I'm not so sure' hung in the air.

THREE

November

As she sat at the table in her kitchen across from her eldest daughter, Pascalle Granderson felt herself getting angry. 'Why can't you and your sister just leave me alone!' she wanted to scream. But she didn't, because deep inside, she knew they had a point.

Although he'd been dead for four years, she wasn't ready to come to terms with the fact that her beloved Trevor wasn't coming back. And truth be told, she wasn't sure she'd ever be. In a way, she was happy in her misery. She'd loved him so much, missed him even more, what was life without him? The only bright spark on her horizon was her little two-year-old grandson Stefan, who she looked after two afternoons a week. Now *he* was beginning to make a mark on her heart. Perhaps there was hope for her yet.

Today, Justine had come round to her mother's house with the express intention of trying to persuade her to join a yoga class at the local library.

'It'll do you good, Mum,' Justine said. 'Get you out of the house.' Pascalle took a deep breath, tried to calm her temper, took a sip of her coffee and smiled over to Justine. 'I do go out of the house you know,' she said, sarcasm in her voice. 'Every day, in fact. I truly am fine. Just as I am.'

'Are you Mum?' asked Justine, with more than a hint of frustration in her voice. 'I don't see how you can be. For the last four years you've been virtually shut up in this house, which frankly is beginning to resemble a mausoleum with all Dad's stuff lying just where he left it. You need to get out Mum. You're only 66 – you have plenty of time left. You have to move on with your life. Get back in touch with your old friends or find some new ones. You can't grieve Dad forever.'

Pascalle had been listening to this lecture from her daughters Justine and Evie ever since Trevor's funeral. Sometimes they'd tackle her separately when Justine came over for coffee or Evie called from her home in northern France. At other times, Evie would get on the Eurostar and arrive on Pascalle's doorstep with Justine as though they were hoping that by ganging up on their mother in person, they'd have more success in getting their message across. Either way Pascalle was fed up hearing it.

At first, she'd put up arguments about how their dad was barely cold in his grave, that they needed to give her time and space to come to terms with his passing, to accept that he'd gone. When that didn't work, she'd decided to take the path of least resistance and nod and agree and hope they'd forget about it for a while.

'Yes darling, you're right,' she said. 'I can't.'

'So will you go to the class?' Justine persisted.

Pascalle nodded her head. 'Maybe.'

Justine threw up her hands in despair. 'You're infuriating, Mum, do you know that? We've been down this road enough times for me to know that your translation of *maybe* is *never*. But I'm not going to stand for it anymore, Mum. I'm not leaving this kitchen table until I get a firm yes. The exercise will do your body good, and seeing new people will lift your mood. Remember how much you used to enjoy yoga and pilates before Dad got ill.'

'That feels like a lifetime ago,' Pascalle replied, sadly. 'I was a different person then.'

She looked down at her shabby jogging bottoms and noticed a coffee stain on one of the legs. Must be there from yesterday. The old Pascalle would never have worn dirty old boring clothes like these. She was colourful, vibrant, lively. Some days the post-Trevor Pascalle felt so bereft of energy she could barely lift her head off the pillow in the morning. Her husband wasn't all that she had lost. She had also lost herself.

'Actually Mum, it was only four years ago, and that's not enough time to destroy the cheeky, hippy Pascalle that we all know…and that Dad loved.'

Pascalle looked up sharply and shot Justine a warning stare.

'We are allowed to mention him, Mum, talk about him,' Justine was firm. 'Talking about him will neither bring him back nor make him any more dead.'

Pascalle's eyes flooded with tears which made Justine soften her tone.

'We miss him, too, Mum. We all miss him enormously. He was our dad. Evie might live in France but she feels the loss of him as much as we do, and it's horrible not having him here. I hate that he never got to meet his grandson, that Stefan will grow up never knowing what a fabulous granddad he would have had. But we miss you as well, Mum. We miss you bustling around the kitchen, baking croissants, stirring your wonderful meat stew, laughing that crazy laugh of yours. We need you back, Mum.'

26

Pascalle wiped the tears from her cheeks and conceded to herself that she missed being that person, too. It had been such a long time since she'd really laughed, felt any kind of joy. Over the last four years - five if you include the year she gave up everything, her friends, her hobbies, her whole life, to nurse Trevor after he was diagnosed with lung cancer – she knew she'd become a very drab, sad, anxious version of herself. But she couldn't seem to get past this grief for Trevor.

'I know yoga isn't a solution, Mum, it's not going to make everything okay, but it's a step,' persuaded Justine. 'Please say you'll go, at least for a few weeks and see. You don't have to speak to anyone. Just go, do the exercises and see if you enjoy it. I'll book it for you.'

Pascalle nodded and took her eldest daughter's hand in hers. While she pondered what answer to give, she studied Justine. Tall, willowy and blonde, she'd definitely taken after Trevor, while petite Evie with her long flowing black hair and dark eyes was the image of Pascalle. They were chalk and cheese when it came to personality, too. Justine was measured and steady, Evie spontaneous and volatile. But they had one thing in common – they were doing their very best to help Pascalle find a path back to them.

'Yes, I'll go, ma petite,' she said nodding. 'Thank you. I'll go, but not yet. After Christmas. I'll start in the new year.'

Justine let out a long sigh. 'It's always later, never now. But this time I'm determined. I won't forget. I'll book you in for the first available free space in January and I'll pick you up and carry you that class if I have to.'

*

The following morning, Pascalle awoke with a start and looked around her. She was in bed and after a second realised she'd been in the longest and deepest sleep she'd had in months. Usually, her nights were spent tossing and turning, reading a little, watching some TV, listening to podcasts or music - anything to get her through the long dark hours. But last night had been different.

She'd been dreaming that she'd been talking to Trevor. She couldn't remember what they'd been chatting about, but she could clearly recall how the conversation ended. She remembered him smiling at her and gently saying, 'My sweetheart, it's time. Let go of me. It's time to move into the future.'

She lay there feeling slightly shocked. His words, hearing his voice again, it had all seemed so real. The last time she'd heard him speak had been in the hospital, just before he'd slipped into a coma. He'd looked so pale and frail lying in the enormous hospital bed. Her Trevor had been a big man, gentle in nature, but well-built like the rugby player he'd been in his youth. In the final months of his illness he'd been reduced to almost a bag of bones by the disease, caught too late and unresponsive to treatment. It had overwhelmed him.

Hours before he died, he'd motioned for her to come closer and when she'd laid down beside him and put her cheek close to his, when she'd taken his fragile hands in hers, he'd whispered, 'I love you, Pascalle. My Pascalle. Never forget it.'

She'd gently squeezed his hands as tears rolled down her face and onto the pillow they were sharing, and he'd drifted off to sleep, exhausted by the effort of such a simple act. She'd carried those words so close to her heart. In her darkest moments, and there had been many of those, she'd recalled them, cherished them, raged about them.

'If you loved me so much, why did you leave me?' she'd screamed, tears of frustration and anger coursing down her face. Deep in her heart she knew the last thing he'd wanted to do was leave her, but sometimes she just felt so angry that she couldn't contain the rage and she'd yell: 'Why

Trevor? Why did it have to be my lovely, gentle, big-hearted Trevor? Why not some murderer or rapist or child abuser instead? Why my Trevor, who'd only ever loved? And who'd loved me…'

Now here he was in a dream, one that seemed so real she was looking round the bedroom for him, with his voice, so familiar, telling her that it was time to move on, to let him go, and get on with her life.

Pascalle got up from the bed and walked over to the chest of drawers where all his clothes still were, clean and neatly folded away. All his sweatshirts and jumpers in the bottom drawer, t-shirts and polo tops in the one above, and socks and underwear split between the two small drawers on top. Shirts, trousers, jackets and suits in his side of the wardrobe. Heavy coats and jackets were on the rack in the downstairs hallway. All still there, just as he left them.

She opened a drawer in the chest and pulled out a jumper. It was a cream cable knit, chunky, cuddly, exactly as he'd once been. She got back into bed, lay down, pulled the jumper close to herself and hugged it for all she was worth. She could smell him on the jumper.

Pascalle turned onto her side and looked over towards the pillow that had been Trevor's. She'd never get used to seeing that empty space. Even after four years it still broke her heart.

Beyond the pillow she could see Trevor's bedside cabinet with his watch, wedding ring and wallet still sitting on the top, a few coins scattered around from the last time he'd emptied his trouser pockets before bed. They'd been there a long time, but the coins and wedding ring gleamed and the leather of the wallet shone, because Pascalle cleaned them religiously every week while doing the housework.

She lay back down, hugged the jumper to herself and played his words back in her head: 'Let go of me, move on.' I know I should, my love, but I don't know if I can. How many times can a person be expected to rebuild their life? I've done it so many times before, I don't know if I have the strength to do it again.

FOUR

December

'How could I have been so stupid? Stupid, stupid, stupid.'
Kate shook her head, took a deep breath, opened her
wardrobe door and continued to curse, under her breath, a
vow she'd made after Jason died to accept all invitations
from friends, even if going was the last thing she felt like
doing. In the last three months she'd been a reluctant guest
at morning coffee, drinks at the local wine bar and dinner
parties.

The dinner parties were the worst because she was usually
the only single person there and had to sit through three
courses of nauseating couples' conversation before she
could politely make her escape. But, since the alternative
was a permanent spot on the sofa, lying under a blanket
sobbing her eyes out surrounded by 30 years of reminders
of her dead husband, she always smiled and said 'Lovely'
when the next invitation came around.

Tonight she was dragging herself to a pre-Christmas drinks party at a friend's house. Kate's heart had sank when the text from her hostess had arrived.

It would be so lovely if you could come. I understand it might be difficult, but you'll be surrounded by friends. Please come

Kate had said a bad word under her breath, then started typing.

Thank you. Of course I'll come. That would be lovely

Now she was rummaging through her wardrobe trying to find something to wear, all the while cursing her stupidity. Why didn't I just say no? They'd have understood. And if they hadn't, well too bad. Stupid, stupid, stupid!
She stifled a growl and pulled out a slinky black dress. Maybe she was being too pessimistic, maybe it would be okay. Who was she fooling? It was going to be awful. Being with lots of people, trying to think of things to talk about. Making conversation was hard enough, but before that was the ordeal of doing her hair, picking the right clothes, putting on make-up, finding shoes that looked good

but wouldn't kill her feet. Everything felt like such an effort. Plus there had been that thing with Luke earlier that afternoon.

She'd been so looking forward to his visit. because she wanted to show off her new living room. The Ikat curtains she'd bought for her bedroom in November had stayed, and Kate had been so inspired by finally being able to make a decision about how she wanted her home to look, she'd tackled the living room – and the offending black sofa. It had been dumped, together with Jason's ugly old brown desk that had sat at the back of the room alongside a filing cabinet and several enormous and untidy piles of books he'd gathered over the years.

She'd had the walls painted a soft blush colour, and bought an elegant grey sofa, cuddler chair, beautiful grey and cream rug, and classy silver curtains. Where the desk and wobbly office chair had been, now sat a very pretty pink velvet chaise longue. Kate was thrilled with it all and she hoped Luke would be too. She was disappointed.

'Mum, I can't believe it!'

'What can't you believe?' Kate asked, taken aback not by the words he used, but by his hostile tone.

'I can't believe what you've done to this room.' Luke had stood in the middle of her lovely room, turning his head in disbelief as he took in the furniture, the curtains, the new wall colour, a look of confusion spreading across his face.

'Don't you like it?' Kate asked feebly.

'Like it?' Luke shrugged, arms up, head turning right and left, scanning the room as though searching for something positive to say. 'Mum how *can* I like it?'

He turned towards Kate and she was stricken to see a steeliness behind his eyes that she hadn't ever noticed before. 'Dad's been dead three months Mum and you've chucked out all his stuff. It's like you're pushing him out of the house, and all our memories with him.'

Kate put her head in her hands and stood there totally confused, lost for words. Her daughter Lila had been so supportive of the changes she'd made that she hadn't thought for a moment that Luke would be any different. Plus, he'd never before spoken to her in this way. She didn't know how to react.

'Couldn't you have waited, Mum?'

Kate lifted her head from her hands and looked up at her son. At 6 foot 2 he was a few inches taller than her and although he'd always been the image of his dad in looks, he had a much gentler, more generous nature. Now there was something about his attitude that reminded her of a part of Jason she'd never liked and hadn't missed in the months since his death. Something that she never wanted to see again. The shock of recognising it in her son helped her find her voice, and when she spoke there was no disguising her determination.

'Waited for what Luke? For him to walk back through the door? If that's what you're thinking, that's definitely not going to happen. So what exactly should I have waited for?'

Luke's face crumpled and Kate softened her tone. 'I know you loved your dad. I loved him too. So much. But your dad was no angel Luke, and everything in this room – in fact most things in this house – reminded me of that. If I'm ever going to be able to move on, they needed to go.'

Kate saw confusion sweep across his brow. 'What are you talking about? Why are you saying he was no angel…?' he started, but Kate stopped him. 'I'm not getting into that now Luke,' she said, firmly. 'Just please take my word that what I've done is what I needed to do.'

Luke folded his arms across his chest and turned away. 'Come on Cyn,' he said. 'Let's go before this gets any worse.'

Luke's wife Cyn, pretty and petite, who'd been sitting quietly on the new sofa, now slowly stood up, flicking her blonde ponytail off her shoulder. As she moved forward to kiss her mother-in-law goodbye, Kate could have sworn she saw a smug smile playing on her lips.

'Don't worry Kate,' she'd whispered as she got close to Kate's cheek. 'I'm sure he'll come round. And if it's any consolation, I rather like what you've done to the room.'

As their faces pulled apart, the smile had lingered on Cyn's lips. What was that about?

For a long time after they'd gone, Kate had stood leaning against the front door, replaying what had just happened, the words spoken, over and over in her mind. Completely drained, she was almost grateful for the feel of the wood beneath her, holding her up. She felt a buzz in one of her jeans pockets. A text from tonight's hostess.

Just checking you're still okay for the party. So looking forward to seeing you

Kate sighed.

Yes, can't wait. See you soon

So now, here she was in her bedroom trying to summon some energy to get herself ready. She looked at the dress she was holding, shook her head and hung it back up. After rummaging around some more, she found a pair of black straight-legged trousers and a red chiffon top with a peplum round the bottom and crystals trimming the V-neck. Her black suede ankle boots had enough of a heel to look dressy but were low enough to make the 10-minute walk to the party comfortable, so they were dug out from the back of the wardrobe.

An hour later, Kate was showered, dressed, mascara and lipstick grudgingly applied. She pulled a brush through her shoulder length blonde bobbed hair and for courage sprayed on some of her favourite Chanel Cristalle perfume - one of her few indulgences - buttoned up her coat and grabbed the bottle of wine she'd placed on the hall table earlier. Taking a deep breath, she set off for the party, intending to be there and back in an hour, maximum.

*

Half an hour in, Kate was disappointed but not entirely surprised to discover that the evening was everything she'd been dreading. Yes, she knew most of the people there, which made chatting easier, and yes everyone was being very nice and friendly, keeping her glass filled and staying off the topic of dead husbands, but everywhere she looked she saw couples.

They were doing those things that people who are intimate with each other do - a steering hand in the small of the back, a light pat of the arm to attract attention, an arm slipped territorially around a waist, two hands interlinked, fingers entwined. All things Jason would do when they were out and she'd taken for granted. Things she used to love and missed like hell now. She'd had enough. Even the Prosecco wasn't taking the edge off her discomfort. It was time to go.

Just then Kate felt a hand on her arm and heard a man's voice beside her. It was the host, Paul, and he was steering someone in front of her.

'Kate, I'd like you to meet a new arrival. This is Rose. Rose, I'd like you to meet Kate. Her husband Jason died a few months ago, August or September wasn't it? Must have been around the same time as Rose's husband Richard was killed in a car accident.'

Kate felt her heart sink and she looked in open mouthed horror at her host, hardly believing that he'd thought it a good idea to shove two bereaved women together as though their respective losses would mean they'd get on like a house on fire. Did he imagine they'd grab some sparkly wine and a couple of chairs and sit down in the corner, out of the way, discussing death experiences, comparing funerals, empathise with respective feelings of loss, devastation, loneliness? She was still staring at him when the other woman spoke.

'Yes, that's right. Richard's accident was at the beginning of September.'

The voice was small but steady, and Kate turned her head towards it. She saw an elegant, well-dressed woman, wearing flowing black trousers and a blue satin blouse. She had short reddish hair that looked as though it had once been styled into a sharp pixie cut but now the layers had grown out. She was tall, around the same height as Kate, and about the same age, and on the outside seemed very composed, but her eyes betrayed terror. She looked exactly the way Kate felt. For a moment both women stood looking at each other, then Kate realised Paul was still speaking.

'Actually, Kate, you might have known Rose's husband. He used to go to the Fairlawn Tennis Club. Aren't you a member there? His surname was Bud.'

'Bud!' Kate exclaimed before she could stop herself. 'Richard Bud?' She most certainly had heard about Richard Bud, or the gossip at least. Wow, so this was his wife. Kate wondered if she'd heard the rumours, too? Wondered if they were true? Looking at this lovely woman standing in front of her, she couldn't imagine they were.

'Um, I haven't been a member there for years Paul,' she stumbled, trying to make up for her outburst. 'I've only recently rejoined, to get out of the house… after Jason, you know. So I never met Richard, but of course I've heard his name mentioned. Everyone at the club seems very sorry about the accident.'

'Yes, these last few months have been pretty shit for both of you, haven't they,' sympathised Paul, patting Kate on the shoulder. Then a beaming smile spread over his face. 'Can I leave you two to chat?' he said, walking off before either had any chance to disagree.

Kate watched Paul's retreating back for a couple of seconds, before turning back to Rose. 'I'm very sorry to hear about your husband,' she said. 'You're very brave to come to this.'

Rose nodded and let out a sigh. 'Thank you, Kate, that's kind. It must be difficult for you too. To be honest, I didn't want to come, but a friend made me. I can't wait until I've been here long enough to be able to make a polite exit.'

Kate smiled at Rose's honesty. 'My thoughts exactly. I set myself a target of one hour maximum.'

'Me too, and when it's up I'm hoping to slip away quietly otherwise my friend Nicky – the one who dragged me here – is very likely to barricade the door and make me stay for a second hour.'

Both women laughed and then Rose nodded towards Kate's almost empty glass and said, 'Since we're both trapped here, do you fancy a refill?'

Kate thought for a moment, and then made a decision. 'I've had a couple of glasses already so wasn't planning on having any more… but I have had a bit of a difficult day, so why don't I have a small one just to keep you company. But you might have to steer me towards the kitchen – these heels may be low but it's months since I've worn any at all and my feet are killing me.'

Both women laughed while they walked toward the expansive centre island where open bottles were lined up, and as Kate was pouring Prosecco into Rose's glass she noticed her eyes wander to the French windows at the end of the kitchen where a small woman with long black hair was standing alone. She looked a little older than Kate and was stylishly dressed in a knee-length, slim fitting black dress which was partially covered by a black wrap emblazoned with red roses.

'I recognise that woman,' Rose said nodding towards the window. 'Do you know who she is?'

'Never seen her before in my life,' said Kate.

'Do you mind if I go and speak to her?' asked Rose.

'Not at all, I'll come with you.'

As they approached, Rose whispered to Kate, 'I've just realised why this woman is so familiar.'

'So sorry to bother you, but I think I know you,' said Rose when they reached the woman. 'Your husband was in the room next to my dad's at Princess Mary Hospital. We got your flowers by mistake and I met you when I brought them round to you.'

The woman hesitated, looking from one woman to the other, as though chatting to a stranger was the last thing she wanted to do. Then her face softened. 'Ah yes,' she said in a soft French burr. 'I recognise you. That was a very sad time for both of us.'

'Yes, it was,' Rose agreed. 'Your husband died just a day or two before my dad. How have you been?'

'Oh, you know,' replied the woman. 'You just keep going, don't you, putting one foot in front of the other….and all the other cliches.'

'Yes I do know,' said Rose. 'My husband was killed just a few months ago. I know just how hard it is to get through the days.'

The woman looked shocked. 'I'm so very sorry. That's very sad, very tragic,' she said shaking her head.

Despite her sadness, Kate sensed a warmth about this stranger and made her feel she'd like to get to know her better.

'I'm Kate, by the way,' she said, leaning over to shake the woman's hand. 'Rose and I have just met - pushed together by our host because we've both recently lost our husbands and he seemed to think we'd have something to talk about.'

'I'm Pascalle,' said the woman, a smile creeping onto her face 'and it's a pleasure to meet you both. As for our host, I'm sure it's not the first time you've experienced insensitivity. Sadly it won't be the last.'

'We're just having a drink to fill the time before we can escape home,' said Kate. 'Would you like to join us?'

'I wasn't going to drink tonight,' said Pascalle. 'I only came because my daughter forced me to. She's next door in the living room chatting with some friends. I'm hoping we can go soon too.' Then something in Pascalle's face changed. 'But you seem very nice ladies and I agree a bit of bubbly would make the evening more fun, so why not.'

All three gathered around the kitchen island and Rose poured Pascalle a drink while Kate asked her about her husband.

'I nursed him at home for almost a year before he went into hospital,' she explained. 'It's been four years since he died, but I just can't seem to come to terms with the fact he's gone. I saw his suffering and I was with him right to the end, but I still expect him to walk through the door at 6pm, and I have dinner ready for us both at that time.'

She looked up at the two women and smiled a sad, defeated smile. 'I've wasted a lot of food in these last four years.'

Kate and Rose both nodded.

'Well, cheers ladies,' said Kate softly, raising her glass. 'Nice to have met you both.'

Suddenly Kate stopped, mid drink. 'Oh my goodness,' she said, a playful smile forming on her lips. 'I've just realised. Rose, if your husband was Richard Bud, you must be Rose Bud. Is that for real?'

'Yes, it's very real,' Rose laughed. 'When Richard proposed to me I told him I couldn't marry him unless we both took my maiden name – Simmons. He wouldn't hear of it, and he got his own way as usual. So, I am forever

Rose Bud. It's a name that torments me – I constantly see people smirking when they read it.'

'I think it's rather sweet,' said Kate. 'Don't you Pascalle?'

'Oui, ma chérie. It's very cute, almost poetic. I rather love it. Definitely more romantic than mine, Granderson. What's your surname, Kate?'

Just as Kate was about to answer a tall, blonde woman rushed into the kitchen. 'Mum, I've just had a call from Peter. Stefan's throwing up. We need to go,' she urged.

'Yes, yes of course. This is my daughter, Justine,' Pascalle told Kate and Rose, putting her glass down on the worktop. 'My grandson's home with his dad and it's obviously not going well. We'd better get back so Justine can attend to him. I'll get my coat. You ladies don't mind, do you?'

'Not at all,' said Kate. 'I've been here longer than my allotted hour anyway, thanks to meeting you both, so I'll head off too. Rose, shall we return you to your friend before we leave?'

'Don't worry about me,' said Rose. 'I'll find her. I'm just jealous that I can't come with you. But best to show a bit more willing. Maybe we'll meet again one day?'

Kate, Rose and Pascalle paused and looked at each other.

'Yes,' they all said at once and then laughed.

'Maybe we can make a date now,' suggested Kate. 'Do you know the café in the library? What about coffee there next Saturday afternoon? About twoish?'

'Suits me,' said Rose.

'And me,' confirmed Pascalle, smiling as she headed down the hallway, towards the front door.

Putting on her coat, Kate realised that not only was she feeling more cheerful, she was smiling. This was the first time since Jason had died that she'd actively wanted to accept an invitation. She recognised that her friends had been doing their best to help her, but none of them really understood, and Kate had always felt that she had to put on a brave face in their company. But with these two women, there had been a different kind of connection. In the very short time she'd spent with them, she felt comfortable, as though she could say anything about how she was feeling and they'd totally understand. She was definitely looking forward to meeting them again.

As she walked back along the road, Kate marvelled at how, despite all her fears, the evening had turned out way better than she could have imagined. Perhaps there was something to this idea of saying yes to every invitation. There was, however, the question of what she knew about Richard Bud and his rather sordid reputation. Of course, it could just be tennis club gossip, and either way it was none of her business, but if she was going to get to know Rose better she needed to be careful to keep her mouth shut.

FIVE

December

The library café was actually a much fancier affair than it sounded and, since Christmas was just two weeks away, had been tastefully decked out in Victorian theme decorations to suit the building which housed it. Kate had arrived slightly early and was filling the time by scanning the menu, which seemed to feature 10 ways with a smashed avocado and not much else. At exactly 2pm she saw a familiar face walk through the door. Rose looked around the room, spotted Kate at the back corner table, smiled and walked straight over.

'So lovely to see you again,' she said sliding into the chair next to Kate. 'I've been looking forward to this.'

'Great to see you too, Rose. And I'm pleased that you look less terrified today than you did at the drinks party. I remember thinking you looked like a startled rabbit!'

Rose laughed. 'That was *exactly* the way I felt that night. Frankly it was the last place I wanted to be. And then Paul pushed us together as though he was thinking, they've both lost husbands, they'll have something to talk about.'

'Actually, he wasn't too far wrong, was he?' Kate smiled. 'I was annoyed at the time, but afterwards the more I thought about it, the more I realised how good it was to chat to someone who had had a similar experience.'

Just then they heard a commotion at the café door and a voice exclaiming: 'Ah there you are,' and Kate looked up to see Pascalle bustling over to the table, a massive smile on her face. She looked so different to the forlorn figure in black silhouetted against the French windows in Diane and Paul's kitchen. Today, dressed in stylish flared jeans, high heels and a black leather biker jacket, she seemed positively dynamic.

'Mes cheries I'm so pleased to see you,' she said embracing first Kate, then Rose, and kissing each one of them on both cheeks. 'Well done for being so quick off the mark in suggesting this.'

Kate laughed. 'I'm glad we could all make today. We were just talking about the party and our host pushing us together. We were both horrified at the time but now we're thinking maybe he did us a favour.'

Their conversation was interrupted by a waitress who wanted to take their order, and once they'd found the hot drinks and cake section of the menu and made their selection, Rose began telling Kate and Pascalle about the well-meaning friend who'd virtually forced her into a pair of smart trousers and top and dragged her to the party.

'I mean Nicky was actually ironing my blouse while I sat there on my bed like a delinquent teenager, scowling at her, with my mother telling me how ridiculous I was being. It's funny now I guess, but it didn't feel like it at the time.'

Kate laughed and added, 'I only went because after Jason died I promised myself that I'd accept all invitations. I was dreading that party. But I admit that most of the time I do feel better for having been out. I'm a magazine writer working mainly from home, so I find that getting away from the house, chatting to other people does take my mind onto other things and gives it a bit of a rest. Sadly, though, I have to go back home and the moment I open the front door, it all comes flooding back.'

As she finished speaking the waitress arrived and when Kate handed over a slice of cake to Rose, she realised she had tears in her eyes. Once the waitress had gone, Rose kept staring at the table.

'I know exactly what you mean,' she said, her voice breaking. 'That's when you remember that he isn't there. That he never will be there again. When it's driven home that you're no longer part of a couple, you no longer have *your* person. You realise a terrible thing has happened, that he's dead and you're here on your own, and somehow you're supposed to keep living.'

Instinctively, Kate and Pascalle each took one of Rose's hands. 'That's exactly it,' Kate agreed, 'but I'm so sorry. I didn't mean to make you cry, especially in a public place.'

Rose shook her head and leaned towards her. 'You know I've been finding it hard to cry since Richard died.' She touched her cheeks. 'Gosh real tears,' she said looking down at the water on her fingers. 'But I don't think it's sadness that's making me emotional, it's relief. It feels so good to be in the company of people who listen and understand.'

Kate turned to Pascalle who seemed more subdued now and was toying with her slice of coffee and walnut cake.

'How have things been for you? It's been four years, hasn't it?'

'Time hasn't healed in my case, not that I think it ever does. It's just a cliché devised by people who don't know what to say.'

'But Pascalle, haven't things got any better over the years?'

Pascalle shook her head sadly. 'Not really. Every morning I wake up and before I open my eyes I think to myself "This is the day I start living again". Then the first thing I see is the empty space next to me in the bed. Trevor's dressing gown is hanging on the back of the bedroom door. My head fills with the thought "he's not here", and my heart breaks with sadness.'

'Have you considered putting all those things away?' asked Rose. 'I gave most of Richard's clothes to a homeless shelter about two months after he died. I couldn't bear to see them around me.'

'I've come very close a couple of times. I pick up his watch and his wallet, or I take a pile of his jumpers out of his drawer to put into a charity bag and then I put everything back exactly as it was on the day he went into hospital for the final time. I just can't seem to let it go.'

'Or let him go,' Kate said quietly. 'It does feel very harsh, getting rid of a person's clothes and possessions, as though you're throwing *them* out with the rubbish.'

'That's it exactly,' exclaimed Pascalle with a shrug. 'And how can I possibly do that to someone I love?'

'Hard as it is, it has to be done,' said Kate. 'No point keeping it all when someone else could use it. They're not coming back to wear it and I know my Jason wouldn't want his clothes to go to waste – every if they weren't exactly the most stylish or expensive. Mind you, not everyone in my family agrees.'

'What do you mean?' asked Pascalle.

Kate let out a long sigh. 'I have two children. My daughter Lila is great, but my son Luke is proving difficult. I've made quite a few changes in the house which has involved getting rid of more than Jason's clothes and my son doesn't like it.'

'Does he still live at home, then?' Rose asked.

'No, neither of my children do. Lila's in a flat share just 10 minutes away, and Luke's married and lives on the other side of town. Our living room furniture was rather old, and there are a few bad memories attached to some of it that I won't bore you with, but not long after Jason died I found myself having a massive clear out. I bought new curtains and a new sofa and chairs that are much more me, and I think the living room looks great. I feel really comfortable in it, and I see it as part of moving on. But Luke doesn't agree.'

'I wouldn't know where to start, with the house, I mean,' said Rose. 'It could definitely do with a refresh. But Richard and I chose everything together, and I've never had to furnish a home on my own. We got married straight out of university and didn't have a huge amount of money so initially we made do with what our parents gave us and the little we could afford. What the house looked like didn't seem important at the time. Not when your mind is full up with hopes and plans for your future.'

'What did you hope for?' Kate asked, forking some of her red velvet cake into her mouth.

Rose smiled. 'Adventure. Travel. Seeing exciting places. Then children. We did the adventure and the travel, but the children never happened.'

'I'm sorry, that must make losing Richard all the more difficult. At least I have my son and daughter to help me.'

'I'd have loved children. But it wasn't to be. Now all I have of Richard are memories, and absolutely nothing to look forward to. We had big plans, you know. When we retired, we were going to go on a great adventure round the world. None of that back-packing lark for us. We were going to visit lots of exotic, out-of-the-way places, travel in style and stay in the best five-star hotels. Now I don't even have someone to go to Brighton with.'

She looked up at Kate and Pascalle. 'I know this seems trivial in the context of what's happened, but who *do* I go on holiday with? My mother has dementia, and her illness means she's not an ideal travelling companion, and most of my friends are in couples. They're hardly going to want a grieving widow tagging along to Bali or the Maldives or Benidorm with them.'

'It's not trivial at all,' Kate replied, thoughtful. 'It's the reality of our life now. Eating alone, sleeping alone, making decisions alone.'

Pascalle had been sitting quietly listening to Kate and Rose, and when they finished she took a deep breath and lifted her head as though she'd made a difficult decision. 'Can I tell you ladies about a dream I had? I haven't shared this with a soul.'

Rose and Kate both nodded at the same time. 'Of course, say anything you like,' encouraged Rose.

Pascalle began the story of her dream and ended with Trevor's line: 'You have to let go of the past to move into the future.'

Tears shone in all their eyes, and Kate spoke first, squeezing Pascalle's hand. 'There it is, your message, your sign. Trevor's giving you his blessing to move on.'

'Yes, and in my heart I know you're right,' agreed Pascalle. 'But you see I don't want to live without him.'

'We none of us want to live without our husbands,' Kate agreed. 'But what a waste it is if we don't. Two lives lost rather than one.'

'If it hadn't been for Mum I'm not sure what state I'd be in,' Rose confessed.

'How lovely that you still have your mother around,' said Pascalle.

'In a way yes, but her mind has deteriorated so much now that she doesn't often recognise me. That's really hard to accept. Shortly after Richard was killed it did cross my mind that there was no point in me living on. We have no children, I have no brothers or sisters. He was my everything. Then one day when I was at my lowest, I looked at my mother and she had such trust in her eyes, and I realised that I couldn't leave her, no matter how hard it is to stay with her. So, here I still am, just getting on with it, on my own.'

Listening to Rose, Kate was struck by how in love with her husband she appeared to have been, and yet if the gossip at the tennis club was true, that love wasn't returned. But then she conceded, you can never tell the state of a marriage from the outside. I mean, take her and Jason, no-one looking in would have guessed what was really going on there, not even their children who still had no idea about their dad.

Her thoughts were interrupted by Pascalle who'd sat bolt upright as though suddenly struck by an idea and was saying, 'Ladies, I know how you can help me. Justine has been nagging me for weeks to join a yoga class here at the library. I don't want to go on my own. But if you two would come with me...' She ended the sentence with a smile.

Kate and Rose looked at each other. 'I've never done yoga before in my life,' Rose said. 'What about you Kate?'

'Not yoga, but I've done a bit of pilates, and I play tennis and swim, so I have a decent level of fitness. Anyway, how hard can it be? Pascalle, I'm in.'

Rose laughed. 'In that case I'd better be in too. When is it, what time does it start?'

Kate spotted a notice on the café wall. 'Looks like it's 9am on a Friday morning. I'll have to rearrange my work diary for that morning, but I can do it.'

Pascalle, who'd bitten into a piece of her cake, choked when she heard the time. 'Oh no, sorry ladies, I didn't realise it was quite so early. Are you sure you don't mind?'

Kate and Rose laughed simultaneously. 'I'll let you know after the first one,' Kate giggled. 'I'll Google the website and see if there are any spaces in the class.' After a couple of seconds she found the relevant page. 'It's not on for the next few weeks because of Christmas, but there are spaces for the first Friday after New Year. I'm booking us on.'

'I guess there's no backing out now,' said Rose wryly as she checked her watch and started to gather her handbag and jacket. 'I'm so sorry ladies, I should be getting back to my mother.' She stopped and looked at both women. 'I'm so glad we've met. I've tried loads of bereavement groups but none of them has helped as much as meeting you has. Speaking to you, has made me feel as though a weight has been lifted from my shoulders.'

'This has been a real pleasure,' said Pasacalle, 'But I'd better head off too. Now I can hardly wait for our first yoga lesson!'

As they hugged goodbye, Kate felt a lightness in her that she hadn't known for the last three months, and if she was honest, for a whole lot longer than that.

SIX

A week before Christmas

Kate picked up her phone to text Luke.

Kate: *Luke just checking that you can still go with Lila tomorrow to pick up the Christmas tree?*

Luke: *No sorry mum I can't. I'm busy*

Kate: *But you always used to go with Dad for the tree a week before Christmas and Lila's really been looking forward to going instead. Start a new tradition, you know*

Luke: *Sorry mum I can't. I'm busy*

Kate: *That's a shame. Oh well can't be helped. Looking forward to seeing you and Cyn on Christmas Eve as usual. I'll have your room all ready for you to stay over to Boxing Day*

Luke: *Ah sorry mum, I should have said. We're not staying. Since Christmas is going to be different this year Cyn wants to spend it at her parents. We're going down on Christmas morning. Maybe we can see you and Lila on the 27th?*

Kate: *I'm going to ring you. I need to talk to you*

Luke: *Don't! I'm in the middle of something. I don't have time to talk*

Kate: *But we always spend Christmas Day together. It's our first without your dad. Luke you have to come!*

Luke: *OK. We'll pop in during the morning on our way to Cyn's parents*

Kate: *Come for brunch. We can open our presents together*

Luke: *Fine. See you then.*

Kate let out a sigh and dropped her phone into her lap. Why was Luke making this so hard? At least he was coming over, she tried to think positively. That was one mercy. A small one.

SEVEN

Christmas Day

Kate woke on Christmas morning feeling like she had a hangover. Despite the fact not a drop of alcohol had passed her lips the night before, she felt groggy and the room was spinning. A look at her clock told her she'd been asleep for exactly two hours. The previous night had been spent tossing and turning, her mind racing between the text conversation she'd had with Luke the previous week and all the memories of the lovely Christmases they used to have when Jason was alive. Nothing, absolutely nothing, felt right anymore.

She dragged herself out of bed and padded down to the kitchen. Maybe a strong coffee would help her feel more alert. On the way, she stopped in the living room and looked at the Christmas tree which stood in front of the bay window. Lila had made it look beautiful, stunning. But even that couldn't lift her heart. Her first Christmas without Jason. As if that wasn't enough to deal with, she also had the puzzle of what the hell was going on with Luke. He was being so negative, so angry. Her heart raced at the thought of what this Christmas Day held in store.

As she spooned coffee into the cafetiere, Kate's thoughts drifted to Latimer Christmases of the past. Normally she loved Christmas, *adored* it. Her aunts and cousins all lived in Scotland and her sister in New York, so she always put lots of effort into making the festive holidays at home in London a special time for her little family.

Usually, the house would be decorated to within an inch of its life, with as big a tree as their living room could hold. Decorating it involved all four of them, a large box of mince pies, a pan of mulled wine, and tunes from a rickety music box first bought when Luke was a baby and which still managed to squeak out a selection of favourite Christmas carols.

'It looks like a fairy has been sick all over it,' Kate said one year, gazing in wonder at the tree. The branches were ladened down with every bauble they'd ever bought or the children had ever made at school. There were angels, their wings half hanging off but still glinting in the miles of multi-coloured lights, sequinned Mickey and Minnie Mouse baubles bought on the two family trips they'd managed to Disneyland Paris, giant glass balls of every colour big and small but always glittery, and two large rather worn 'Baby's First Christmas' baubles jostling for space alongside an unlikely collection of 'Surfer Dude' Santas sent by a friend in New Zealand. Settled on top was a sparkling gold star and a ton of tinsel.

'That fairy must have had a severe case of gastroenteritis,' joked Jason, and they all howled with laughter.

The rest of the house would live up to the tree with swags of faux holly, mistletoe and eucalyptus entwined round the banister, a light-up Rudolf in the conservatory, a small golden tinsel tree in each of the children's bedrooms, and a line of sparkling mini trees on the window ledge in the kitchen.

They'd all loved it. Thought it was great fun. Even if the year leading up to this time had been a difficult one, Christmas always brought them back together. Jason was in his element, in charge of games, the TV remote control and selecting the films to watch across the holidays, and even when Luke and Lila were teenagers and more interested in their friends than their parents, they still loved the family

Christmas traditions. But this year…. Well, who knew what this year would be like.

The cards pouring in through the letter box had sent Kate into an emotional slump, which got even deeper when Luke's texts had arrived, and it had taken every one of Lila's powers to lift her out of her gloom by telling her how much *she* was looking forward to a happy family Christmas.

'I truly believe that Dad would want us to keep going with the family traditions and to have a fun time. He always loved Christmas, he wouldn't want us to stop or be miserable just because he's not here.'

'Yes love, I'm sure you're right,' Kate had replied lamely. 'It just all seems such an effort.'

'Don't worry Mum, I'll help. Everything will be just as it always was… with one exception.'

'Well two if you include Dad not being here and Luke only coming for brunch.'

'Actually, I was thinking more of the tree,' said Lila, looking slightly shifty.

'What about the tree?' Kate asked, eyeing her daughter suspiciously.

'I know you love the multi-coloured extravaganza we usually have, Mum, but do you think for one year we could have something a little more…stylish?'

'Stylish,' spluttered Kate. 'What's style got to do with Christmas?'

'Well exactly, Mum!' exclaimed Lila. 'It was never our priority. But look round this living room Mum. It's so elegant and tranquil now – it needs a new Christmas look. Plus, how are you going to feel unpacking and hanging all those familiar decorations without Dad?'

The last comment hit home. 'Extremely sad,' conceded Kate. 'Okay, we'll go for something more stylish, whatever that means, but I have to come with you to choose the new decorations…and I have the right of veto!'

'It's a deal!' replied Lila laughing.

They'd treated themselves to a day in Oxford Street, and had visited all the big stores, checking out their Christmas departments, and choosing the theme Lila thought would work best in Kate's new-look living room. They'd gone for a very soft and pretty blush pink with hints of silver and lots of sparkle and gleam. The end result was gorgeous. The baubles were like soft puffs of pink cotton wool hanging from the branches, the warm white lights glowed, and on top sat a new angel with a golden crown and the sparkliest of wings. Rudolf was allowed to take his usual place in the conservatory, but most of the rest of the decorations were culled leaving just a tasteful scattering. The scratchy music box was retired and in its place was a Christmas playlist which Lila created on Kate's phone so that she could listen whenever she wanted. Kate thought the whole effect was lovely. Very stylish. She also rather liked the tranquillity having just two colours created - it seemed to go with the calmer atmosphere that was descending on the house.

Now sitting, coffee in hand, gazing around the living room on this Christmas morning she had to admit that while it looked great, it didn't feel right. Kate sighed, closed her eyes and tilted her head up towards the ceiling. Why aren't you here, Jason? You should be here with me. With us.

Just then Lila rushed into the room, still in the trackie bottoms and t-shirt she wore to bed, her long, dark wavy hair flowing down her back. Kate saw the look of excitement drain from her face when she realised that her mum was close to tears.

'Oh Mum,' she said giving Kate a hug.

'Thanks love. I needed that. And thanks too for staying over last night. It helped knowing you were in the house with me.'

'No worries, Mum,' said Lila, giving Kate an extra squeeze. 'I guess this Christmas is about making new traditions while holding onto the best of the old ones. Or at least the ones that make us cry the least.'

'I wish your brother felt the same.'

'He'll come round.'

'Will he, Lila? I'm growing increasingly unsure that he will. I wasn't convinced that he couldn't spare one morning to buy the tree. His "No" was pretty firm when I asked if him and Cyn were going to come on Christmas Eve and stay until Boxing Day as usual. It felt like agreeing to brunch was just placating me.'

'Well, maybe he thought that as things would be different anyway without Dad, why not do something different for Christmas dinner,' ventured Lila.

'Yes I do understand that,' said Kate, 'but I also thought that as this was our first Christmas without your dad it would have been good for us all to be together, to support each other. He didn't even speak to me about it. I can't deny that I do feel a bit hurt. Anyway, I always thought that Cyn couldn't wait to get away from her family at Christmas time. From the way she usually describes them, they sound like real misery guts.'

'I agree she always seemed to love the Christmases she's spent here, but people change. At least they're coming for part of the day.'

'Yes, and I shouldn't be greedy or expect to have everything the way I want it,' conceded Kate. 'We'll just have to fill them with lovely breakfast treats so that if the festivities at Cyn's family are dull they won't feel they've missed out.'

Kate paused and looked around the living room again. 'What do you think he's going to say about the tree?'

'Truthfully, I think he probably won't like it,' said Lila. 'But it's not for him, it's for you. Does it make you feel cheeerful Mum?'

'Yes it does.'

'Then that's all that matters.'

'I hope you're right darling, I really do.' Kate shrugged. 'Come on, let's get ready. I'm dying to see you in your new green dress. I think you're going to look gorgeous.'

Upstairs, Kate put on a purple sequinned top she'd had for years, tamed her hair, and slapped on some make up to cover up the dark shadows from her sleepless night. One of many. She'd hoped that as time went on she'd start sleeping better, instead most nights were spent lying awake trying to make sense of everything. Was it only three months since

Jason had died? Some days it felt like she'd only seen him that morning, on other days it seemed like years.

She was checking herself in the mirror for the final time when the doorbell rang. Lila got there before her and Kate heard Luke and Cyn's voices in the hall. She hurried downstairs to greet them.

'Merry Christmas darling,' she said, moving into her son's arms to kiss him on the cheek and hug him. Did he resist slightly or was she being oversensitive? 'Why did you ring the doorbell?' she asked. 'You have a key. That's what you usually use.'

Luke took a breath to answer, but Cyn got there first.

'Oh, we just thought that as it's Christmas Day we'd be more formal,' she said with a smile. 'Didn't want to catch you out.'

'Doing what?' Kate was confused. 'This is still your family home Luke. I know that you and Cyn have your own flat, but this will always be your home and you can come and go whenever you like.'

Luke looked a little bit sheepish and mumbled a soft 'Sure thing' as he walked into the living room leaving Kate to hug and kiss Cyn.

'Oh Kate, that tree looks stunning! What gorgeous colours,' exclaimed Cyn catching her first sight of the tree.

'Thanks Cyn,' Kate smiled. 'It was all Lila's doing really. She chose it and did most of the decorating. I was just her humble assistant.'

'And this room, Kate, it really does look amazing. I can hardly believe it's the same room.'

She turned to Kate with a smile that seemed more malevolent than warm. Kate detected insincerity in her voice and looked over to see how Luke was reacting. He hadn't said anything about the room or the tree and her heart sank when she saw him sitting on the edge of the sofa, clasping his hands in front of him, staring intently at the floor, as though desperately trying to keep his face neutral.

'Oh, it's just tidier and with a few softer colours,' said Kate, carefully selecting her words. 'Really I've just made it look less like an office and more like a living room.'

'Well, I think it looks truly lovely Kate,' Cyn gushed on. 'I can see you everywhere in here - you're definitely making it more of a reflection of you.'

Innocent though her comments sounded there was an undertone that started an alarm going off in Kate's head. It wasn't like her to be so opinionated, so challenging. Cyn usually just went with the flow. Was she trying to stir things between Luke and his mother? And if so why? Especially on this day when all Kate wanted was for them to have a nice time. She drew on her years of experience of making the best from a difficult situation, shook off Cyn's comments and announced, 'Time for champagne, I think.'

'Oooh lovely, but just a small one for me,' replied Cyn. 'Remember we're off down to my parents and the police are always pretty hot with drink driving at this time of year.'

'Yes of course, Cyn, I didn't think,' said Kate. 'We don't usually have to worry about that on Christmas Day do we, because you usually both stay.'

Nerves and frustration were pushing Kate towards an argument, but she stopped herself just in time and summoned a happy, welcoming smile. 'A small glass for Cyn it is then. Lila would you mind doing the honours sweetheart?'

They all followed Lila into the kitchen and while she poured the champagne, Kate started cooking breakfast. Luke had visibly relaxed as he left the living room and chatted almost normally while they sat round the breakfast bar tucking into a full English Christmas breakfast. He spoke as he always did about his work, playing football with the local team, and a concert he'd been to with Cyn, and seemed back to himself again. He even teased Kate about how she'd managed to burn both the bacon and the sausages – her ability to burn anything that went into the oven or under the grill was a family joke.

'Usually it's one or the other, Mum, but today you've excelled yourself.'

'You can never be too careful with pork,' she stated with a smile. 'Better charred than riddled with salmonella. If we're all finished, let's open the presents.'

'Sure,' Luke agreed. 'We have some for you, too. Where are yours?'

'Under the tree,' said Lila. 'Come on into the living room. We'll sit round the tree and I'll pass out the gifts.'

Luke's face stiffened. 'Can't we stay in here?'

'Don't be silly Luke, all the gifts are next door under that glorious tree,' said Cyn in a sweet voice. 'Let's go in there and enjoy it.'

As the three women walked down the hallway to the living room, Kate noticed that Luke was lagging behind. 'Are you okay, son?' she asked.

'Yes Mum, fine,' he answered, but his mouth was tight and his voice strained.

Luke, Cyn and Kate sat on the sofa while Lila handed out the presents which they opened one at a time so everything could be admired. Luke's face was like thunder, while Cyn couldn't have been more chirpy. She uncharacteristically squealed in delight at every gift and when Luke opened the parcel from his mum, which was a state-of-the-art Bose speaker he'd been coveting for the last year, Cyn exclaimed: 'Oh that's a wonderful present. You can put that in the living room and get rid of those old speakers your dad gave you years ago.'

Kate cringed at Cyn's comment and glanced over at Luke who was admiring the speaker while nodding and smiling, but his eyes told a different story. They looked furious and Kate could tell he was trying hard to control his voice.

'Yes this is a wonderful gift, thank you Mum. It was exactly what I wanted. But perhaps we can just put Dad's speakers somewhere else.'

'Course we can,' replied Cyn, still all bright and breezy. 'Whatever you think is right, Lukie.'

The minute the last present was opened, Luke stood up. 'Time for us to go Cyn. Your parents will be expecting us.'

Kate was taken aback at Luke's abruptness and tried to hide her disappointment by rushing to the kitchen to find them a bag to take their gifts home in. Luke followed her.

'Mum, I need to speak to you,' he said in a low voice.

Kate closed the kitchen door behind them.

'I'm sorry Mum if this day isn't turning out the way you'd hoped,' he said.

'Darling I'd be lying if I said it was but I'm just grateful you both came over for part of it.'

'It's just that I find it really difficult to come to the house now. It's not so bad when we're in here because the kitchen's the same as always, but that living room is totally different and I can't stand to look at it. I hate that Dad's desk has gone, and as for that tree! If Dad was alive we'd never have a tree that was colour co-ordinated, and definitely not one that's pink.'

Kate felt she almost had to take a step back to cope with the force of his fury. Luke never spoke to her like this, he'd never been this angry at her, not ever. Yet here he was standing in the middle of the kitchen, his face getting redder by the second, his jaw tight, his hands in fists.

'When I come home now it's as though Dad never lived here. Where is he in that room, Mum? This house? I accept that you have to move on. I *know* it because you've told me often enough. But it feels like you've shoved him out. It's not the family home I grew up in. I don't feel I belong here Mum.'

Kate stood wide-eyed with shock, trying to summon the words to respond. 'Son, I'm so sorry that you feel this way, but at the end of the day it's just a room, it's just a tree,' she tried to reason. 'It's people who make this house a home, our home. Surely you can see that you're coming here now for me and for Lila?'

Luke looked up to the ceiling and Kate could see all the rage leave his body. 'No Mum I can't see that, not yet anyway,' he answered, letting out a long breath. 'All I can see is you wiping my dad out of my life, and I hate it.'

Just then they heard Cyn calling: 'Lukie, Lukie, are you ready?'

'I'd better go, Mum. I hope you and Lila enjoy the rest of your day.'

'Will you come at New Year?' asked Kate.

'No, Mum, we won't. I'm not sure when I'll next be over.'

Kate must have looked as crestfallen as she felt because he added quickly: 'I'll text you. Love you, Mum.'

By the front door Cyn was all smiles and hugs and wishing everyone a lovely day and Kate could have smacked her for taking her son away from her. She could see he was hurting and she wanted to envelop him in a hug, but Cyn was shooing him out of the door and down the path towards the car.

'You should be so proud of yourself,' Cyn told Kate as she turned back to give her a hug, her voice dripping in syrup. 'It's obvious that you're quite determined to move on with your life, leave the old one behind, and good for you. The rest of us will just have to be quicker at catching up.'

The words sounded encouraging but her tone was snide.

'I'm not intending to leave anyone behind. Especially you and Luke.'

'Oh, don't worry about Luke,' said Cyn, breezily. 'He'll be fine. I'll make sure of that.'

Before Kate could say another word, Cyn rushed down the path, into the car.

'Well,' said Lila, as she and Kate stood on the doorstep, waving her brother and his wife away. 'That was intense. I think that calls for another large glass of something alcoholic.'

'Make it two,' replied Kate, sagging against the door frame. 'I think I'm going to need one for each hand.'

Bereft and confused, Kate watched the car drive away. What on earth was going on with those two? She wished that Rose and Pascalle were here with her right now. Maybe they could help her work out how to make Luke understand.

EIGHT

Boxing Day

Rose dropped two teabags into the teapot and filled it with boiling water from the kettle. She was making her mum a cup of tea, nice and strong, just the way Violet liked it. 'It's my Irish heritage,' Violet used to say proudly. 'Strong enough to stand a spoon up in it. Just like my Irish grandad took his.'

Christmas Day had come and gone in Rose's house with no tree, no decorations or celebrations, no lavish meals. Her first Christmas without Richard was not something she wanted to mark and since most of the time her mother didn't know what day it was, it was easy to fall out of step with the rest of the world and just treat December 25th as one to get through, like every other.

One bright spot was a text from Kate on Christmas morning, wishing her strength and courage, and a funny message from Pascalle that was all emojis of fir trees and gifts. Other than that, Christmas had been cancelled in the Bud household.

Nevertheless, much as she tried to ignore the festive season, memories of fun times from years past with Richard kept swimming into her mind. She'd never forget the look in his eyes on every Christmas morning when he spied his gifts, carefully wrapped and piled under the tree.

'Are they all for me?' he'd always ask in fake wonder, knowing fine well that they were.

Rose loved to treat him and seeing him so happy was worth the several hundred pounds the gifts always cost. That for her was the greatest gift of all. This year there were no presents, no one to treat and make happy. She was grateful that today Violet was having one of her more lucid spells, which meant Rose didn't have to explain who she was 10 times every hour or answer the same questions time and time again.

'Mum, did Richard talk to you much about your finances? Show you your bank statements or discuss the rental agreement on your house?' Rose asked airly while she set out mugs for the tea.

'No, not really. Well, yes he did at the beginning when he was setting everything up. I had to sign some documents. Remember, you were there too. But nothing much after that. Why?'

'Oh, just curious. I had a quick look over your bank statements earlier and there are a few things that don't seem quite right. I haven't checked them closely or had a chance to speak to the letting agents, but I thought I'd ask if he'd talked to you about making any changes to your bank accounts or the house rental.'

'No love, not that I remember anyway,' Violet replied laughing. 'Oh, I'm sure it's all fine. With two accountants in the family how could it not be? I know that Richard was never as diligent as you, but I'm sure he did a fine enough job with my finances. It was a real blessing when he suggested that we rent out my house and I come to live with you.'

'It would have been difficult for you on your own, Mum.'

'Oh yes I know,' agreed Violet. 'It was great having Richard to advise me. You must miss him so much love. Especially now. He did so love Christmas, didn't he.'

'Yes, Mum he did,' said Rose sadly. 'He was like a little boy at Christmas. Yesterday was hard without him. But I'm grateful I still have you.'

'Was yesterday Christmas? You know I have no recollection of it at all!'

'For someone with a bad memory you managed to pack away quite a bit of dinner,' laughed Rose. 'Not to mention two helpings of trifle. Fortunately, I'd made it with as little sugar as possible so it wouldn't affect your diabetes.'

'Christmas always did give me an appetite,' smiled Violet, almost blushing. 'Shame I can't remember your trifle. I'm sure it tasted lovely.'

Rose put down a cup of practically black tea in front of her mum and a plate containing a few chocolate biscuits. While Violet tucked in, Rose's mind strayed to the statements she'd looked at this morning. There was definitely something odd about them that merited further investigation, but she hated herself for being suspicious and was trying hard to convince herself that there would be a simple explanation behind it. She'd trusted Richard with her mother's money. Had she done the right thing? After all, she hadn't trusted him with their own earnings.

Right from the start she'd known he was a spender and that their joint money would easily slip through his fingers. Reasonably good at managing other people's money, he was less efficient when it came to his own. In their relationship Rose held the purse strings but always made sure Richard had enough in his bank account to feed his love of nice clothes, good food, and golf and tennis with the boys.

Violet reached across the table and took Rose's hand. 'Will you be okay, love? Moneywise I mean,' she asked all concerned. 'I imagine you will because you always were careful. Richard less so I know, but you were. But if there's anything you need just take it from my accounts Rose. Take anything you want. It'll all be yours one day anyway.'

Rose smiled at Violet's kindness and squeezed her hand.

'Thank you, Mum. But I'll be fine. I have a good pension and as long as I invest the money from Richard's life insurance wisely, I'll be comfortable. Let's face it, we spent most of our money on holidays and travel. I don't think I'll be doing much of that in the future.'

As she said the words, the image of the two of them, laughing and carefree, standing on that far flung beach during their honeymoon flashed into her mind, closely followed by the realisation that there would be no more of those trips, no more excitement as they packed their cases ready for a great adventure, no more strolling along palm-fringed white sands hand in hand, or snorkelling in warm, azure seas feeling as though it was just the two of them in the world. No more of the life she had looked forward to.

Rose felt herself fold forward, as though everything inside her, all her organs, her bones, her muscles, had melted and her body was collapsing into itself, exhausted with the grief of it all.

'Oh Mum…' she managed before her throat choked and the emotion she'd been holding inside for all those months burst through. Rose the woman who seldom cried was sobbing.

Violet rushed round to her side of the table, mortified that she'd said something that had made her daughter cry, and put her arm around her shoulder. 'I'm so sorry love, so sorry to make you sad. I know how hard this is, believe me I do. After your dad died I thought I'd never smile again, but I did and I have and you will too. You *will* be alright. You're strong and clever and you will survive this. If I can, anyone can.'

Still the tears kept flowing. Rose felt they'd never stop. She grasped onto her mother's hands, pulling them to her as though their touch was the only thing keeping her alive.

Gradually her tears subsided, and she managed to say, 'You're right Mum. We're survivors. And I have you to look up to, to give me confidence to keep going. I know how much you loved Dad and how much you miss him, but you've kept going, and so must I.'

Rose stood and hugged her mother. 'Now,' she said, tears still on her cheeks but her lips trying to smile. 'Let's have another cup of tea. Maybe even another biscuit.'

'What about my diabetes?' countered Violet.

'I got some new special ones for diabetics in Boots the other day,' said Rose. 'Let's have one of those - push the boat out!' Violet giggled as Rose moved to refill the kettle.

'I'm going to have a detailed look at your statements soon, Mum,' she said.

'That would be lovely dear, but there's no rush. It's Christmas after all.'

'Yes, I know, but best to keep busy. Anyway, I need to start getting my head around it since I'll be managing everything now.' Rose held up three teabags and dropped them into the teapot. 'This cup's going to be super strong, Mum,' she said with a smile. 'I hope you're ready!'

As Violet drank her tea, Rose hoped she was ready too because if all was not well with those accounts, she'd need all the strength she could muster. What on earth had Richard been up to with her mother's money?

*

Next afternoon Rose was relieved to be sitting in the church hall at a meeting of the bereavement group. She'd felt so grateful to hear that as the festive season was such a difficult time for the bereaved, they were having a special meeting between Christmas and New Year. After the difficult couple of days she'd had, Rose was so full of emotion and worry she was ready to explode. When she found herself tidying, tidying, endlessly tidying everything in the house she realised she needed to get out and talk to someone, but who?

There was her friend Nicky, but she was more a client than a friend, not really someone to open up to, and anyway she'd be with her family and it didn't seem fair to disturb her. Maybe Kate or Pascalle? They too had their own families so best not disturb them. Then she found a message on her phone about the bereavement group meeting. So here she was, telling them about her morning.

'It's now getting to the stage where I finish my cups of tea at the sink so that I can wash, dry and put the mug away immediately. My poor mum's empty cup barely lands on the coaster than it's whipped away and washed,' Rose explained. 'I can't stand a pleat of a curtain out of place, I'm constantly straightening them. I hoover really thoroughly every morning and then if I see a bit of fluff or a stray hair on the floor, I get the hoover out again! Honestly, my house is immaculate - but I can't seem to stop myself neatening, washing up, straightening.'

Rose looked around at the other group members. Some couldn't hide their surprise that their quiet colleague was saying so much, others were nodding.

'Control,' ventured the elderly man sitting to the left of the meeting leader, Maria. 'Since your husband died you've felt out of control, and this is your way of bringing some back into your life, by controlling your environment. It'll be even worse because of the time of year.'

Previously, Rose had dismissed this man as a bit of an attention seeker because he was always the first to speak and kept interrupting others to tell some story about him whether it was relevant or not, but perhaps she'd underestimated him. What he'd said made some sense. Since Richard had died, she'd felt as though she was on a rollercoaster, shooting down and around at breakneck speed, with no brake or safety belt. Her heart was constantly in her mouth, and it took only the smallest thing to be out of line or to go wrong, for her pulse to race and her hands to shake. Sometimes she could hardly breathe. The feelings were getting worse not better, and since things went wrong a lot, she was in a constant heightened state. It only took the toast to burn or her mum to drop a plate and Rose's reaction was immediate and extreme.

'I find myself doing all manner of unnecessary chores just to get through the day. Maybe that's what's wrong with you, too,' ventured a woman sitting opposite Rose.

Wrong? Rose felt her hackles rise as she took exception to the word 'wrong'. That didn't seem fair. Here she was, feeling vulnerable and fragile and worried enough to open up to this group of strangers, just to be told she was wrong. She wanted praise for her bravery, and some help, not to be told there was something *wrong* with her.

Then another voice piped up.

'Those empty hours are difficult. I'm always looking for things to do. Always feel I *have* to be doing something.'

This from an elderly lady who sat slightly behind her neighbours in the circle as though she didn't really want to be there. The woman went on, 'It wasn't so bad when my Cyril first died because lots of people came round to see me, and I had plenty to do sorting out the funeral and all that terrible paperwork. But once I'd got myself straight, once the funeral was over, people drifted away. It was as though they'd either lost interest in me or decided that I didn't need help anymore. No-one called round or even phoned, and before I knew it I'd had a day when I hadn't spoken to anyone at all. I mean I know death is to be expected when you get to my age, but it still hurts. There's still a great gaping hole in your life.'

The group leader Maria leant towards the woman. 'Do you have a family, Rita?' she asked.

'Oh yes, two lovely daughters and four grandchildren,' replied Rita. 'They live nearby, and at first one of them would pop in for a cuppa and a chat every day. A different one each time, sort of on a rota. But that's drifted. The children have to be taken to this club or that activity after school, so they don't have the time to come. My girls are always apologetic when they give me a quick call to let me know, and of course I don't let on how disappointed I am.

'I *have* offered to help out with the grandkids. but the girls always say, "Don't worry Mum, we can manage. You focus on you and getting over Dad. On building a new life for yourself." Because I mean I'm only 72 - plenty of years left. But frankly a life without my Cyril, and with my girls and my grandkids only popping in every now and then, and not that many friends to speak of, hardly worth living, is it?'

Another man, to the left of Maria, started talking about his sister and brother who hadn't been near him since his wife died, and then a few more people revealed how lonely they too were feeling, and before she knew it Rose realised that they were all so busy saying things about themselves no-one was talking about the things *she* wanted to talk about, that *she* needed help with.

Gradually a low groaning sound filled the room. Maria looked around, trying to detect the source of the noise. When she realised it was coming from Rose, she leaned over and patted her knee.

'Are you alright?' Rose had her fists clenched tight, eyes glued shut, tears streaming down her cheeks, and was making a keening sound. Maria knelt in front of her, taking both her fists in her hands. 'Breathe Rose,' she said calmly, 'breathe.'

Suddenly Rose's eyes popped open and she snapped: 'Breathe! Breathe! Is that all you can say to me, all the help you can give me!'

Rose jumped up out of her chair which fell backwards and clattered onto the floor, the crashing sound drawing everyone's attention and forcing Maria back into her own chair. Rose stood, face flushed with anger and frustration, looking round the circle of astonished faces all turned towards her. Teeth gritted, she lashed out.

'I've had enough of listening to you lot. All you do is drone on about your kids and your grandkids, and how horrible they are to you. Well at least you have them. At least *you* have a sister,' she barked, pointing at one of the men. 'And *you* have children and grandchildren,' she ranted, pointing at Rita. 'What do I have? Well, I'll tell you what I have! I have nothing and no one!'

By now Rose was verging on the hysterical, and she knew it. A little voice deep in her centre was telling her to stop, that she was humiliating herself, and that no good would come of this outburst. The voice sounded strangely calm, as though the real Rose was still there buried in her core, still measured in her thoughts, still reasonable in her approach, but had been overwhelmed by a furious Rose whose weeks of desperately looking for hope, help, answers but finding nothing had built a wave of frustration and resentment that was now bursting to the surface. This red faced, boiling hot Rose couldn't be controlled.

She was standing now in the middle of the circle pointing at each person and throwing out insults and rage.

'Oh, I have money,' she then heard herself say with ugly sarcasm in her voice. 'I have a very nice house, and I have a mother. But she's mad as a hatter, and I have nothing else! No kids. Couldn't have them and wasn't allowed to spend the money on getting them. We're fine on our own, Richard would say. Think of all the great times we'll have together, just you and me. Kids would only get in the way. IVF? That's just throwing good money after bad, and there's no guarantee it will work. No, let's reconcile ourselves to it being just us and the amazing future that we'll have together.'

Rose paused, breathing heavily. Everyone else was silent, looking stunned. She went on in the same angry voice.

'Except now there is no us. And no future. Now it's just me and a mother who doesn't know what day of the week it is. Soon she won't know who I am, and what happens then? What happens to poor lonely, no-family, no-husband, no-mates Rose then? That's what I want to know! That's what I thought maybe you could help me with! But instead you're telling me I have something *wrong* with me.'

By now, Rose was running out of steam, standing still, shoulders slumped, eyes downcast looking at the floor. Maria, who'd been pinned to her seat by the force of all this anger, took her chance, walked over to Rose, slid her arm around her shoulders, and guided her across to the tea table at the back of the room.

'A cup of tea, Rose,' she said cheerfully, 'with plenty of sugar. I reckon we could probably all do with one of those.'

92

Rose shook her head, her voice now quiet, her energy spent.

'Tea with sugar won't help me,' she said weakly, and then turned back to face the others in the room. 'I need more than tea. I need answers. I'd thought maybe I'd get some here. But no. I guess I'll just have to find them on my own.'

Rose shook herself free of Maria , stormed over to her chair to grab her coat and bag and strode out of the hall shouting, 'I'm off. Enjoy your tea.'

NINE

Day after Boxing Day

Rose heard her phone ping and noticed a text from Kate.

Hi Rose, just wondering how you're doing? I hope Christmas wasn't too tough.

Rose sighed. Tough? That was an understatement. But in some ways not as tough as this morning had been. She'd awoken with a terrible headache after a night spent sobbing, but even the pain of the pounding in her head couldn't mask the tremendous shame she felt about the way she'd lost control yesterday and shouted at everyone at the bereavement group.

She'd tried phoning Maria three times to apologise but there had been no reply and no option to leave a voicemail. So, Rose had sent a text to say how sorry she was, how she couldn't understand what had come over her as she'd never had an outburst like that in her entire life, and that she hoped everyone in the group wasn't too traumatised.

'It's probably best if I don't return to the group,' she ended the message. Maria hadn't responded.

She'd been prowling the house searching for something that was even remotely out of place so that she could straighten it up when Kate's text arrived. Rose looked at her phone again. A wave of something approaching relief washed over her as she read Kate's words. She remembered being surprised at how in tune they'd been when they'd met at the party. Rose wasn't one for making friends, her life had revolved around her work, Richard and her parents. Any friends she had were really long-standing clients that she sometimes saw socially. She didn't often feel an affinity with people, especially on such a brief meeting, but Kate and Pascalle seemed different.

Rose started texting. After yesterday's humiliating fiasco what did she have to lose?

Rose: *Terrible day. Terrible few days to be honest. I'm so looking forward to that yoga class. Maybe we could stay afterwards for a coffee in the library café?*

Kate: *Pretty terrible here too. And yes to the post class coffee. That's always assuming we can still move after all that flexing! And well done for surviving your first Christmas*

Rose smiled as she read Kate's message. Surviving. Yes, she'd survived. Just. She walked into the living room and looked around, and in the far back corner of the room, mostly hidden by a cabinet, she spotted the flap of a cardboard box. Sympathy cards. She'd never got round to opening them, just piled them up and then swept them into that box which she'd tucked in the corner and forgotten about. Rose took a deep breath and decided that perhaps today, more than three months on from the terrible day that changed her life, it was time to tackle the box. After all, she couldn't feel any worse than she did now.

She settled herself on the couch, opened the box lid and inside found about 30 cards, a pile of leftover Orders of Service from Richard's funeral, and a memorial book that the tennis club had given her, signed by all the members who'd known him. It had hardly been the biggest of funerals. The funeral director had estimated 40 or so mourners in total, but Rose suspected it was fewer than that and he was being kind. Either way, she didn't care.

Nicky had kindly driven her and Violet home after the small wake, chatting about this person she'd spoken to and that.

'From what I could tell there were about five people from his office,' she'd said. 'I'd imagined there would have been more with it being a biggish firm and him always seeming so popular, but Julia - you know the nice lady who I think is the secretary for the team he worked in – she said they were all so busy not many could get the time off to attend the funeral. Then she mentioned something about that famous charm of his working with the ladies and not so much with the men in the company.'

Rose had noticed Nicky shoot her a look at this point, but when she didn't respond Nicky kept talking. 'Jealousy, I expect. Did you see that a few men had come from the tennis club? A couple of women too. Apparently, they both worked there, swapping between the bar and the reception. One of them seemed really upset. Did you see her? She was the one in the navy jacket with the fancy Hermes scarf?'

Rose had shook her head.

'She was breaking her heart!' said Nicky. 'Poor soul. Although I'm not quite sure that a flashy scarf was an appropriate item to wear for a funeral.'

At the time Rose couldn't have cared less what anyone wore. Now she pulled out the memorial book from the tennis club and flicked through the pages. Some names seemed familiar, and she read their messages. Others she skated over. She stopped at one message, tucked in a corner of a page, and written in small writing as though the author didn't want it to be seen. Rose squinted to read it.

'My darling R. I'll never stop loving you, Sx'

Rose felt herself go hot and cold all at once. S? She racked her brains. The only people she could remember Richard mentioning with the first name S were men. Who was this S? Why would they never stop loving her Richard?

Rose felt her heart thud and her hands shake as she dropped the book back inside the box as though it was made of boiling hot lava. She couldn't look at this now, couldn't deal with it. First her mum's money and now this. It was all too much. She jammed the lid back on the box and took it out to the bin, dropped it inside and slammed down the lid all the while silently screaming: 'What the hell Richard? What next am I going to find out about you?'

TEN

New Year's Eve

It was the week before the first of the yoga classes and Pascalle was rummaging through her chest of drawers looking for something stretchy to wear. She was cursing under her breath in French at the state her body had got into since the last time she'd done any exercise and at the lack of suitable clothes that would fit.

Pascalle had hoped her eldest daughter would feel satisfied to hear that not only was her mother booked into the class, but she'd persuaded some new friends to go with her. Justine, who was hosting the Christmas lunch, had looked suitably impressed at the news, which had boosted Pascalle who was trying to muster some festive spirit by focusing on her grandson who was having the happiest day of his life.

When she spoke about Kate and Rose, she looked positively cheerful.

'Good for you Maman. I'm very happy for you,' said Justine. 'I'm also amazed that you've agreed to go to something that starts at 9am.'

Pascalle's face fell and she nodded sadly.

'That will indeed be difficult,' her mother agreed. Although she didn't sleep much at night and always awoke early, she treasured her mornings in bed, drinking coffee and reading until at least 10am. That was something she'd done since she retired. Her guilty pleasure, she called it. Even when Trevor was ill, she'd loved the mornings when he'd had his pain medication and seemed settled and calm, and they could both lie in bed, snuggled up, just as they used to do in the old days, pre-children. Getting out of bed in time to get to the library and start exercising at 9am was going to be a challenge, but every time she thought about it, Trevor's words would float into her mind and she would shrug off any doubts.

'But of course, darling, I will go,' she reassured her daughter. 'For you.'

Now there were just a few days before the class was due to start and Pascalle needed something to wear. She sighed and pulled out a pair of fuschia pink leggings. They'd definitely seen better times, but then so had she, so perhaps they were well matched. All she needed now was a t-shirt. She spotted a bright blue one right at the bottom of the drawer, and as she tugged at it, a piece of paper came flying out with it. Pascalle bent down to pick it up and was surprised to see it was an old black and white photograph of her as a child, on a beach in France. She was sitting on the sand in the middle of a circle of sandcastles, each one with a French flag sticking in the top, and she was grinning so hard in the picture, so proud of her achievement in building all these castles.

Sitting beside her was her papa, Mattieu, shirt off but long trousers on, covered in sand, beaming equally as proudly at both the little chateaux he'd helped to create, and at his clever daughter.

Pascalle stroked the photograph gently with one finger, confused as to how it had ended up there, but also happy to see her papa's lovely face again after all these years.

He'd died when she was 19, from a massive heart attack. When she'd heard the news, Pascalle had been completely crushed. Uncomprehending. Sitting on the floor looking at the photograph now, Pascalle recalled that day as though it was yesterday. She'd just come back from a usual Wednesday at college, skipped upstairs to her bedroom to unpack her bag of books, when her mother, Evangeline, came in and told her the terrible, terrible news. She'd screamed at her mother, 'How dare you make up something so horrible to tell me! Go away! Get away from me you terrible woman!'

Then Pascalle lost control, picking up objects in her room and throwing them, trashing books and magazines on the floor. Eventually when there was nothing else to destroy she turned her fury on her mother, who'd been sitting on the bed quietly sobbing. As Pascalle raised her fists to hit Evangeline, she felt her wrists grabbed, looked down at her mother's sweet hands on hers, sensed Evangeline's warmth as she was gently guided to sit at her mother's side, an arm go round her shoulders, and then the tears of rage turned to ones of total devastation. Papa, her lovely papa. How could it be that he was gone?

Just the memory of that time had Pascalle welling up, the tears spilling as she recalled the horrible days that followed, the disbelief, frustration, anger that she felt, and the tenderness her mother showed her, despite her own sorrow and despair.

'She's always been so open emotionally,' Pascalle had overheard her mother tell a neighbour a few days after the funeral. 'You always know exactly how Pascalle is feeling.

She hides nothing. And she so loved her papa. I don't know how she will recover from this.'

'It will be hard of course,' replied the neighbour, an older woman who always wore black, a sign of the past traumas that she'd suffered. 'But she will recover with time and patience. Don't despair Evangeline. Pascalle will come back to you.'

Lying on her bed, tears streaming into her already sodden pillow, the teenage Pascalle hadn't been so sure the old lady would be proved correct. She felt desolate, abandoned. Her two elder brothers were being kind, although keeping her at arm's length as they had no idea how to deal with their sister's dramatic shows of emotion, and her mother was being soothing and patient, but Pascalle felt incredibly alone. Betrayed almost. How could her beloved papa have left her? His *petit chou*?

Weeks went by. Some days she raged, other days she felt so weighted down by sorrow that she couldn't muster the energy to cry. She dropped out of college or rather, as she attended so little, they dropped her. She didn't care, she just wanted to be alone. Occasionally she'd go for a walk to the park where her papa had taken her as a child, but mostly she stayed in her bedroom, coming out only to eat. Her mother begged for help from Pascalle's friends, the family doctor, the priest, but her daughter refused to see anyone.

After three months, she decided she had to get away from the house, the village, the family. They all held memories of Papa and she couldn't stand seeing any of them anymore. She planned her escape, withdrew money from her bank account, looked up train times, and early one the morning she sneaked out of the house, boarded the first train to Paris and was gone. She left behind no note. 'They're better off without me, and I'm better off without them,' she'd told herself.

How naïve and stupid I was then, Pascalle thought now getting to her feet. Still holding the photograph in her hand, she made her way down the stairs and into the kitchen to make herself a coffee. On the way she recalled how big and terrifying Paris seemed at the time. She'd visited it before on a school trip, but she'd never been there on her own and although she'd been full of confidence that she was right to get away from the constant reminders of her papa, from her brothers' anxious looks and her maman's soft patient sighs, there was also a part of her that was afraid.

I can't believe that I managed to find a job and make a life for myself there, Pascalle mused to herself while stirring her coffee. For a whole year I was on my own. I had my job and made a few friends, yes, but for 12 months I just thought about Papa and how much I loved him and missed him. Then I met Noah...and everything changed.

Pascalle felt a shudder go through her body at the memory of Noah, a man she trusted enough with her love to marry him, but who would ultimately set her against her family and take her mother away from her. She looked down at the photograph of her and her papa on the beach, memories of those innocent childhood days rich in her mind. From a different time, she thought, and a different life.

She set the photograph down on the table just as she heard her phone ping. Where had she put it? After a search of the kitchen, she found it in her handbag sitting on the chair by the window. It was a message from Kate inviting her to join a WhatsApp group – YogaBunnies. Pascalle laughed. She'd never considered herself a bunny, but perhaps that was part of this new life she was venturing into. With Kate and Rose to help her. Two lovely women. But more than that. Two women who seemed, in the very short time they'd been together, to know exactly how she was feeling. She looked down again at the photograph. My lovely Papa. My lovely Trevor. Perhaps now is the time to say au revoir to you both.

ELEVEN

January

'Good lord, I need to sit down after that. Do you ladies have time for a coffee?' asked Pascalle.

Rose and Kate nodded thankfully and trudged behind their friend to the café. They were emerging from their first yoga class. It had been held in one of the rooms of the library, a grand Georgian manor house which had once been a rich family's mansion and had been bequeathed to the local council more than a century before. It sat in its own gardens, which were now used as a park. The ground floor of the house was used as a public library, smaller rooms on the top floor were rented out to local teachers, and a café was on the first floor, housed in what would have been the grand sitting room with tall windows overlooking the park. The women found an empty table by one of the enormous bay windows and collapsed into the chairs.

'That class almost killed me,' said Pascalle.

'I didn't think it was that bad,' said Rose. 'I feel lengthened and relaxed.'

'Lucky you,' said Kate, slumping further into her chair. 'You know I thought I was quite fit, but that was *really* tough. I did notice, though Rose, you doing a rather elegant Warrior pose. Are you sure you haven't done yoga before?'

Rose laughed at her two exhausted friends. 'No I haven't, and I guess since I'm the only woman standing that means I'm getting in the coffees.'

Kate and Pascalle managed to smile and nod, and while Rose walked over to the counter to place their orders, Kate considered what a lovely woman she seemed to be and how she couldn't believe that Richard would have behaved so badly towards her.

When Rose returned with a tray containing three coffees and three Danish pastries – 'we need something to give us energy,' she informed them – Kate and Pascalle had been discussing their fellow classmates.

'I found them rather intimidating,' confessed Pascalle. 'They looked very professional in their snug Sweaty Betty leggings and little racer back tops. But I must say, while my body feels exhausted, my mood is a bit brighter. You know,' Pascalle stopped and looked over the table at her two friends, 'I think this might be the first time I've had coffee with friends in months. Maybe even years.'

'How can that be, Pascalle?' asked Kate, biting into a succulent cherry Danish. 'Surely you must have lots of friends.'

'Well I did,' she replied. 'Before Trevor got ill I had lots of friends. We were always meeting up, at least twice a week, and we used to have such a good time together. Or we'd go to the cinema, sometimes even dancing! Trevor wasn't much for going out, so I mainly socialised with girlfriends. Then when Trevor got ill, I couldn't bear to leave him. The chemo made him terribly sick. He just faded before me and I was so terrified something might happen while I was out that I just stayed at home.

'Very occasionally I'd meet a friend for coffee, but I was so anxious, all I wanted to talk about was Trevor and how ill he was and how panicked I felt at the prospect of losing him, and they didn't want to hear that. They wanted bright, lively Pascalle. They wanted to tell me about their lovely holidays with their lovely husbands, their new grandchildren, all the wonderful things they were up to.

They were bright and colourful and I was dull and grey. So one by one, they stopped asking me out.'

'But Pascalle, that's so sad,' said Kate. 'Just when you needed them most.' She thought for a moment. 'Mind you that's pretty much been my experience too since Jason died. I mean, people do invite me to things, but they don't want to hear how I'm feeling. Not really. They ask, but if I start to talk about how sad I'm feeling they're quick to change the subject.

'There was one friend who asked me over for coffee and since she was a really good friend I felt I could open up to her. She asked the usual "How are you?" Normally I just say "I'm fine" and move the conversation on, but that day I felt safe enough to answer truthfully. I thought maybe telling her would help me. So I said, "Actually I'm feeling really sad today." And do you know what she replied? "Oh, never mind. I have something that'll cheer you up", and she produced a holiday brochure and proceeded to tell be about the wonderful three-week trip she'd booked for her and her husband next summer to the Maldives. I mean why did she think I would want to know that?'

'I think it's embarrassment,' suggested Rose shaking her head. 'I've had a few strange reactions from people too. There was this one woman called Bernadette, she was actually the wife of one of my clients, and although I'd met her a few times, I can't say we were close. When she heard that Richard had died, she came round to say how sorry she was and brought me a home baked cake.'

'That was nice of her,' ventured Pascalle.

'Yes it was, but then I met her a few weeks later in the street and she was all gushing with apologies saying, "I'm so pleased to see you! I've been meaning to call you to arrange for us to have a coffee and a chat but I haven't got round to it yet. I've just been so busy." I don't know what she expected me to say to that. Did she think I'd been sitting around at home waiting, wishing upon wish that Bernadette would spare an hour in her extremely busy schedule to take poor sad little me out for a coffee?

'Someone looking in from the outside would think she meant well. But in the months since Richard died I've encountered more than a few people who haven't been able to set aside their own embarrassment at being faced with a bereaved person who might at any moment burst into tears and sob all over them. I want friends who hear how I really am, not just feel relief when I say I'm fine. I want friends who see that I've not only lost my person, but all those things that attach to that person. My companion. My status. My future. Trying to come to terms with those realities is what taxes my mind every day, not whether Bernadette has phoned for a coffee.'

Rose's face was pink with emotion by the time she finished. Kate leaned across and slid her hand over one of Rose's. 'We'll always listen,' she said quietly.

Rose nodded and grasped onto Kate's hand. 'And it's a relief to know that,' she replied, a smile forming on her lips.

'I think we should tell each other one thing about our husbands,' suggested Pascalle. 'If I'm going to get to know you ladies, I'd like to know something about your other halves. I'll start. My Trevor was what you British call quiet and retiring, and quite shy. He was the total opposite of me. Tell us about Richard.'

Kate took an internal deep breath. What was Rose going to reveal?

'It's hard to find just one thing,' she answered, editing her thoughts as she spoke. 'Okay, so I guess the most obvious thing is that he loved expensive things – clothes, cars, holidays. And he could wind me round his little finger.'

All three women laughed. 'Now you Kate.'

Kate thought for a moment. What was she going to reveal? Although she hadn't known these women long she felt she could trust them, but she wasn't ready yet to say out loud her true feelings about Jason. Not to anyone. And maybe never. Instead she decided on one small detail that made her smile. 'Well, he was my toy boy…'

'Ooooh,' said Pascalle and Rose simultaneously, both laughing. 'That makes you a cougar,' pointed out Rose.

'I guess it does,' Kate giggled. 'Never thought of it like that. He wasn't that much younger than me – just four years – but I rather enjoyed being the older woman.'

'Kate that's wicked…but I can see that I'm going to get on well with you,' said Pascalle. 'You know I haven't had as much fun in years as I've had this morning.'

'Maybe it's the endorphins from the yoga class, but I'm feeling more cheerful too,' agreed Rose.

Suddenly Kate looked at her watch and then grabbed her bag and yoga mat.

'I'm so sorry ladies but much as I have loved this, I need to get back to work.'

'I'd best go too,' said Rose. 'I need to get home for my mum. So I'll see you both next Friday at 9am?'

'Absolutely!' chorused her friends.

As the others stood up to go, Rose paused. 'Are you okay, Rose?' asked Kate.

'Yes, yes, I'm fine. It's just that I feel a bit happy inside. And I like it.'

Long may that last, thought Kate.

TWELVE

Later that day

'Rose, are you listening to me?'

Rose had just come in from the yoga class and had made a cup of tea when she realised her mother was talking to her. Today she seemed to know who she was and Rose felt her heart soar.

'Yes Mum of course I am,' she replied smiling. 'Now what were you saying?'

'I was just asking if we still had any of those diabetic chocolate biscuits. I'd like one with my tea.'

'We certainly do, Mum. I'll pop the kettle on and put one on a plate for you.'

As Violet ate her biscuit with relish, Rose sat gazing at her wondering how on earth this could have happened to them both. Her mother losing her mind and Rose becoming a widow at 63. How could her life which had been fun and happy and full of promise have descended into this bleak half-life, with nothing to look forward to but more dark, sad and lonely days?

She tried very hard to remember the mother from her childhood, the one who'd always put her only daughter above everything, who took pride in all her achievements, and who'd only ever wanted her to have more than herself and Vernon had ever had. Suddenly Rose reached over and took Violet's hand making her flinch with surprise.

'Rose?' she asked, confused.

'Mum, were you *very* disappointed that Richard and I didn't have the big wedding you wanted us to have?'

'That's a funny thing to ask me after all these years,' said Violet.

'Yes, I suppose it is. But I was thinking about it the other day and I did wonder.'

'Truth be told, yes I was, we both were, your dad and I,' said Violet wistfully. 'We'd saved up for your wedding from the day you were born. Your dad didn't earn much as a bus driver, but we put away what we could every week for your big day. We had it all planned. You looking beautiful in a big white wedding gown, as expensive as you wanted it to be, flash cars to take us to the service, and a sit down dinner for all our friends and relatives afterwards. We wanted it to be a day to remember. It was our dream, Rose. But when it came to it, it wasn't yours.'

'No,' agreed Rose, emotion rising in her chest. 'Well, that's not quite true. It wasn't Richard's dream. He thought that instead of spending all that money on one day, it would be better, mean more to us, for you to pay for our honeymoon. At the time it seemed to make sense. What was one day compared to three weeks of luxury in the Bahamas, just the two of us? I remember him saying, "Surely the way we start our life as man and wife on our honeymoon is more important, more worth spending the money on? Start as we mean to go on".

'Then when the day came, I did wonder if we'd done the right thing. That register office was very drab and dark. All a bit too understated.'

'But you did look lovely in your cream suit,' Violet reminisced. 'All those tiny amber coloured roses scattered over your hair, and that beautiful posy of flowers. So simple. You really shone that day, you know. It was just a pity there were so few people there to see you and celebrate with us.'

'It was a shame his sister couldn't come, but at least his mum and dad were there. Did I tell you at the time that Richard's mother couldn't believe her wayward son was settling down?'

'You certainly seemed to have a good effect on him, love. He worked hard when he was with you.'

'He still had plenty of nights out with the lads, though Mum. Lovely clothes, a flash sports car, and plenty of holidays. There was definitely a lot of fun in his life.'

'So, I suppose that honeymoon really was the start of the life he wanted,' said Violet.

'Was Dad very heartbroken?' asked Rose tentatively. She wasn't sure she wanted to hear the answer.

Violet smiled and looked at her daughter. 'I'd be lying if I said he wasn't. But the moment he saw how completely happy you looked standing at the end of the aisle in that registry office, smiling into Richard's face, he realised how wrong he'd been to be disappointed. He told me, "We had our wedding day, Violet. It was Rose's today, and it was right that it was exactly as she wanted it to be". So don't worry love. Your happiness was worth more to him than a big wedding day.'

'Thanks Mum,' said Rose, moving round to give Violet a hug. 'You really are the best mum, you know.'

'Get away with you!' Violet exclaimed and roared with laughter.

The two women sat smiling at each other for a couple of moments and then Rose saw her mother's eyes change and a strange look gradually wash across her face.

'Right then,' said Violet. 'Best get those potatoes peeled. Your dad'll be in for his dinner soon and there won't be anything in the pot.'

As Violet rummaged in the cupboard for potatoes, Rose felt her heart break in two. Her mother was gone. Would she get her back again? Would she ever have another normal mother and daughter conversation? Perhaps if it never happened again, it would be for the best. Then her mother need never know that her daughter's happiness wasn't quite as complete as she and Vernon imagined.

THIRTEEN

A few days later

It was Sunday afternoon after the yoga class and Pascalle had brought a chair from the dining room into the hallway and positioned it opposite the coatrack so that she could contemplate the clothes hanging there in comfort.

The rack was like a long pegboard, cream coloured, Shaker-style, and on it were hanging three of her coats, and four of Trevor's. There was the leather biker style jacket he bought at vast expense that she hated on sight, but he thought was super trendy. Alongside it hung a black jerkin, one of those padded puffa-style jackets that always made him look weighty on top but skinny at the bottom, and a fake Barbour.

They'd been hanging there for the last four years, untouched, and now a little dust covered, Pascalle noticed from her perch.

She'd done a great job of keeping all his possessions in the bedroom clean and neat, not such a good one with these. Still, it was a lot to keep track of. She literally hadn't got rid of anything, not even the novel he had been reading before he got too ill to concentrate, or the handkerchief on his bedside cabinet. She'd washed it and placed it back there.

Anytime Pascalle had thought about moving her things into Trevor's bedside cabinet or had accidentally strayed onto his side of the bed in the middle of the night, she felt like a trespasser. She couldn't face having only her things in the wardrobe, no need of his chest of drawers, an empty bedside table, just her coats hanging in the hallway, all of them the final visual representation of the fact that Trevor was never coming back.

It was a fact, of course. Her head had known that for four years, but it also knew that the heart often takes a while to catch up to the head and Pascalle's heart had been dragging its metaphoric heels. Until now. Her dream and talking about it with Kate and Rose had persuaded her that her heart was ready.

'It's time,' she said out loud as she leaned over to pick up the roll of black plastic bin bags lying on the floor by the side of her chair. She took a deep breath. 'Désolée, mon chéri,' she whispered as she stood, took the leather jacket from its peg on the coatrack, folded it up and placed it gently into the opened bag. 'Désolée.'

*

That same Sunday afternoon, Rose was sitting in her friend Nicky's cafe waiting for her to have a quiet enough 15 minutes so that she could join her for a chat. With her mum at home on her own, she knew she couldn't stay too long, but she needed to get out for a bit, speak to someone who wasn't her mum, and café owning Nicky had been a long-time client and as close to a friend as Rose got.

Nicky was on her own and dealing with a fairly lengthy queue, so Rose was just gazing round at the other customers to pass the time. She noticed a couple sitting side by side at a table to her left. They were in their early 50s, she estimated, he had close cut greying hair and a short beard speckled with grey that looks so handsome on middle-aged men, and she could have been Spanish with long, lustrous dark hair which was tied straight back off her face by a cherry red scarf. She had a confident air that said, 'I know I'm beautiful'.

It was obvious that they were intimate. He was leaning close into her, bopping her playfully on the nose, dropping kisses onto her cheek. She was fake fending him off, interspersing her looks of exasperation with giggles. As Rose watched, he took the woman's hand in his and kissed each finger, all the time looking into his companion's eyes. He was rewarded with a look every bit as intense as his, her acknowledgement that despite her protestations, she was enjoying every single second of this play.

In their eyes, Rose could see it all, everything that had gone before, and everything that would come afterwards, and she felt a lead weight drop from her chest into her stomach. It was exactly the way Richard would have made things up to her after an argument or won her round to his way of thinking. But never again. She couldn't stand to watch the couple any longer, so before Nicky could get to the end of the queue, Rose got up and left the cafe.

*

While Rose was walking home, fighting to hold back her tears, Kate was in the shower. She had spent the morning shredding piles and piles of Jason's unopened bank statements, pay slips and letters from the Inland Revenue she'd found stuffed into the filing cabinets and the drawers in his desk when she'd emptied them ready for the charity pick up back in the autumn.

Unable to face dealing with them then, she'd chucked them into several plastic bags to shred later. When she got up that morning, she decided that today was the day. She wasn't sure whether it was because she was in a new year, or if it was the conversation she'd had with Rose and Pascalle about moving on, but something had given her the strength to open the bags and take out the envelopes. She hated what she found inside, the truth in black and white of the man that Jason had really been, the man only she knew. After she'd opened a few letters she realised she didn't have the strength to deal with it after all, so she got out the little shredder and started feeding in unopened envelope after unopened envelope. The real Jason being ripped to ribbons.

After two hours she couldn't tackle any more. She threw the remaining bags in the loft and stepped into the shower, desperate to wash away all her grief and anger and find a way to replace it with feelings that were softer, more tolerant. Yes, Jason had been an extremely difficult man to live with, yes he was selfish and thoughtless most of the time, but at the end of the day he had lost the most precious thing of all. He'd lost his life. How could she stay angry at a man who'd died in the prime of his life?

Despite the sound of the shower she could hear the doorbell ringing and ringing, but she didn't even attempt to step out of the warm, comforting water to go and answer it. She knew it wasn't Lila or Luke because they had keys and could let themselves in, and nothing else could be that urgent. Probably just a neighbour, or a charity collector. They'd come back if they were desperate to speak to her.

Instead, she stood in the full force of the hot shower, steam billowing around her, tears streaming, crying so hard that she thought her lungs would never be able to take in another breath again. Then I'll be dead too, she thought. Dead from crying. But I don't want to be dead, she told herself. I want to be alive. Jason had lived his life to the full and always on his own terms. Not enough years, but each one of them grasped and lived. I have to do the same. Because death is the end. And I'm not ready to be at the end.

FOURTEEN

Mid-January

The next Friday, Pascalle couldn't wait until the yoga class was finished to tell Kate and Rose about the massive step forward she'd taken.

'It was hard ladies, very hard. It felt more like a leap than a step. But you know, when it was all gone, when I'd handed those bags of Trevor's clothes over to the charity shop, I did feel like I'd achieved something.'

Kate smiled over at her. Although she'd cleared almost all of Jason's furniture from the living room and most of his clothes from the bedroom, she'd held onto a few of his things. A favourite t-shirt. His football scarf and beanie hat. His wedding ring and watch. A massive, thick sweatshirt he loved to cosy into on really cold days. None of it was valuable, but she couldn't bring herself to part with everything because it would have felt like cutting a cord that attached him to the family, cutting him adrift. She knew exactly how much Pascalle's actions had cost her.

'You've done so well, Pascalle. Giving away Trevor's things was an extremely difficult thing to do, but you've done it. I'd say that you're definitely moving on.'

'Exactly,' agreed Pascalle. 'I've been stuck for the last four years, not able to see that there could be a future for me. Although I don't have Trevor to share things with, I still have my daughters and my grandson and in the last couple of weeks I've come to see how little I've been in their lives. I've pushed them away. Now I want them back, close to me, living life with me.

'I've learned that you can't know what life without someone is truly like until they're gone. Not just moved out or emigrated but still at the end of a phone or able to respond to a letter, but totally gone. I had time to prepare for Trevor's death, to say our goodbyes in a way that you ladies didn't have, and for that I'll always be grateful, but I still wasn't prepared for the aftermath of him dying. For four years I haven't been able to accept the fact. Now I'm beginning to.'

Rose nodded. 'I remember one of the bereavement counsellors I saw telling me that everyone has their own timeframe, their own route to acceptance, and some people never get to that point. Then more tragedy happens, more grief is heaped on top, and they become almost paralysed, unable to help themselves, or the family around them.

'One client she told me about had lost her daughter 10 years before and was so focussed on her own grief that she couldn't see that her grandchildren were suffering too and needed her. They wanted to spend time with her because she was a link to their mum. Instead, the woman wasn't open to them, didn't go to them, but waited for them to come to *her*, to comfort *her*. But they were young and didn't understand, and anyway when they did go to see her, Nan just sat there sad and crying. It was as though she believed her grief was greater than theirs. But Pascalle, unlike that woman you've realised that your family needs you, and you're on the road to being there for them.'

At Rose's words, Kate felt a stab of pain to her heart. It had made her think of Luke and the fact that the only time she'd heard from him since Christmas was an abrupt text wishing her a Happy New Year.

'I wish I was making as much progress with my son,' Kate sighed. 'He doesn't even phone me anymore. He replies if I text him but he doesn't make the first move and he used to always text and call me.'

'Oh Kate that's sad. What's happened between you?' asked Pascalle.

'It wasn't just Jason's clothes that I sent to the charity shop. He had a rather messy home office at the back of our living room and I've got rid of his desk, filing cabinets, bookcases and a lot of his books as well as our old sofa which I've hated for years. I've repainted and refurnished the whole room and, even though Luke lives elsewhere, he hasn't taken it very well. He told me at Christmas that he hates coming to the house now because he can't see his dad in it anymore and he can't stand being there.

'My daughter Lila is more understanding and keeps reassuring me that it's my house and I need to feel happy there. But it's a terrible feeling to have your son so angry with you. Luke's always been a very sweet boy, and we used to have a really lovely relationship. In the past, he'd have done anything for me, anything. He also absolutely worshipped his dad and so I do see how difficult things are for him. But I just imagined he'd see what was best for me and support me in my choices.'

Pascalle smiled a gentle smile. 'I know a thing or two about children being angry with parents. I also know that when we are grieving we often only see things from one point of view, and that's usually our own. You're doing what's right for you Kate, and that's absolutely as it should be, but you have to understand that it may not be right for your son. What you're doing by clearing away Jason's things is adding to his sense of loss, but the lovely sensitive side of him will not want to tell you how much you're hurting him because he'll also want you to find happiness. All of that adds up to a lot of hurt and frustration.'

'I know you're right Pascalle. And from the way you're speaking it sounds as though you have some personal experience of this kind of situation.'

The smile on Pascalle's face grew sadder. 'I may sound wise now, but I haven't always been that way. I've seen and caused enough hurt to know what it feels like and how it can twist the mind and the emotions. Beware Kate, tread carefully, because if you lose your son, it could be very hard to win him back.'

In Pascalle's eyes, Kate saw fear and regret and she hoped against hope that she could heed her warning. She also knew the best way to help her son understand was to tell him the truth, and she knew that would devastate him. Telling him might mean losing him completely.

FIFTEEN

February

It was mid-afternoon and Rose was sitting in her kitchen going over some old statements from the joint credit card account she'd held with Richard. Violet came in and asked for some tea.

'Of course, Mum,' said Rose. 'Good idea. I'll just put the kettle on.'

'And I'd like a chocolate biscuit,' her mum stated firmly.

'You know you can only have one a day and I'm afraid you've already had today's ration.'

'But I want a chocolate biscuit now, I don't care about this morning,' her mother replied. There was an anger in her voice that made Rose feel unnerved because she knew where this discussion was going. She tried to keep her voice light.

'Remember what the doctor said - with your diabetes getting worse we need to limit your intake of sweet things and I'm afraid that includes chocolate biscuits. But we have loads of those nice crackers that you like. Have those.'

As Rose turned from clicking on the kettle she saw her mother's face grow red, her eyes blaze and her mouth become a slit of rage.

'Who the hell are you to tell me what I can and can't eat!' she ranted, grabbing Rose roughly by the arm. 'In fact *who* are you anyway? Some carer, I bet, left here by my stupid daughter to babysit me. Well, I can make my own decisions and I'm bloody well having a chocolate biscuit!'

The rage in her mother's voice made Rose feel so afraid - this was the angriest she'd ever seen her. They both reached for the biscuit jar sitting on the worktop at the same time, and so intent was Violet on getting there first that rather than pick it up, she swiped at it and it went flying onto the floor, smashing on the hard tiles. Rose instinctively leaned forward to try to catch the jar before it fell and because of that she didn't see Violet's arm still swinging and it connected with Rose's face, smacking her across the cheek.

'Mum no!' she yelled, grabbing both of Violet's wrists. The older woman startled and stopped. She looked at her wrists, then up to Rose's face where an angry red wheal was beginning to form on her cheek. Rose looked straight into her mother's eyes, seeing her own terror reflected there.

*

Later that day, Rose was sitting alone. Her mother was asleep on the sofa and she was looking at some pictures of Richard taken on their last Christmas Day together. He had his arm round Violet and they looked as though they'd just shared a very naughty joke. They were always colluding about something. They'd got on so well, Richard had been so patient with her, and could always defuse any growing annoyance between mother and daughter with a funny comment or a joke. Rose had depended on him so much.

'She's your mum and she's given you a lot over the years,' Richard would say soothingly, 'Now it's your turn to care for her. And she is grateful - or at least she would be if she could remember to be!' They'd both laughed at his joke.

'Caring for her is the very last thing you can do for her. I know it's rough, but she can't help it. Try to take a deep breath every time she asks the same question a million times, stick on a smile, and answer again for the million-and-first time!'

Then Richard put his arms around her and within that circle, Rose felt safe, restored, ready to tackle anything.

Since his death, Violet's mind had deteriorated so much and in recent weeks her dark moods and violent swings were becoming more frequent to the point that Rose wasn't sure how much longer she could keep her mother at home, for both their safety. Equally, the very thought of her dear, kind mum in a home made her stomach churn. She'd hate it, and she'd hate me.

Rose gazed down at the photographs and pleaded, oh Richard why aren't you here to help me? Why have you left me alone to deal with this, make all the decisions, and carry the guilt? How could you die and leave me all alone…?

*

The following Friday Rose, Kate and Pascalle were settled around what had become their regular table in the library cafe when Rose took a deep breath and announced, 'I think the time has come for my mum to go into a home.'

132

'Why, has something happened?' asked Pascalle all concerned.

'Sadly yes, well a lot of things actually,' nodded Rose. 'They were small at first but in recent weeks she's had no lucid moments at all, she's constantly confused and she's becoming really angry. The other day she slapped me. I know it was an accident, we were having a big of a row over whether she could have another chocolate biscuit and she just lashed out, swiped at the biscuit jar sending it flying and caught me on the face. It was really frightening because she seemed to turn from my confused mother into this angry, raging woman who I didn't recognise. Ordinarily my mum wouldn't hurt a fly, but in that state I don't know what she might do.'

'That must be really tough to deal with,' sympathised Kate.

'And putting her into a home is a difficult decision…not to mention an expensive one,' said Pascalle.

'It certainly is,' said Rose. 'But I can sell her house - we currently rent it out - and the money raised from that plus her pension would cover the cost for a while at least. Plus there may be ways of investing the money from the house sale that would pay the bills. I'd need to look into it a bit more.'

'It's lucky that you have your accountancy skills to help you,' said Kate. 'I wouldn't know where to start.'

Rose shrugged her shoulders. 'They don't help with the guilt, though. I feel so selfish even considering it. When Richard was around he was such a help but now, even with the support of carers who come in and sit with her while I'm out, I just don't feel I can cope with her. Sad to say, I don't feel safe around her, and I'm not sure she's safe around herself either. But I feel so *guilty*. My head says it would be better for both of us - Mum would be safe and get proper care, and I'd be more free to do other things, but my heart realises that is if she goes into a home, I'm left on my own, and that's not something I want either.'

'That's one of the many ironies about Jason dying,' revealed Kate. 'During our marriage there were a few times when I felt we'd reached the end of the road, but apart from the damage that may have done to our children and my reluctance to throw away all those shared years, the thing that kept me away from the solicitor's office was that I didn't want to be on my own. I knew exactly what that was like - I was 27 when I met Jason and although I'd very much enjoyed the single life in Glasgow, by then I was looking for someone special to share my life with. Someone to grow old, crumbly and grumpy with. Someone who'd look out for me. Even when he drove me to anger I decided that a future together was more important than a less frustrating life alone, and I put the effort into working it out so we'd stay together. Then he went and died.'

Kate looked down, toying with her coffee cup. 'I knew what widowhood looked like. My mum was widowed at 60 and my granny at 48. I never for one moment thought that would happen to me...' she trailed off.

All three were quiet for a moment, each woman considering how fate had changed the course of their lives.

Then Pascalle took a deep breath and turned to Rose. 'My darling Rose, do what's right for you and that will be right for your mum. You have life left. Make her comfortable and safe, and then get out and enjoy that life.'

Rose knew that Pascalle's words were wise and true, she just hoped she had the strength to carry them out.

Kate piped up, 'We've gone all sad. You know, I think it's time we had some fun! It's my birthday in a couple of weeks so why don't we have a girlie night out?'

'It's my birthday soon, too,' said Rose. 'Let's make it a joint celebration. What shall we do?'

A cheeky smile grew across Pascalle's face. 'I haven't been to a bar for years. Let's go to one of those places that young people go to – let's live a little.'

'Gosh Pascalle you really are coming out of your shell,' laughed Kate. 'But I'm not so sure about us going to a club – I couldn't stand the droning music and all that young flesh. But I'll ask Lila for some ideas of places that are lively but where we three wouldn't look too out of place. What date would work for you both?'

All three were busy checking dates on their phones when suddenly Kate's pinged. It was a reminder that she had a meeting due to start in 10 minutes.

'Shit, totally forgot about that again,' she said, leaping up. 'I need to run. I'll have to do the meeting in my yoga clothes - still it's on Teams so people only ever see your top half anyway. I'm around most nights and weekends, so I'm happy for you two to choose date and time and I'll get some ideas about place. I can't wait!'

She dipped to kiss each friend's cheek and was about to rush off when she stopped. 'You know if it wasn't for the money I'd definitely give up work. I'm much more interested in what life has to offer me now. You two are a good influence!'

Rose burst out laughing. 'Glad to be of service,' she called out to her friend's retreating back. Then she turned to Pascalle, growing more thoughtful.

'I can see that Kate still has some issues to sort with her son, but it sounds as though she's beginning to see a bit of a future for herself. It's making me realise that I've been floundering about for too long, questioning everything in my life, questioning things in Richard's life but never actually doing anything about finding the answers. I need to get a grip, take back control. I need to understand some things, put them behind me and then get on with being me again. I must confess I'm not one for nights out, but this one with you two, could be the start for me.'

'Good for you Rose,' said Pascalle opening the diary on her phone again. 'How does two weeks on Friday sound?'

'Perfect. Absolutely perfect.'

Pascalle had taken her first step in clearing Trevor's clothes. Now it was Rose's turn to make a move. She wondered where it would lead her.

SIXTEEN

March

By the time the date of the girls' night out came around a couple of weeks later, Rose's courage at setting out on a road to a new life had faded, and instead she'd spent days fretting about this evening. They'd planned a night at a new upmarket cocktail bar which had opened locally, where they could get dressed up and enjoy some food, cocktails or wine and lots of chat. While it was relatively low key, it was way more excitement than Rose had had in her life for a very long time.

Part of her felt up for a bit of fun but most of her was in a fluster for all sorts of reasons. She was worried about leaving her mum for so long, even with a trusted carer. Then there was the question of what people these days wear to bars. But what was panicking her most of all was that she just wasn't a girls night out sort of person.

Occasionally her and Richard would go out to dinner with other couples, but it wasn't that often, and she wasn't much of a one for having close female friends. Having her own business meant there was never any danger of going to an office party. When she did go out it was usually just her and Richard having a nice meal or going to a play or a film.

Much as she liked Kate and Pascalle, and was already valuing their friendship and feeling comfortable with them, she hadn't totally committed herself. She'd shared a huge amount with them, opened up to them in a way she hadn't done to anyone else, but there were still some thoughts and emotions she was keeping to herself.

Perhaps that was a consequence of being an only child, living in her own head, not fully giving of herself, even with people she trusted. Richard was the only person she could say truly knew all of her, all her thoughts, emotions, fears, opinions. Not even her parents completely understood her. She believed that if someone knew too much about you, you became weak, and she preferred to stay strong. With others she built a steel wall around herself, keeping everything inside. But with Richard, she'd loved him and trusted him so much that she'd completely opened herself to him, body and soul, and allowed herself to be vulnerable.

In the months since Richard's death, the walls of steel around her had been stronger and more impenetrable than ever. The only way to survive this terrible event, the shock, the reality of discovering how much her life was having to change without him, was to close every metal door, bolt them fast, and sit safe within them. Emotionally alone, but safe. Now her mother was so ill she'd put up even more barriers. If she fell to pieces, what would happen to her Mum?

Deep inside, Rose knew she couldn't keep people out forever, but she was so out of practise that allowing people help her was a slow process. That was part of the problem at the bereavement groups she was now beginning to realise, and even with Kate and Pascalle, two women she'd felt an instant connection with and who often said exactly what she'd been thinking, she wasn't totally comfortable.

She was also a bit worried about what they'd talk about all evening. Rose was inherently shy, didn't have any hobbies, and as no-one was ever interested in the work of an accountant, she didn't have many topics of conversation. With Kate and Pascalle, she could talk about how she felt about life without Richard or with her mum, but they were hardly fun subjects for a girls night out.

Rose looked around her perfectly ordered kitchen and sighed. Maybe she could talk to them about her growing realisation that there wasn't nearly as much money in her mother's accounts as she'd expected there to be, but the consequence of that being true was way too enormous for her to face it. Or the strange message from the mystery 'S' she'd found among the remembrance cards that she kept trying to push out of her mind because she couldn't bear to consider even for a second what it might mean. No, they weren't appropriate topics either.

Instead, Rose took a deep breath and decided to do what she always did – mainly listen and nod. She walked upstairs to her bedroom, opened her wardrobe doors, pulled out a pair of black trousers, and four tops.

'Which one tonight?' she asked herself. 'I wonder what the others are wearing?'

She grabbed her phone, opened YogaBunnies, their group WhatsApp chat, and typed out:

Can't decide what to wear. What are you wearing tonight?

*

A mile away, Kate was also scanning the contents of her wardrobe, looking for something to wear. Part of her was really looking forward to having a bit of fun, but another part of her was tense - her birthday in two days' time would be her first since Jason's death, and it was making her feel anxious, although she didn't really understand why.

She couldn't say hand on heart that birthdays with Jason had always been great. Most of them had involved some input from her. If she'd wanted anything specific she'd either have to organise it herself and he'd pay for it, or if she wanted him to be the one to do the buying, she'd have to drop heavy and very directional hints well in advance. Therefore, her fears weren't that she was going to miss being treated or made to feel special. Maybe it was more that this was yet another reminder that he was no longer in her life? Well she hardly needed reminding about that. No, this was more about her no longer having her special someone to share her day with. No more anticipation that maybe this year he'd get it right, no more badly wrapped gift, or little message written in her card.

She loved those messages. Granted they were seldom very prosaic, more along the lines of a simple 'To my darling Katie, with all my love always, Jas.' But she loved that he called her Katie, the only person who ever used that pet name for her. He'd said it the first time he'd met her, and when he used it, she always felt special to him. Seeing it written in her card used to take her back to those early days of their relationship, when life was full of romance, and reminded her why she loved him.

She opened a drawer in her bedside cabinet and pulled out the birthday card from last year. Always sentimental, she'd saved most of them over the years, but this one she kept close to her because it was the last she'd ever receive from him. She opened it and inside saw that familiar writing and the usual message, with one large X for a kiss. She smiled to herself. He never was overly demonstrative. When she'd tease him about that, he'd always say she should just know that he loved her without him having to say it all the time. Sometimes would have been nice though.

Kate ran her fingers over the words. There would never be a new one of these messages. The handwriting would never grow shaky with age. There would never be another birthday kiss or celebratory hug. Never again would he take her hand in his and lead her towards whatever birthday cake he'd been able to find at the last minute. He was pretty good at remembering to get the card and wrapping paper for the gift, but the cake was always a panic purchase.

She recalled his offerings over the years. Colin the Caterpillar one year, an expensive looking creation lavishly decorated with pink and white sugar roses another, and then the year she had to blow out candles on a giant tray bake with jelly rings strewn across the top.

'All they had Babe,' he'd said, not in the least bit shamefaced. 'I thought you'd see the funny side.'

She'd blown out the candles, trying very hard to stay jolly and not show her disappointment at his forgetfulness. Then she'd opened his card and seen the message. She was his Katie, the one who'd shared all those happy times when they were young and carefree, and she forgave him. Just as she was still forgiving him now. Her mobile buzzed and a text interrupted her thoughts. It was from Rose.

Can't decide what to wear. What are you wearing tonight?

Kate shut down the memories, put the card back into the drawer, turned towards her wardrobe and got back to the matter at hand.

*

'Fifth time lucky,' said Pascalle out loud as she slipped yet another dress from the pile on her bed over her head. She had been so excited for this evening that she started getting ready mid-afternoon, having a shower, shaving her legs and underarms, and taking time to carefully blow dry and then curl her long dark hair.

Last week she'd had the colour done for the first time in well over a year, having booked an appointment as soon as they'd set the date, and she loved the rich, deep shade of black she and the hairdresser chosen to flatter the golden tones of her Gallic skin. Although Pascalle was 66, she still had great cheek bones and a pretty, almost elfin face. Trevor used to say she reminded him of Audrey Hepburn, and she'd beam at the complement. She was so grateful that her skin had barely aged, which meant she could easily carry off a hair colour that would be too harsh on other women of her age. Tonight, she was wearing her hair loose, curls bouncing cheekily around her face.

Deciding what to wear was proving more difficult than she'd imagined. Last night she'd pulled out six brightly coloured and patterned dresses, all of which had been favourites in past years, and hung them in a row on her bedroom door so that she could see them all and take her time mulling over which one to chose. Twenty four hours later, she still hadn't selected one. She was definitely out of practice at going out.

This was going to be the first really fun night out she'd had with a group of women since Trevor died. Four years of long, boring nights in. The old Pascalle, the Pascalle who existed before Trevor's cancer diagnosis, would never have believed it possible that she'd go four *weeks* without a night out never mind four years. So here was a chance to rekindle the spark of that old Pascalle, and she needed an outfit that not only looked amazing but also made her feel right, and tonight she wanted to feel fun. Maybe even a little flirty. Not that she'd be hunting for a man, she just wanted to recreate the excitement of the old days when she had a bunch of great friends who all loved a laugh and a night out. Friends who melted away during Trevor's illness.

At the time she couldn't understand it. Surely friends were supposed to support you in your hour of need, not desert you as though you're some sort of sinking ship? Which of course in a way she was, sinking further and further in the mire of caring for a dependent and terminally ill man. A man who seemed to have lost half a stone overnight every time he got out of bed in the morning, whose skin gradually turned yellow, whose remaining hair fell out thanks to the harsh chemo treatment, leaving him bald and chubby cheeked because of the steroids he took daily. A man who changed from her strong, gentle, doting Trevor into a frail almost skeletal figure, weak, vulnerable.

He had been grateful for the care she'd insisted on giving him at home until almost the end but wasn't really aware of the terrible toll it was taking on her spirit. In lots of ways, neither was she. Not until the inevitable happened and she was left alone. By the time of Trevor's death, the fun-loving Pascalle was a memory. But tonight, Pascalle was ready to feel funny and flighty again, and who better to share her re-entry into a social life with but her new friends Rose and Kate. She smiled at the thought of them.

The fifth dress still wasn't right, so she took the sixth one off its coat hanger and carefully slipped it over her head. The fabric was jersey and the shape bodycon. With a wide V-neck, ruching down one side of the skirt, mid-length sleeves and in a bold floral print of giant red roses on a black background, it announced that Pascalle was back and ready to party!

She pulled on a pair of vertiginous heeled shiny red pumps and thought, 'This is exactly how I want to feel tonight.'

She picked up her phone and with a wide smile on her face, wrote a text to the YogaBunnies group chat:

Just leaving. Can't wait for you both to see what I'm wearing!

SEVENTEEN

That night

Later in the bar they were waiting for their third round of cocktails to arrive at the table and were agreeing that the evening was going very well indeed. They'd started with mojitos, moved on to cosmopolitans and were about to sample some pina coladas, and they'd talked and talked and laughed. Even Rose! They'd discovered quite a few more topics they agreed on ranging from not missing their late husbands' snoring to the dress choices of the other women in the bar.

'If that woman looked in the mirror tonight and thought that dress was flattering then she needs a new mirror,' said Kate not too subtly pointing out one particularly tight and revealing creation. Pascalle had howled with laughter, then added, 'But her shoes, now those are my kind of shoes.'

'The heels are at least six inches high!' protested Rose. 'I'd be like a giraffe with extremely painful feet in those.'

'As I say, perfect for little me,' laughed Pascalle.

Then their attention turned to a young woman carrying the tiniest of handbags, so small it couldn't even fit her phone, which she was holding in her other hand.

'Not sure I see the point of a bag that small,' Kate tutted, then she laughed. 'I really sounded my age there, didn't I!'

'That was extreme old lady talk,' teased Pascalle. 'You have to be more with it, the two of you. Like me.'

'Pascalle, you're the oldest of us all,' Kate pointed out while handing out the newly arrived pina coladas. 'Mind you, you look years younger than us in that amazing dress and with your gorgeous hair. Maybe we do need to be more like you.'

'Now ladies, we're all three of us gorgeous so let's give a toast to that, and then I have a serious question to ask you,' said Pascalle.

They took a sip of their cocktails, savoured the taste for a long moment, each one nodding with pleasure, and then Kate and Rose turned to their friend, ready for the question.

'What should I do about my wedding and engagement rings?' she asked.

Kate and Rose looked at each other, confusion written on their faces. Pascalle went on. 'You see, wearing them signifies that a person is married, and technically I'm no longer married. Neither are you two. If we'd got divorced,

150

we'd probably have had some sort of ceremonial removal of our rings, a first step to freedom. Maybe we'd even have sold them or given them away.' She stopped and looked at her two friends, both of whom were now deep in thought.

'A friend of mine who went through a particularly harrowing divorce sold her ring and gave the proceeds to a cats' home,' Kate said finally. 'Her ex-husband always hated cats and she thought it was funny that something he'd spent so much on was now financing several month's supply of Kit-e-Kat!'

They all three burst out laughing.

'Actually it's true,' said Rose, brushing away tears of laughter. 'These rings put us in a kind of limbo, don't they. We want to be married but we're not. We want to wear our rings because they symbolise what that person meant to us and the ultimate commitment we made to each other, but now that person is no longer here. We're married, because our marriage hasn't been dissolved, but without someone to be married to.'

'Widows,' said Kate with a grimace on her face. 'Such an ugly word. Black and deathly. That's not us. I mean look at you Rose, all tall and elegant with your gorgeous glowing skin. And Pascalle with your stunning dress, and that giant crimson rose pinning back the curls at the side of your head. You're the antithesis of black and deathly.'

Rose absent-mindedly stroked her cheek, and Pascalle flicked her hair off her shoulders, obviously thrilled at her friend's complement. A cheeky smile came over her face.

'What if one of us, or maybe all of us, wanted to get married again?' she asked.

There was an audible intake of breath from Kate and Rose.

'Don't look so shocked ladies. I know I'm in my mid 60s and I'm only now beginning to accept that Trevor has gone, but *I'm* not dead yet. I could have another 20 or 30 years ahead of me. Do I want to spend them on my own? Maybe not. And you two ladies are younger than me. We each have decades of life left. How sad if there was no-one to share it with.'

'I do feel a bit shocked,' admitted Rose. 'Richard was the only man I've ever wanted, ever considered. We met at university. He was my first boyfriend and my last. I would have no idea how to start looking for another husband, or who I'd be looking for. Of course, I do miss being hugged and kissed and having someone who loves me, but I can't imagine loving anyone as much as I loved Richard. Still love Richard...'

As Rose tailed off, Kate began nodding. 'I agree it would be lovely to have someone to snuggle up with again, someone who's always looking out for you, but I wouldn't know where to start either,' she said. 'I can't imagine being with anyone who isn't Jason. Anyway, let's face it, most men our age are fat and balding with a lot of emotional baggage and who knows what health issues ahead of them. I could imagine nursing Jason as you did Trevor because we'd spent all those years together and given so much to each other, but I don't fancy spending my remaining life looking after someone who, by comparison, I hardly knew.'

By this time the three glasses were empty again and Rose suggested they move onto prosecco on the basis that a bottle would last longer. While she was trying to attract the attention of the waitress, she asked, 'Have you been looking, Pascalle? For a man I mean?'

Pascalle smiled and looked quite coquettish. 'No, not really. I haven't signed up to any of those dating websites or anything like that, but I have noticed in the last few weeks that when I'm in the supermarket or even at church, I have a look around to see if there's anyone I might fancy.'

'Has anyone caught your eye?' asked Rose.

'Mmm, well there was someone…' Pascalle had a cheeky grin on her face.

'Pascalle! Do tell! Who?' demanded Kate.

'About half an hour ago there was a man over there, standing at the bar. A what-do-you-call-them, grey wolf?'

Rose laughed. 'You mean a silver fox.'

'Yes, that's it!' exclaimed Pascalle. 'A silver fox. He was tall, elegant, slim, had a full head of white hair and looked as though he was on his own.'

All three women looked over towards the bar but the only men standing there were anything but silver foxes.

'Where is he now?' asked Kate looking around for a distinguished figure.

'Sadly, I think he left,' said Pascalle, shaking her head, her mouth breaking into one of those cute pouts that the French are so good at.

Just then, the door pushed open and in walked a tall man, white haired, tanned, maybe in his late 50s, wearing jeans and a blue and green checked flannel shirt.

'Alors!' Pascalle blurted out. 'That's him! And don't look now ladies, but he's coming over here!'

Kate and Rose flicked a glance to each other, and against Pascalle's advice they both turned round to see this man who'd caught their friend's eye.

'Definitely tall enough,' said Rose out of the corner of her mouth. 'Not bad looking either.'

'No paunch,' whispered Kate under her breath, nodding appreciatively. 'That's a plus.'

'No wedding ring,' noted Rose. 'But then that doesn't mean anything. Richard never wore one of those.'

'Good skin colour,' Kate added. 'Probably not a smoker or a big drinker.' Both women looked at each other and then down at the table in front of them that held the debris of several cocktails and bowls of salted peanuts.

'Oh my god, I think he's actually coming over to us!' exclaimed Pascalle. Suddenly she didn't feel so coquettish.

Despite all her brave talk about finding another man, she hadn't meant it. Everything was still so raw, her steps out of her grief still so small and new, but the rings *had* been bothering her. She'd sat night after night looking at them, recalling the day they'd bought the engagement ring. How as a little girl she'd imagined when the time came she'd try on hundreds of rings until she was sure she'd found the right one. Instead, she'd been so excited about marrying Trevor, she'd picked the second one she'd been shown - two blue sapphires lying on their side with a flash of diamonds running diagonally between them, in the shape of an infinity symbol.

It wasn't at all the ring 10-year-old Pascalle had dreamed of, but she'd loved it and Trevor had loved it, and when he slipped it on her finger his look of pride made her love the little ring all the more. To set it off, she'd chosen a plain gold wedding band. Two rings endowed with such precious memories and meanings…and yet at the end of the day both just rings. Perhaps, she'd mused, removing them would be a sign of her readiness to accept Trevor's death and move forward with her life. Now, however, she had more pressing matters to deal with in the shape of a handsome man, striding towards her, looking directly at her, *smiling at her*.

The Silver Fox stopped at their table, which was nestled in a booth, edged by a horseshoe shaped, bright blue velvet covered padded bench. The three women had arranged themselves on the plush seating so that they could see each other, but now all three faced forward, eyes like saucers looking up into a face which was smiling down at them. Inwardly each one of them gasped.

'Evening ladies,' said the Silver Fox. 'I hope you're having a good time.'

All three nodded in unison.

'I wonder if one of you ladies would do me a favour?'

All three nodded again. Who was going to be the chosen one?

'I was in here earlier this evening, sitting just where you are now before I moved to the bar,' he explained. The women were agog. 'I was with my good lady wife...'

'Wife!' Kate exclaimed. Rose and Pascalle glared at her, leaving Kate blushing in seeming embarrassment at having spoken out loud.

'Yes, my wife, and she seems to have left her mobile phone here. Maybe dropped it on the floor? I wonder if one of you would mind looking to see if it's there.'

The three women dived under the table at the same time, hands down on the floor, searching for the missing phone, all of them thankful for a moment away from the handsome stranger's gaze.

'Found it!' shouted a triumphant Pascalle, emerging from under the table and brandishing the phone. She was aware that she touched the man's hand as she placed the phone in his palm. Nothing, not a single spark.

The man thanked them profusely on behalf of his wife, and as he strode away from the table and towards the door, the three women breathed a loud sigh of relief. Then they looked at each other and dissolved into giggles.

'That was an unexpected bit of excitement,' said Rose, beaming.

'Indeed,' agreed Kate, sighing in relief. 'Let's get that waitress over here -- we need a drink to calm us all down. We also definitely need to order some food. My head's spinning and I don't think it's entirely due to our encounter with the Silver Fox.'

Just then a waitress came over and they placed their order before sinking back into the plush seats.

'Actually, that was quite fun,' said Kate, still laughing. 'Both your faces were an absolute picture when that man walked over. I expect mine was too. And Pascalle, he was a good choice. You obviously have taste. I know, let's play that game Lila always plays with her friends, where you give the men in the bar marks out of 10.'

Rose was shaking her head. 'That's a terrible game,' she said. 'Very demeaning.' She paused, then went on, 'But I'm definitely up for it! And as for the wedding rings, well I rather like mine so I won't be taking them off just yet.'

Just then the bottle arrived. Rose filled each glass and then picked up her own saying, 'Cheers to us! To being wonderful, with or without a man!'

Kate and Pascalle returned her cheers. And as she sipped the wine, Pascalle could feel her heart begin to slow down. It had been fun, to feel that frisson of excitement about a man again, but it had told her that that's all it could ever be.

Trevor was the last, he had to be the last. The others? Well, we're all entitled to make some mistakes, but Pascalle's had cost her dearly and she had to respect her vow that those mistakes ended with Trevor.

EIGHTEEN

March

Two days later, Kate, Lila, Luke and Cyn were sitting around a table in their local Chinese restaurant. They each had a glass full of bubbly in front of them, and beside Kate was a pile of envelopes and a few bags with ribbons and 'Happy Birthday!' written on the side. Kate was telling them about her night out with Rose and Pascalle and their encounter with the handsome stranger.

'Honestly, it was so funny,' she said laughing. 'Especially the moment he looked into Pascalle's eyes and she thought he was about to kiss her. Her face went all pink.'

All of them laughed and Kate's heart soared. She'd been so looking forward to this family meal to celebrate her birthday. After the disaster of Christmas this was the first time she'd seen Luke and Cyn in the flesh. Lila had been over to theirs a few times but had refused to go into much detail with Kate about what they'd talked about. All she'd say was that Luke was still struggling to cope with their dad's death and she was sure he'd eventually come round.

Kate texted Luke regularly and he did reply, but the responses were terse. Kate had hoped they might have their usual family meal to celebrate his birthday at the beginning of March, but he chose instead to go out to dinner with Cyn and some of their friends. Kate had reluctantly resigned herself to sending him a birthday card through the post and transferring money into his bank account as his gift.

So when she'd texted him to ask if he and Cyn would like to get together to celebrate her birthday she'd hadn't held out much hope. Much to her astonishment, he'd said yes they would, but he'd insisted they go out to a restaurant and all meet up there. Kate imagined it was so that he didn't have to come near the house, and while she would have preferred something at home as she was still feeling anxious about her birthday, she decided it was best to accept his conditions. Just having her son, daughter in law and daughter together for her birthday was a massive step forward, so she felt optimistic. He was her son, her firstborn, he couldn't shut her out forever.

'Let's order,' suggested Lila, breaking into Kate's thoughts. 'Now what does everyone fancy? I vote we have starters AND a main course, and there might be a little surprise for dessert.'

Kate grinned from ear to ear. 'What do you mean a little surprise?'

Lila grinned back, flicking a conspiratorial look towards Luke. 'Just wait and see Mum, wait and see.'

This was their first visit to this particular restaurant, so it took several minutes to study the menu and chat about what to order. Kate surveyed the table - all her children around her, and for the first time in months, all of them looking happy and relaxed. The evening couldn't be going better.

While Jason had been alive, they hadn't had the money to go to restaurants much as a family, but when they had, selecting the dishes was usually the most fun because Jason would usually make everyone laugh with witty comments about their choices. He had a great sense of humour and knew how to tease people without them taking offence. Everyone loved his company. Only Kate knew what he was like away from other people, and only she'd be fretting about the bill at the end of the night, but she was always willing to overlook that for the fun he brought to their family. Tonight, the atmosphere as they tucked into their food felt almost as good as in the old days. What a relief, thought Kate. Jason, you've finally answered my prayers and had a firm word from beyond the grave with your son. Hurrah. Once the main course had been cleared away, Lila suggested that Kate open her presents.

'I can see you've been itching to get at them,' she said. 'We won't keep you in suspense any longer. But don't start with mine because I just need to nip to the loo and I don't want to miss you opening it. You can open the card, but not the gift!'

Lila was obviously up to something, but Kate felt sure all would be revealed in good time, so she picked up the parcel nearest to her which was from her Scottish aunt, then moved onto a card with a gift voucher from her sister in New York, a few cards from friends, and then one each from Lila and Luke.

Inside Lila's card was a thoughtful handwritten message, acknowledging how difficult this day would be for her mum and wishing her a happy time and a better year ahead, complete with a host of kisses.

Luke's card simply said 'Happy Birthday Mum' and had obviously been written by Cyn. Not a kiss in sight. Kate wanted to cry with disappointment. Instead she swallowed hard, looked at both Cyn and Luke with a smile on her face and said, 'Thank you it's lovely.'

Lila arrived back at the table, closely followed by a waiter bearing a giant birthday cake. They all clapped as he placed it down on the table, and Kate could see that the cake was decorated with a smooth white icing topped by a sea of tiny pink sugar roses in the middle of which sat a sparkling fountain firework. Kate was thrilled. They'd obviously made an effort to make this day a happy one, and she couldn't have been more grateful.

When the waiter went off to find a knife to cut the cake, Lila pointed to a rose gold bag with a flurry of ribbons foaming around the top.

'That's my gift, open it now!' she insisted.

Inside was a box containing a beautiful long silver chain from which hung three silver rings, each one of which was engraved with the name of a family member - Jason, Luke, Lila. Tears sprang to Kate's eyes as she clasped the chain around her neck. All of her family, together in this piece of jewellery to be hung close to her heart.

'Thank you so much, Lila.' Her voice was thick with emotion as she reached over to kiss her daughter. 'This is gorgeous, perfect. I love it.'

Then Cyn, who'd sat happily joining in the festivities of the evening, leaned over to Kate. 'Now for our present. I hope you love it too.'

She handed Kate an envelope with a shiny gold bow on the front. Kate opened the envelope and inside found a £50 voucher for John Lewis. Not knowing exactly what to think, Kate held up the voucher. As Luke saw it his expression changed from one of anticipation to confusion.

'Why did you get that?' he asked Cyn.

Cyn smiled rather smugly as she replied, 'Well your mum's been making the house look so lovely and most of the things have come from John Lewis that I thought she'd appreciate being able to buy even more from there. I mean, there's so much more of the house to redecorate and we don't know enough about your new style Kate to choose something for you, so I thought you'd enjoy selecting things for yourself, from what has obviously become your favourite shop!'

The atmosphere round the table changed in an instant. Kate's heart went shooting down to her boots. She felt confused and hurt by the gift and was dreading what was coming next. Luke was glaring at Cyn, rage in his eyes. Lila sat looking down at her hands. Cyn beamed at everyone round the table, her smile never faltering, looking rather satisfied with herself and completely at ease with her purchase.

Luke spoke quietly, obviously barely managing to control the anger in his voice as he said through gritted teeth, 'When you said you'd take care of a gift for Mum this year I thought you meant perfume, or maybe a pair of earrings. I didn't imagine you'd give her something that would reduce Dad's presence in the house even more! How could you Cyn? How could you do something like this when you knew it would hurt me, not to mention Mum? Sometimes I just don't understand you.'

Kate, realising that her family celebration was fast turning into another disaster, tried to calm things down. 'It's fine, Luke,' she said. 'Don't worry. Maybe I'll use it to buy some frames and I can hang up those family holiday pictures I got printed years ago but never did anything with. We all look so happy in them. I know just where to hang them so they'll be really visible. It's a perfect gift and really is very generous of you both. Now, where is that waiter with the knife so we can cut this delicious looking cake?'

But Luke wasn't to be distracted or placated. He pushed back his chair roughly and jumped up. 'Cyn, get your stuff,' he ordered. 'We're going.'

Kate and Lila gasped in sync and Kate could feel the tears in her eyes. It was all going wrong again and there was nothing she seemed able to do to stop it.

'Luke please stay,' she pleaded. 'It's fine, honestly. We're having a lovely evening, and I'm so grateful that you came and have made such an effort for me. Just stay and eat some cake and we can talk about happier times.'

'Sorry Mum, but no, we're going.' Luke was firm. 'I'm sorry about the cake, I'm sorry about your birthday. Lila please will you pay for the whole meal and let me know how much it came to and I'll transfer the money to your account. Now Cyn, please move!'

With that, they sped out of the restaurant leaving Kate, Lila and a rather stunned waiter staring after them. Lila reached out and slid her arm around Kate's shoulder. 'I'm so sorry Mum. Your birthday's been ruined.'

For a few seconds Kate couldn't speak. She just sat there immobile, tears streaming down her cheeks, feeling only despair that once again what she'd hoped would be a lovely time together, where they could chat and reminisce, laugh together and make new memories, had turned into a disaster.

Finally, she found the strength to speak. 'It's not your fault, love. You gave me the most beautiful gift and I will treasure it. More than that, you give me a wonderful gift every time you come to see me or spend time with me, because you're giving me your support, helping me to feel better, to make sense of your dad's death and this terrible situation with Luke. And that, darling, means more to me than anything.

'I just wish, though, that I understood what is going on with those two. They seem like totally different people since your dad died. I just don't get it.'

Lila sighed, and Kate could see that she too was struggling with her emotions. 'I know Mum, I don't understand either, but I still believe that he will come round, I honestly do. He has to.'

Kate squeezed her daughter's hand. 'I hope you're right, love, but if the events of the last six months are anything to go by, getting there isn't going to be easy.'

NINETEEN

April

Rose was sitting at the desk in her office at home, staring at her mother's bank statements with a sinking heart. She'd put off dealing with them long enough. Now she had to face the fact that there should be way more money in her mum's account than there was here. Where was all the money from the rent on Violet's house?

She'd made an appointment to see the letting agents next week – this was a matter that needed to be dealt with face to face. In the meantime, she was looking at the detail of her mother's accounts.

What the statements seemed to show was that Violet's pension had been paid into her current account, and very little else. Only a fraction of the rent the letting agents were supposed to charge showed, and there seemed to be quite a few large withdrawals. Her ISA investments also seemed to be lower than when Vernon died and Rose imagined that they should have grown as interest was added every year. Instead, the interest had been regularly withdrawn, together with a few other significant sums. But by whom? Certainly not Rose or Violet? Why on earth would her mother have needed £6,000 last year? And £4,000 the year before?

She gave her head a shake. Perhaps she was just tired. She'd looked at two potential care homes that morning for her mum and had liked one of them. While she was there, she spoke to the manager about how her mum's stay could be funded. She hadn't yet broached the subject with Violet because she wanted to be absolutely sure in her choice of home, and to have the financial side of it all sewn up. Plus she knew it was going to be a difficult conversation and she wasn't convinced she had found the right words to explain it to herself yet. Now looking at these accounts, the guilt she'd felt this morning at getting close to making this major decision for Violet had been replaced by bafflement.

Some of the money had just been withdrawn. Other sums paid to companies. Rose got out her notebook and wrote down the company names. She turned to her computer and typed them into Google. The first one came up as a cruise company. Violet had never been on a cruise. She'd barely left Rose's home in the last four years, and anyway she used to get seasick when they went on the rowing boats in the park when Rose was a little girl, so she definitely wouldn't be setting foot on board an ocean liner.

The second name came up as a luxury holiday company, offering long haul and weekend breaks to five-star resorts around the world.

'Nothing is too much trouble for us,' boasted the website. 'No detail too small to be overlooked.'

Well, Rose thought to herself, they have one detail wrong - they've taken a lot of money out of the wrong account. Why hadn't Richard noticed this? And if he had, why hadn't he done something about it?

Rose picked up her mobile phone to call them but when she looked again at her computer to find their phone number she realised that they were closed for the day. Instead she clicked on 'Email us' and composed a message asking for details of a payment for £3,000 from Violet Simmons' account on a date last year, and included her own contact details.

She was just about to repeat this with the cruise company when she noticed an email in her inbox from Richard's tennis club. A few days previously she'd remembered that he usually audited their accounts for them as a favour, so she'd found the name and email address of their treasurer, contacted her and asked if she'd like Rose to audit them this year. The treasurer, Valerie, had replied saying she'd love to take up Rose's offer but only if it wasn't too much trouble, and she was sure she felt up to it. After today she didn't feel up to anything but going to bed, but she'd offered, so she'd follow it through.

Rose sent a reply saying she'd be happy to and that she'd come to the club to pick up the books the following week. Once she'd pressed send she sat for a while staring at Valerie's message.

'The books are all ready for you now,' it had said. 'Richard always made sure we kept the financial side of things well up to date.'

Impressive, Rose thought. She was glad to see he was up to date with something.

*

Five days later Rose found herself sitting in the car in the tennis club car park. Richard had been the tennis fan, not her, so she'd very rarely come to the club. In fact, the last time had probably been Christmas drinks in the December before he was killed. He'd dragged her along, or rather he'd guilted her into going.

'Honestly Rose, my friends at the club think I've murdered you and buried you under the patio,' he'd grumbled. 'They hardly ever see you - some of them have never met you.'

Rose had been surprised at how insistent he'd been that she go. Usually he was keen to go to social events on his own, always coming up with a valid reason why she *shouldn't* go. Normally he'd persuade her that Violet couldn't be left that long on her own, or he'd be mainly with the guys so she'd be bored without another woman to talk to, but this time he was practically begging her.

'Tennis is *your* thing,' she'd argued. 'I'm rubbish at sport and that's all they talk about. I have no idea what they're going on about so I never know what to say to them.'

'You could talk about your job. Or your mum.'

Both suggestions were so ridiculous Rose had almost laughed out loud. 'Oh yes, those are absolutely riveting subjects,' she'd countered sarcastically. 'We might think that being accountants is interesting but most people go blank when they hear that word. And what is there to say about an octogenarian who's slowly losing her mind? Hardly ho-ho-ho jolly Christmas conversation.'

Richard had held up his hands and relented. 'Yes okay, you have a point there, but please don't get so worked up about it.' He'd moved over to her and tried to bundle her into a hug, but she pushed him away.

'Don't. I'm feeling annoyed with you and I want to keep this feeling because today you are being *very* annoying!'

At that he'd smiled one of his charming smiles and dropped his voice to a soothing croon, 'I know, I know, but I'm also pretty lovely and so are you, very lovely in fact, and I want to show you to all my friends at the club so they can see what a lucky chap I am.'

By the time he'd finished speaking Richard's lips were inches from her cheek and he was beginning to slide his arms around her waist. Rose had felt her anger dissipate and had melted into his embrace.

'So will you come? Pretty please? You'll make me the proudest man in all of London if you do.'

Rose, utterly disarmed but trying to sound as though she was only grudgingly agreeing, had nodded her head. 'What time and what's the dress code?'

On the night she'd worn a cherry red cocktail dress - it was Christmas after all - black patent peep-toe sandals with a medium heel, and her best smile. As she'd anticipated, people started a conversation with her but the chat quickly dried up so she spent most of the evening sitting at a table in the corner largely ignored by everyone, including Richard. He was schmoozing his way round the lounge, a few words here and there. So, this was his idea of showing her off. Rose felt furious at herself for agreeing to come.

Every now and then Richard would go to the bar and bring her a drink, but he didn't stop with her for long. This time as he ordered drinks for them, Rose noticed that there was a different woman behind the bar. This one was younger than the previous woman, probably mid 30s, petite with long blonde hair pulled into a ponytail, massive mascara rimmed blue eyes, plum coloured lipstick and a figure-hugging top showing off a curvaceous figure. She was pretty, no doubt about it, and she seemed to be giving Richard short shrift. No smiles, just business.

Then as she was pouring a glass of wine for Rose, Richard said something to her that made her burst out laughing. She looked up from the glass, smiled an enormous smile, took his hand and squeezed it. When she turned to the till to ring up the order, Richard glanced over to Rose and winked, picked up their glasses and walked across to her table.

'Cheers,' he said, sitting down.

'Cheers,' she replied, taking her wine. 'What was all that with the barmaid?'

Richard took a long drink of his lager. 'Oh nothing,' he said, putting down his glass and wiping his mouth.

'It didn't look like nothing. Whatever you said must have really tickled her. I've never seen anyone's mood change so fast. What did you say? It must have been a great joke to make her laugh like that.'

Richard shrugged his shoulders and kept a steady smile on his face. 'Oh, it was just that I'd heard she'd had a difficult day, something going on with the man in her life, and I was trying to cheer her up. I told her if she smiled I'd nip round and beat up her man for her. That's why she laughed.'

'No wonder she laughed. The thought of you beating someone up. You can barely beat an egg!'

'I know, right,' Richard agreed. 'Wouldn't want to ruffle this expensive haircut or damage my baby-soft complexion.'

Then they'd both laughed, until Richard spotted someone new arrive at the bar and went off to chat to them leaving Rose alone. She looked over to where the barmaid was standing gazing at her, a very neutral expression on her face. Rose smiled, trying to look friendly. The clipped smile the barmaid returned unnerved Rose slightly. She was remembering that look while she was sitting in the car park, trying to pluck up the nerve to go inside. Eventually she took a deep breath, opened the car door and got out.

As tennis clubs go, this one was relatively small. Richard had preferred it over the bigger, more expensive clubs because he said it was more friendly, more intimate. It had a tiny reception area which was usually only manned during the day, so in the evening new arrivals headed straight to the lounge bar. As Rose was about to open the door, she heard a voice behind her calling her name. It was Valerie, the club treasurer, who was coming out of a little office, carrying a large envelope.

'Rose, how are you?' she asked effusively, taking Rose's hands. 'It's so good to see you, so good of you to come in. Let's go into the bar, I'll get us a drink and you can tell me how things are with you. What would you like? Please have something because I'd love to sit and have a chat.'

Rose had intended to grab the books and run home, but she felt pressured into accepting Valerie's hospitality. She asked for a white wine spritzer and as she walked over to the table her hostess had indicated in the corner, she suddenly froze in her tracks.

The bar was busy and above the hubbub of everyone chatting she heard Valerie call in a loud voice: 'Sally! Sally, when you're ready, I'd like a couple of drinks.'

Rose looked over at the bar and saw that Valerie was chatting to the same barmaid Richard had made laugh at Christmas. So *she* was called Sally! The memory of the mystery message and the letter 'S' with a kiss flashed into her mind and she felt her heart rate climb. Was this the 'S' who had written that message?

When Valerie arrived with the drinks, Rose was still shaking and could only manage to smile her thanks. Her hostess didn't seem to notice anything was wrong with her as she settled into her chair.

'So Rose, tell me how are you? Richard's death was such a shock, I can't imagine how you're dealing with it.'

It was a question that Rose hated being asked. Kate and Pascalle too. Absolutely hated it, because the truthful answer was, 'How do you think I'm doing? My husband is dead, I have no future, my nerves are in tatters, I only have one emotion - devastation - and I feel like the loneliest person in the world.' That was what Rose *really* wanted to say, but she'd been asked the question so many times, she'd developed a stock and more diplomatic reply.

'Yes, yes it was a massive shock. But I'm okay, thank you. I'm doing as well as one would in the circumstances. Taking each day as it comes. Putting one foot in front of the other...'

Valerie nodded and leaned a little closer to Rose. 'It must be so difficult,' she sympathised. 'And how is your mum? She has dementia, doesn't she? I remember Richard telling us about her and how hard it was for you to get away especially in the evenings, because you are her carer.'

Rose was taken aback with this statement. She'd never thought of herself in that role, they'd never described her as such and there was no formal arrangement. She was just Rose looking out for her mum. She hesitated before replying.

'Em, yes, well I suppose you could describe me as such. Although before Richard died she wasn't quite as bad as she is now. His death has had a major effect on her and her mind has got worse in the last few months.'

Valerie was all sympathy. 'Oh, you poor thing. Does she have someone with her tonight?'

Rose shook her head. 'No, so I mustn't be too long. I left her watching her favourite programmes on the TV and she'll get upset when they finish and she notices I'm not there.'

'Of course,' said Valerie, and she picked up the envelope that she'd laid on the table and handed it to Rose. 'Here are the books and the relevant information. It should all be there - Richard had us well trained! We are so grateful to you for offering to do this. Auditors are expensive and small clubs like ours need to save all the money we can.'

Rose took the envelope, stood up and started walking towards the door, with Valerie following behind her. Just as she got to the door, Rose glanced over towards the bar and saw Sally standing there, glaring at her.

Rose turned to Valerie. 'While I'm here, can I ask you something? Do you have anyone at the club with the letter S as their first name initial? I only ask because I was looking through that lovely remembrance book the club sent me – so thoughtful – and trying to picture the faces of everyone who signed it and there was one signature I couldn't read. It looked as though it began with an 'S' and was probably a woman's handwriting.'

Valerie looked thoughtful. 'Gosh we have so many members, but it was really only the ones who knew Richard well who signed the book. Let me think…we do have a Sheila, but I don't think it would be her because she tends to play during the day and Richard usually came in the evenings. Oh, it could be Sonia. She always used to have a laugh and a joke with Richard. We celebrated her 90th birthday just last week and she was saying how much more fun it would have been if he'd been there.'

180

Rose smiled. 'Yes I imagine it would have been. He always had a way with the older woman. Did I hear you calling the barmaid Sally earlier? Could it have been her?'

'Yes, yes of course,' said Valerie. 'How silly of me. I was only thinking of players. Yes, Sally and our other barmaid Barbara were so upset when Richard died. He was always teasing them and making them laugh. It probably was her. You can ask her if you like.'

'Oh no, I won't bother her, she looks busy. I just wondered. Wanted to put a face to all the names in the book. Well, I must go, I'll bring these back in a few weeks.'

'That would be so generous of you, but if you'd prefer I can arrange to have them collected once you're finished,' suggested Valerie. 'It would be the least we can do. Especially with your mum needing you to be with her virtually all the time.'

'I do go out!' Roses shot back, then realised she'd been rude and softened her voice. 'I'm sorry Valerie, I shouldn't have spoken like that. Whatever impression Richard gave you, I'm not at home constantly, and if I know I'm going to be a while I arrange for a sitter for Mum. Anyway, that spritzer slipped down rather well. Maybe when I return the books I'll bring my friend Kate Latimer. She's a member here I believe. We could have a drink together.'

'Ah Kate. Yes, of course I know her,' said Valerie. 'I hadn't realised that you two were friends. You'd both be very welcome. Just let me know when you're dropping by and I'll make it my business to be here.'

As the two women parted company and Rose walked back to her car, she kept thinking about the barmaid's glare and the message in the book. Could there a simple, innocent explanation for both of them or was Rose's view of the life she'd lead for the last 30 years about to be completely shattered forever?

TWENTY

April

That Friday Rose and Kate were sitting in the cafe after yoga waiting for Pascalle. She hadn't been to the class but had texted to say she was going to join them for a coffee. Kate had just been mulling over in her mind what could have kept Pascalle away from yoga when suddenly Rose asked her if she knew the barmaid at the tennis club. Kate felt herself stiffen. Where was this conversation going to go?

'Which one? I think there are two or three working on a shift system?' she asked.

'The one who was there the other evening was called Sally. Do you know her?'

Panic rose within Kate and she hoped it wasn't obvious to her friend. She'd heard the stories about Richard and Sally, but didn't know for sure if they were true, and she certainly didn't want to say anything that would hurt her friend. So she opted for an evasive, 'Sorry Rose, I have seen her but I don't really *know* many people there. I've only been a social member in the past few years – it's much cheaper than a full tennis membership – so I don't go that often. To be honest, I didn't know Richard either. I heard about his accident and that everyone was shocked because he was a regular, but I'd never met him. Anyway, why do you ask?'

'Oh, she just looked at me a bit funny as I left the bar, that's all,' recalled Rose. 'There was nothing I can put my finger on, it was more something in her manner – made me feel a bit uneasy. Why would she look at me that way when we don't know each other? Will you come to the club with me when I take the books back next Tuesday? I'll get a sitter for Mum and we can have a drink at the bar and you can tell me if I'm going mad.'

Oh my God, thought Kate, trying to work out what to do next. If she said no, Rose would probably go anyway and there was a chance she'd speak to someone there about Sally and they might hint at the rumours. But if Kate went with her, then at least she could try to steer her away from the gossips and deflect her interest in Sally. This was such a dilemma. She didn't want her friend to be hurt. And equally, she didn't want to lie to her. Kate could see that Rose was puzzled by her hesitation, so in the end she felt she had no choice but to say, 'Of course, I'd be happy to. I can't have you going on your own.'

Just then, much to Kate's immense relief, Pascalle came rushing up to their table, all of a fluster. 'Ladies, ladies, oh my goodness, I have something to tell you! C'est terrible. *Terrible*!'

While Pascalle settled herself at the table and Rose tried to calm her down, Kate got her a coffee. They had both become used to Pascalle's Gallic dramas, but there was something in her eyes that told them that this time the drama was serious. Finally, with a strong coffee in front of her, Pascalle took and deep breath and told them what had happened.

'It's my daughter, Justine. The one who lives here,' she started. 'She came to visit yesterday and I knew something was bothering her the moment she walked through the door. I was so worried something had happened to my little Stefan. Was he hurt? Or was it her husband Peter? And then I thought oh no, is something terrible going on with my Justine? Was she ill?

'She kept saying, no, no nothing like that. Then she sat down at the kitchen table and gave this great long sigh. I was so worried! She looked at me and said, "Maman, you're right in that I do have something difficult to say".

'Ladies,' continued Pascalle, grabbing each of her friends by the hand, 'at her words my heart dropped to my feet. I was so afraid. And then she said, "We're moving Mum. Away. To the countryside".'

Pascalle stopped, tears filled her eyes, and she shook her head so sadly. 'They're leaving me,' she whispered. 'Ma chère Justine et mon très chèr Stefan. How can they leave?' Then one by one, the tears dropped into her undrunk coffee.

Kate and Rose looked at each other, as though trying to work out how best to console their friend who was obviously devastated.

'Oh Pascalle, that is awful news,' said Kate. 'But maybe they're not going too far away, maybe you could still see them regularly.'

Pascalle took a small, embroidered hankie from her pocket, sniffed and wiped her eyes.

'No,' she said sorrowfully. 'I don't think that will be possible. They're moving to Yorkshire. Peter's company is opening a new office there and they've offered their London employees the opportunity of relocating. They get a good financial deal, and the company also helps them to find a house. And of course, property there is so much cheaper than here so they'll be able to afford a bigger house with a lovely garden for little Steffie.

'I can see why it's so appealing to them. The air is cleaner there and it will be easy to get into the beautiful countryside. They'll be able to afford to have another child, so everything for them is right. But sadly, not for me…' and as her voice tailed off the tears began again.

'Yorkshire's not *that* far. You can visit often,' suggested Rose, hopefully. 'With one of those senior railcards it won't cost much either.'

'But it won't be every day. I won't be able to look after Steffie twice a week as I do now. He won't be close enough to come for tea or Grandmaman sleepovers. No, it just won't be the same. And wait, ladies, there's more!'

Kate flashed Rose a look of alarm. 'More?' they chorused.

'Yes more. They want me to go to Yorkshire with them!' At that Pascalle broke into full blown sobs.

Now it was Kate and Rose's turn to look devastated. Kate had only known Pascalle a short time, but their shared experiences meant she was as dear to her, and she was sure to Rose, as a lifelong friend. Neither wanted to ask the obvious question. Finally Kate haltingly broke the silence, 'Are you going to go?'

Pascalle sighed, freed her hands from the caring hold of her two friends, sat back in her chair and said quietly, 'Je ne sais pas, mes chères. I really don't know.'

'What would it involve for you?' asked Rose. 'I mean, where would you live for a start? Justine and Peter will have the relocation package from his work but you wouldn't.'

Pascalle shrugged her shoulders. 'Justine says she has it all worked out. They'd buy a house with an annexe or with enough land to build me a granny cottage. If I sold my house here, I'd have enough money to invest in the property with them so she envisages my space being quite sizeable, not just a little shed at the end of the garden. I'd be near them, able to see Stefan every day, take him to school, and help look after any new baby if they had one and Justine decided to go back to work. I'd be close to them all, but I'd still have my own space.'

'It sounds as though Justine definitely has done her homework,' said Rose, 'but I'm not hearing a great deal of enthusiasm in your voice for the idea.'

Pascalle threw her arms in the air in a typical French gesture of despair. 'I truly don't know what to think or what to do. It all sounds very neat and thought out, and it would be lovely to be that close to my beloved Steffie every day. If there was a new baby, it would be wonderful to see it all the time, too. And Yorkshire looks beautiful. I've never been there but I Googled some pictures of the area they're thinking of moving to and it seems gorgeous. Judging by the houses for sale on Rightmove, we'd definitely be able to afford a big property with plenty of space for me. We could do lots of family things, and I'd be near my Justine, which is so important to me because I don't often see my other daughter Evie.

'But…and this is a very big but, where am I in all of this? Where is Pascalle? Where are my needs and wants? I spent months nursing Trevor and I don't regret a single day of that - and I'd happily do it all again if I had to - but I lost *me* during that time. My sense of fun, adventure, I stopped doing all the things I loved doing like painting and crafting. I could barely shower let alone get my hair done or wear make up or shop for new clothes. I became dull, dull, dull!'

'You have us now,' said Rose.

'Yes, I do, and that's the point,' said Pascalle, becoming more animated. 'I do have both of you, and in the short time that we've been friends you've helped me so much. It's thanks to you that I'm now facing up to Trevor's death, and I can see that there is still a life for me. You've helped me find the old Pascalle again. The woman my daughter describes as "my hippy dippy mum". She's just starting to come to the fore, just started to craft and paint again, and I don't want to lose her. If I go to live in Yorkshire and do all those things to help Justine, I'm afraid she'll disappear forever.'

'You'd make new friends,' suggested Kate. 'You're very sociable and lovely and you'll have new friends in no time. They have a thriving craft industry in that part of the world. You might find you fit right in.'

Pascalle shook her head. 'Maybe that's the problem. Maybe I don't want to "fit in". Maybe I want to be free to be exactly me while I have the health and energy to do it. Plus, I have all the friends I need and could ever want sitting here, at this table.'

At Pascalle's words Kate felt such a rush of emotion for her, for all of them, for the great friends they'd become so quickly. She felt she could tell them almost anything, talk to them about most things, and rather than judge, they'd do what they could to help. She could see that would be a very hard thing to give up, and she felt her own devastation that the trio could be broken up if Pascalle did move. Still it wasn't her decision.

'So, what are you going to do?' she asked.

Pascalle shrugged again. 'I will do as Justine has suggested and I'll go up to Yorkshire with them in a couple of weekends time to see the place they want to move to and look round some properties with them, and I'll see how I feel about it. Then I will pray to God, to Trevor and to my papa Mattieu to help me decide. Hopefully all three of them working together will lead me to the right decision.'

At that Pascalle managed a wry smile, but Kate could see that behind her eyes lay worry and fear. She was feeling some fear of her own. Would their little trio soon be broken up, just when she needed it most? And would she be the cause of the pain that might push one of them away for good?

TWENTY-ONE

May

Rose had completed the tennis club books and everything
seemed in order. Unlike with her mother's accounts. The
holiday companies had responded by email. Their records
showed that holidays had been booked in the name of
Richard Bud and money had been paid for by bank transfer
from Violet Simmons accounts. Rose read the messages
and felt her heart rate rising and her hands shaking. She
took some enormous deep breaths to try and control herself.
She couldn't think about it now. The concept of the mystery
'S', Richard's secret holidays and his embezzling her
mother's money was just too enormous and overwhelming
to contemplate. She'd think about all of that later. She

turned her thoughts to a more pressing situation. The care homes she'd visited for her mother wouldn't wait forever so she had to make a decision soon.

Adding to her worry was the fact that she had yet to broach the subject of a home with her mother. To be honest, she didn't really know how to do it. Violet was seldom lucid these days. She was mainly very angry and sharp with Rose, and left taps, lights and cooker rings on and unattended almost every day. There never seemed to be the right moment, and Rose didn't feel confident that she had the appropriate words to explain her plan. She'd made an appointment with her GP for next week in the hope that he might be able to help her.

On the Tuesday evening, Rose picked Kate up from her home and they both drove to the tennis club where she'd arranged to meet Valerie and return the accounts books. Rose felt nervous and drove in silence, listening quietly while Kate chattered away about her busy day at work, and how a quiet drink might be just the thing she needed.

'The last time I was out for the evening was my birthday dinner, and I can't think about how that ended without shivering,' she told Rose. 'I'm hoping that tonight will be altogether more pleasant.'

Rose glanced over at her.

'I know you're worried about that barmaid,' Kate sympathised, appearing to sense her friend's tension. 'I'm sure it was nothing and we'll be able to just have a quiet drink and a good chat.'

They drove into the club car park and Rose pulled into a parking space, turned off the engine and then sat very still. Kate was halfway out the door when she noticed her friend wasn't moving. She looked across at her and smiled.

'You're nervous. Don't worry, I'm here.'

Rose cleared her throat and kept looking out of the car windscreen for so long that Kate sat back inside the car again and closed the door. Finally Rose spoke.

'I haven't been entirely truthful with you Kate, and I'm sorry about that. I've realised that tonight might become embarrassing for you so it's best that I tell you why I'm really concerned about Sally and then you can decide if you still want to come with me.'

'Rose you're sounding very odd and I'm a little bit nervous now too. But I do still want to help you, so yes, I think you should tell me everything.'

Rose nodded her head and turned to face her friend.

'I suppose you got cards and other messages of support after Jason died. Did you look at them all?'

'Oh God we got loads. Letters and cards. I read them all. I put the cards up all round the living room. After a couple of weeks I couldn't stand to see them any more so I put them in a box in the loft, out of sight. Why?'

'I got some too, not as many as you I imagine, but I couldn't face looking at them at the time, so I put them in a box and forgot about them until a few months ago when I came across them while I was tidying. At the bottom of the box was a small memory book with messages from Richard's friends at the tennis club.'

'That sounds nice,' interjected Kate. 'What was wrong with that?'

'It wasn't the book, Kate, it was one of the messages. Oh my God, I can hardly bring myself to say it.'

'Just take a deep breath and take your time. What did it say?'

Rose paused, took another breath and continued. 'It was in a woman's handwriting, and it said: "My darling R. I'll never stop loving you." It was signed just with the initial 'S' and a kiss. Kate, I'm terrified that the S could be Sally the barmaid?'

Rose saw Kate's eyes open in shock. 'Ah,' she said.

Rose felt the blood drain from her face and she began to shake. Kate leaned over and put her arm around her friend.

'Well, yes, I suppose it could be Sally the barmaid. But there must be other women with that initial at the club.'

'Yes, there are, I asked Valerie, but they're both at least 20 years older than Richard and while older women loved him, he wouldn't have been attracted to them.'

'So you think this S was having an affair with him?'

'Yes! I mean what else could it mean?'

'It could mean lots of things, Rose. People use the word love all the time when they're not actually in romantic love. They could just have loved playing tennis with him.'

'Oh, come on Kate, of course it means romantic love! Hell, I really hope it doesn't, but I'm so afraid that it does.'

'If Sally the barmaid is the S it would certainly explain why she was so off with you last time you were here.' Kate let out a long sigh. 'Gosh, Rose, this is a can of worms.'

'I know,' Rose acknowledged. 'And I've dragged you into it now and I'm so sorry. I haven't known what to do about it, haven't been able to talk about any of this even to you and Pascalle. I've been so afraid. Look, I don't know what's going to happen in there, so if you want to go home now just say and I'll drive you and come back alone with the books.'

'Are you planning on speaking to Sally?'

'Yes, I am. It might sound mad, but I've had this on my mind since just after Christmas, wondering who this could be, what it could mean, and I need to get to the bottom of it now. You see Kate, if he was seeing this Sally it makes sense of some of the questions I've had since he was killed. Why was he on that road when he should have been 10 miles in the other direction, and why was he driving at that time when he should have been sitting in a restaurant having dinner with his golf mates? Was he with her? Plus it would explain some of the strange withdrawals he made from my mother's bank accounts. Much as it absolutely kills me to think of him having an affair, I just need to know. I need some answers.'

Rose noticed that Kate too had grown pale.

'Yes I can understand that you do,' Kate nodded as though she was weighing things up in her mind. Then she looked Rose straight in the eye as she said, 'If what you fear is true, then this next hour is not going to be a pleasant one. But I agree it will be best to find out one way or the other. And don't worry I'm not going anywhere except with you.'

'Oh, thank you Kate,' said Rose, slumping with relief. 'I know this is turning out to be more than you bargained for, but I'm so glad you're going to be with me. Right, let's go before I change my mind.'

Rose opened the door and stepped unsteadily out onto the tarmac. 'My legs are shaking.'

'Just grab the accounts books from the back, I'm on my way round to your side.'

Kate took Rose's arm and together they walked slowly into the club reception and made their way to the lounge bar area. As Rose scanned the room looking for Valerie, she saw Sally standing behind the bar. At first the barmaid's face registered surprise, then seemed to harden.

'Rose!' called Valerie walking towards her. 'And of course Kate. So lovely to see you both. Come have a seat over here.'

Valerie led them to an empty table right by the bar and took their drinks orders as they sat down. All the while Rose was looking under her eyelashes towards Sally, whose face was by now thunderous.

'She doesn't look very happy to see you,' Kate whispered to Rose.

'I know,' Rose whispered back. 'Let's just have this drink with Valerie and I'll go and speak to Sally on the way out. I hope my courage lasts that long.'

Just then Valerie returned with a glass of white wine for each of them and a gin and tonic for herself. Rose patted the envelope containing the books.

'Everything was in order,' she managed to say more brightly than she felt. 'Well done. Looks like the club is thriving.'

Valerie looked very pleased at Rose's comments and went on to talk about the committee's plans, how they were going to spruce up the dressing rooms and bar area, and their bigger ideas to rework some underused the land surrounding the club to create more courts. All the while Sally was sitting on a stool behind the bar glaring at Rose.

The three women finished their drinks and Rose signalled to Kate that they should be going. There were no customers around, so as they were walking towards the door Rose seized her chance, took a detour over to the bar and stood in front of Sally. Desperately trying to contain her nerves, she said quietly, 'Hi, I believe you're Sally. I notice you keep looking over at me with a scowl on your face. Given that I don't know you, I don't understand why that would be. Have I done something to offend you?'

Sally's face flushed and Rose noticed that her hands had started to shake. 'I don't know what you mean,' the barmaid shot back.

'Well, I've been in here twice in the last couple of weeks and both times I've had the feeling that if you could fell me with a glance I'd be prostrate on the floor by now. I can't imagine what I could have done to provoke such a reaction, but there's obviously something about me that bothers you, and I'd like to know what it is.'

Rose could feel her whole body shaking and it was taking all her strength to keep her voice under control. As she spoke, she looked directly into Sally's face, refusing to break eye contact. Sally stared back, a look of defiance spreading over her face. 'I think you must be imagining things.' At that she turned and walked away through a door in the back corner of the bar.

'Everything okay?' interjected Valerie who'd seen Rose speaking to Sally.

'Yes, yes,' replied Rose, turning around and fixing a smile on her face. 'I was just asking the name of the wine we had. It was very nice.'

The white lie seemed to satisfy Valerie who ushered Rose and Kate towards the front door of the club and out into the car park, all the time reiterating her thanks.

'I hope things go well with your mum,' she said, 'and if you ever fancy dropping by for a drink you'd be most welcome. There's bound to be someone here who'd have known Richard and will take care of you. And Kate, please come and see us more. Safe home.'

With that Valerie walked back inside the club and Kate turned to Rose.

'Did you ask her if she was "S"?'

'No, I couldn't find the right words. I couldn't just come out and ask, "were you having an affair with my husband?" could I?' said Rose looking deflated and disappointed with herself.

'Why not?'

'I panicked. Instead, I asked her why she had been glaring at me, I thought that might give me an in, but she just turned and walked away.'

Kate brought her hands up to cover her mouth, thought for a long few seconds, and then turned to her friend.

'Okay, okay. Rose please don't hate me for this, but *I* haven't been entirely truthful with *you*.' Kate let out a sigh, then seem to muster some courage before continuing. 'I have heard some gossip involving Richard and Sally.'

Panic shot across Rose's face and her heart started to race.

'What are you talking about Kate? Do you know something?'

Slowly Kate nodded. 'I don't know anything for sure, but I've heard rumours, strong rumours. I'm so sorry Rose. I couldn't say anything to you before because I don't know how true any of it is, but I'd say the way that woman has been glaring at you makes me think there is some foundation to the gossip. I think you should go back in, ask to speak to Sally somewhere private and make her tell you.'

Rose couldn't believe what she was hearing. There had been rumours, and Kate, her friend, knew about them and didn't say anything. She was so confused, her knees were buckling and her body was shaking.

'Tell me what?' she asked, her voice hoarse with anxiety.

'Tell you about her and Richard.'

TWENTY-TWO

A few minutes later

Sally and Richard? Rose was distraught at the very thought of it. She'd suspected this for months but now she was confronted with it, she couldn't take it in. What was more, one of her friends, one of only two people she trusted, had been hiding it from her.

Kate was still holding Rose's hands, and asking, 'Are you ready?'

'Ready? No, I'm not ready. I feel sick and my legs are like jelly. Kate I don't understand. Why have you been keeping this from me all these months?'

'Not keeping it from you, Rose, just not saying anything, which I admit is still bad. But I barely knew you, or Richard or Sally, and for all I knew the stories I'd heard could have been idle tennis club gossip. I mean you always talk about how much Richard loved you and cared for you. Why would I believe them rather than you? Look, I'm here for you now, if you still want me to be. Lean on me. It'll help to steady you.'

Rose felt her body weight sag over towards Kate. To be honest at this precise moment she hardly knew what to think about Kate. But one thing she was sure about, she wasn't going home until she'd spoken to Sally and discovered the truth behind the message and those rumours.

'Ok Kate, I am annoyed with you, but I do need to speak to Sally now, and it would help me to have someone with me. If you're okay to come with me, I'd appreciate it.'

Kate offered her arm to Rose again for support, and the women made their way back into the club and into the lounge bar. As they walked, they made a plan that if Valerie spotted them they'd pretend that Kate had left something behind so that she could go and search while Rose tackled the barmaid.

Fortunately, Valerie was nowhere to be seen, but there was no-one behind the bar. Kate deposited an unsteady Rose on a bar stool while she called out for service. Sally appeared from the door at the back of the bar, took one look at Kate then Rose and stopped in her tracks, a shocked expression on her face. Kate leaned over the bar and said very quietly to her, 'My friend Rose needs to speak to you now please. Where can we go that's private?'

Sally started to shake her head as though she was about to refuse when Kate added, 'Or we can do it here. Either way, it's going to happen.'

Sally pursed her mouth, frowned and reluctantly nodded her head towards the doorway she'd just come through.

'Behind that door is the office. There's a side entrance to it in the corridor. Come in that way,' she said.

Kate nodded, collected Rose from her bar stool and they headed along the corridor to hear what Sally was going to say.

*

The office was small, with giant boxes of crisps and nuts piled against one wall, and a desk with two office chairs tucked under it along another. On the desk were some empty mugs indicating that this was where the staff popped in for a cup of tea when the bar wasn't busy. Sally stood near the doorway which led to the bar as Rose and Kate walked in from the corridor as instructed. With all three in the room, there wasn't much space. Sally indicated for Rose and Kate to sit on the two chairs, while she stayed standing where she was.

'It's only me on tonight,' she explained brusquely, 'so I need to keep an eye on the bar.' She folded her arms across her chest defiantly. 'So, what is it that you want to say?'

Rose felt her stomach turn over and her heart race so much she could barely breathe, but she managed to get out, 'It's more what you're going to tell us.'

Even she was amazed at how calm she sounded when her insides were churning and her mind was in turmoil. She could barely take in that she, Rose Bud, who'd always had a life that followed the straight and narrow, achieving but hardly adventurous, non-confrontational and definitely undramatic, should be sitting in the back room of a tennis club bar about to hear something that she knew was going to break her heart. Yet somehow she was keeping her voice steady. Once she'd got the words out, she took a deep breath, sat up straight and waited.

Sally folded her arms tighter to herself and looked towards the wall, avoiding any eye contact with Rose or Kate.

'I loved him,' Sally said, almost in a whisper. 'Richard I mean. I loved him.'

The words fell on Rose with all the weight of a cascade of heavy rocks. Her head spun and she thought she was going to faint. She took a deep breath, cleared her throat and replied, 'Lots of people loved him.' Her whole body braced as if for physical impact.

Sally dragged her eyes away from the wall and looked first at Kate and then at Rose. 'Not the way I loved him. And what's more he loved me.'

'Don't be ridiculous,' snapped Rose.

'Ridiculous?' Sally laughed. 'I'm not the one who's ridiculous. If you want to see ridiculous, just have a look in the mirror. You believed that he loved you? All you were to him was money, fancy holidays and a boring life.'

Kate gasped and turned to see Rose flinch as though each word was a bullet shooting straight into her heart. But Rose was determined to stay dignified and calm.

'How dare you!' she said. 'You knew nothing about Richard. He was *my* husband and he loved *me*. Only me.'

Sally smirked and shook her head again. Then she looked very long and very hard at Rose. 'Actually, I feel sorry for you, because I can see in your face that you believe that to be true. And I feel sad for you because the truth is you didn't know him at all.'

Rose made as though to stand up and leave, get out of this place, away from this horrible, horrible woman who was spouting lies about her Richard. Why on earth had she thought it was a good idea to confront her? Why hadn't she just gone home and forgotten all about it? Her mind was still racing when she realised that the strength had gone from her legs. She couldn't walk, couldn't even move. All she could do was sink into the back of her chair, breathing heavily, sweat breaking out on her brow, and try to clasp her hands together to stop them shaking.

Kate reached over to her. 'Rose, I think you've heard enough. Let's go home.'

But Rose shook her head, because deep inside she knew this was all true. She sat there defeated as Kate tried to deflect the barmaid.

'You don't know what you're talking about. Richard was devoted to Rose.'

'That's where you're completely wrong,' Sally countered. 'I know a lot, and top of the list of the things I know is that Richard was never devoted to Rose. In fact, he was the complete opposite. Just answer me this question - Rose have you looked at your mother's bank statements yet? Yes, I can see from your eyes that you have. You'll have noticed that there's quite a bit of money missing. Richard took that. He used the money to take us on a cruise. For 10 days. Remember the series of conferences he said he had to attend as part of his induction at work? Well, there were no conferences. He was with me. In the Caribbean.'

Sally seemed to have warmed to her subject now. Without waiting for any answers, she unfolded her arms, leaned on the desk and continued.

'Then there was the long weekend we had in a luxury hotel in New York. Flew business class too, of course. All thanks to your mother. I also imagine that there's not quite as much money as you'd expect coming into her account from the rental of her house. That's because most of it went on rent for *my* flat. That money never touched the sides of your mother's account.'

Rose felt catatonic with shock. She couldn't move, think, speak. She felt she might pass out. Yes, she'd had her suspicions about him and another woman, but the rest of it was utterly unbelievable…and yet, Sally was right about the bank statements. Money *was* missing. There *were* big payments to holiday companies. She could feel Kate's hand on her arm, urging her to stand up, to leave, to get them both out of this nightmare, but she knew she had to stay and hear everything. With a great effort of will she eventually managed to stutter, 'But why? You already had a man. He told me.'

Sally thought for a moment and then smiled. 'Ah yes, that night he brought you to the club for Christmas drinks. I was in a foul mood because he'd persuaded you to come, sort of parade you in front of me - and vice versa, I suppose. His little game - to see both his women together, with one having absolutely no idea about the other. I imagine it gave him a cheap thrill. He said he'd told you he was trying to cheer me up because I was having man trouble. He didn't tell you that the man I was having trouble with was him.'

Suddenly Rose found strength from somewhere, put both hands on the table and pushed herself up to standing. She was considerably taller than Sally and noticing that made her feel powerful, back in control.

'I've heard enough,' she said. 'Come on Kate, let's go. This woman is a fantasist and I won't let her say any more ridiculous things about Richard.'

As Kate stood up and the two women gathered their things to go, Sally shrugged her shoulders and leaned on the doorway.

'On you go, that's fine with me. But you know in your heart that everything I've said is true. Richard was the fantasist, the liar, and if you go now you'll never know how big a liar he was. You'll never know how your marriage, in fact your whole life is built on one big fat lie.'

Rose stopped and felt tears rush into her eyes. She blinked hard to stop them from falling, feeling desperate to get away, but also knowing if there was more, she had to hear it, otherwise the imagining what it could be, would gnaw away at her for the rest of her life. So, she turned, sat down slowly, took out a paper hanky, wiped her eyes, and calmly and quietly said, 'You have my attention. Go on.'

*

Sally turned and walked into the bar, returning with a stool. She put it down opposite Rose, sat on it, and began in a softer, gentler voice.

'You wanted children, am I right?' she asked.

'What's that got to do with you?' Rose countered.

'Did you ever go for tests to find out why you never got pregnant?'

'How is that your business? That was way before Richard met you.'

'Just answer,' Sally urged. The harshness and ferocity had gone from her voice, as though she could see how hurt Rose was, and with more to come, wanted it to land gently.

'No, no, we didn't go for tests. Richard said there was no point. We were happy as we were, just the two of us, and we could still have a wonderful life. He said children would complicate matters. He convinced me not to have tests.'

Rose stopped. She slowly lowered her eyes from Sally to the desk in front of her, as though reliving the heart-breaking moment she gave in to Richard. 'But I never stopped longing,' she said quietly as though to herself. 'Hoping for a miracle.'

Sally slowly shook her head. 'Well, it would have taken a miracle, or a failure of modern medicine, for your dream to come true,' she said.

Kate interjected, 'What on earth do you mean?'

Sally looked at her and then back at Rose. 'Exactly what I said. Rose, just after you and Richard were married, he had a vasectomy.'

Kate's hands flew to her mouth in shock and Rose felt a rushing in her ears as though she was going to pass out. What was this woman talking about? Richard would never do such a thing to her. A vasectomy?

Kate spoke first. 'Sally what you're saying is wicked and enormously hurtful. I hope you're sure of your facts.'

'Oh, I'm sure alright,' the barmaid replied. 'I discovered it about three years ago. I thought I was pregnant. One part of me was devastated because I didn't think Richard would leave you - you and your mother were his cash cows after all - so I knew I'd have to bring up a baby on my own. But another part felt hopeful - perhaps the prospect of becoming a father would be the push that would make him walk away from you, force him to rethink his life, inspire him to change, to come to me. I was so nervous telling him because I didn't know how he'd react.'

'What did he say?' asked Kate.

'Nothing. He didn't say anything. He just laughed. Laughed and laughed. When I asked him what was so funny, he said I couldn't be pregnant, or if I was it was someone else's and he wasn't going to be responsible for another man's child.

'I was so hurt but furious, too, because he was being so cruel. Then he explained that it couldn't be his because he'd had a vasectomy. He told me that he'd never wanted children, but he knew you were desperate for them. Children to him would have meant the end of his lovely life, where everything revolved around him, where the money flowed in because you worked so hard and he did the absolute minimum. He seemed almost proud of it. You know this is true, Rose, don't you? You know he never really contributed much.'

Rose just nodded her head. She felt utterly defeated. Stricken. Because she knew every word Sally said was true.

'He decided not to take any risks and a few weeks after you were married, he had the snip. Then over the course of the next few years he had to do an enormous charm offensive to persuade you that neither of you should have tests. Instead, he painted this wonderful picture of just the two of you, happy with each other, having the best life together, funded mainly by you. And you fell for it, Rose.'

Sally paused, picked up a can of coke that was sitting on the side and took a sip. When she finished she put the can down, stood up and walked around behind the stool.

'I know all of this Rose because he kept me dangling for years with promises to leave you. Over time I came to realise that he never would, but I kept hoping. Then after your father died and he began looking after your mother's financial affairs, he realised that he had a very lucrative seam of money at his disposal. Probably that was why he offered in the first place. So he set me up in a rather lovely flat in a much nicer area than I could have afforded on my own, and he treated me to expensive meals in town and luxury holidays abroad. Typical Richard, he was treating me, but he was also treating himself. He loved luxury and it made him feel great to be able to splash cash around - even better that wasn't his.'

Sally stopped and thought for a moment. 'If he hadn't come to see me that night, he'd still be here, bleeding your mother dry.'

It took a moment for Rose to register what Sally had said. She was so battered down by the night's revelations that she was barely processing anything now. Had she heard the barmaid correctly?

'So he'd been with you that night?' she asked weakly.

Sally stood tall, shook her hair back and took a deep breath, as though preparing to deliver the hammer blow.

'Yes, he was with me. His work hadn't been going brilliantly. People there had rumbled that he wasn't as effective as they'd hoped. He'd basically been hauled in by his boss and told he had to buck his ideas up or he'd be out. Richard was incandescent. He couldn't tell you - you thought everything in that particular garden was rosy - so he came to me. He vented, ranted, threw a few ornaments. I did my best to calm him down but he was still pretty het up when he left. Oh God....'

Sally suddenly buckled, lost her self-control and tears started to flow down her cheeks. 'I should never have let him get in that car,' she sobbed. 'I'll never forgive myself for that. You see Rose, I really did love him.'

The silence in the room was broken only by Sally's sobs. After what seemed like an eternity, Kate put her arm under her friend's elbow and said, 'Come on now Rose. Come home. You've heard enough.'

The two women rose unsteadily to their feet, and Kate guided Rose out of the room, down the corridor and out into the car park. Rose was ashen faced and silent.

When they got to the car, Kate took Rose's handbag, found her car keys and guided her into the passenger seat. Kate got in the driver's side and said, 'I'll drive. We'll go to mine. We'll have a cup of tea, or maybe something stronger. Then we'll think about what to do next.'

Next? How could there be a next for Rose? She'd always suspected she loved Richard more than he loved her, but she had never, ever thought he'd betray her in this way. For her, there could be no next.

TWENTY-THREE

Later that same night

Rose's hands shook when she took the mug of tea laced with brandy from Kate. They were both sitting in Kate's kitchen. Rose hadn't said a word since they'd left the tennis club, she'd just sat in the passenger seat and sobbed as though her heart was breaking. She'd allowed Kate to steer her from the car into the kitchen and position her on one of the kitchen chairs with a giant box of man-sized tissues in front of her.

'I have dozens of these boxes all around the house,' explained Kate. 'I find I need them quite often.'

Rose pulled a handful of tissues from the box and blew her nose hard. She'd been crying so much her nose was swollen and she could barely breathe. 'I'm so sorry Kate, that you had to hear all of that.' Then she stopped and thought for a moment. 'But then I guess you knew quite a bit of it already. I can't imagine what you were thinking about me, going on about my lovely husband Richard, and all the while you knew he was having an affair.'

Embarrassment and guilt swept through Kate. Why hadn't she told Rose, prepared her gently? But then she had no idea if the gossip was true, and she had never seen Rose and Richard together to work out which was the real situation. On top of that it didn't seem right for her to be revealing something this big to Rose, someone she really didn't know that well. But still she could see betrayal in her friend's eyes, and not just from what Richard had done to her.

'Rose, I'm the one who's sorry. I didn't say anything because I didn't *know* anything. It was all gossip. But you have every right to feel angry with me.'

Rose allowed a smile to pass over her lips as she spoke, her voice still quivering with emotion.

'I don't really know what to think at the moment. But one thing I'm sure of is that I'm sorry you had to hear all that horrible, sordid, venomous stuff that woman was spouting. It wasn't your business and I apologise for dragging you into that, and for you having to have me here…in this state.

If you could give me just another few minutes, I'll finish this tea, pull myself together and get back home to Mum.'

Kate sat down opposite Rose. 'I say again that you have nothing to be sorry for, and I hope one day you'll be able to forgive me because the fact that we've experienced something very similar gives us a special insight into how we each feel. Just as we do with Pascalle. And that special insight fast tracks a friendship.

'I'm here to help you just as much as someone you've known for years. So don't worry or think you're imposing on me because you're not. Don't imagine what happened tonight will push me away because it won't. We all have our secrets, Rose, or things about our husbands we may not want others to know. Some small, some bigger.'

Kate paused and smiled. 'What we heard tonight fits into the bigger category, I'd say, but the point now is what to do next. Let's not go into whether what she said is true or not, let's just get you through tonight. Now, you're not in the right emotional state to go home to your mum. Will the sitter do a night shift?'

Rose shook her head. 'I'm afraid not. She's just a neighbour that Mum knows and feels safe with. No, I need to go home. I need to spend time alone to process what Sally said, get my head around it all, because very sad to say there's a lot of truth in her story. She was right about Richard spending Mum's money, and of course there was the mystery message. I just need time to sort it all out in my head, and home is the best place for me to do that.'

Kate started to protest, but Rose stopped her. 'It's okay. I *will* be okay. I just need time alone.'

Both women drank their tea in silence and then Kate walked Rose out to her car. 'You're sure you're okay to drive?' she asked. 'Because I could drive you home and then walk back. It's not far, it wouldn't take me long.'

'Don't worry,' said Rose. 'That's very kind of you but I'm fine, honestly.'

As she opened the driver side door, Rose turned to Kate.

'You know, I thought the worst thing this world could throw at me had happened when Richard was killed. Turns out I was wrong.'

She leaned over, gave Kate a hug, got in her car, started the engine and drove away.

*

Violet was in bed by the time Rose got home, and the neighbour had left a note saying she'd gone back to her house because all seemed calm and settled for the

220

night. Rose locked the front door, turned out all the lights downstairs, and walked upstairs to her home office. She sat at her desk in the dark for a very long time, replaying everything Sally had told her. About the holidays, the flat, the vasectomy. The vasectomy! Could that part be true? The money she could work out now that she knew what she was looking for, but could Richard really have been so devious and cruel to her? Could the man she'd loved with all her heart and soul, who she thought was her soulmate and who loved her back with everything he was worth, could he really have done something so calculating, so deceitful as to deliberately rob her of her chance to have a child, to be a family? It seemed so brutal. Why would anyone do that to someone they loved?

Rose thought back to all the conversations they'd had before they were married about how many children they'd have, what they'd call them, who they'd look like. They'd seemed so in tune with each other, both so excited at the prospect of starting a new life together, and all the happy times they'd have ahead as a family.

She remembered the disappointment of her period arriving every month, how she grew more worried and more desperate for a baby. How Richard had appeared equally as distraught, had seemed to share in her disappointment, but had always managed to soothe her, telling her that next month would be different, that one day they would have their child.

It was Rose who had suggested they go for tests, maybe look into the possibility of artificial insemination. Looking back, she now saw that Richard had been quick to shut down that idea. He wasn't keen on artificial means, he'd said, let nature take its course.

'And if it never happens we can still have a great life together,' he'd said. 'Just you and me. Do we need anyone or anything else? Think of all the fabulous times we can have together. Children would be wonderful of course, but think without them, we'll have the money to do what we want, go where our dreams take us.'

Then he'd smile, take Rose in his arms and smother her neck in kisses until she was giggling and melting into his arms, and they'd make love and all the disappointment would be forgotten…until the next month.

On and on it went, month after month, year after year, punctuated by thoughtful gifts for her, expensive gifts for him, luxury holidays in plush hotels in idyllic, faraway locations for them both. Each month Rose's disappointment grew less, and her acceptance of the situation increased, as did Richard's…or so she thought. Now she realised it was never disappointment and it was never acceptance, it was always relief.

As she sat in the dark, combing over all those memories, she had to admit that she'd been fooling herself her whole married life. In her heart she'd always known the real Richard. Deep down she'd known that he couldn't bear the idea of sharing his life with any more people than he absolutely had to, because each person meant less for him. Unless of course they had something he wanted.

He'd beguiled her so she gave him everything, and he tolerated her because she was malleable but smart enough to earn lots of money, and too much in love to question. She had pushed aside any doubts, blocked them from her mind because she'd loved him with everything she had and was willing to trust him and believe that he loved her. Now she could clearly see that he'd spent their married life betraying her. Everything she thought was true about their life together was a lie. Everything. Rose covered her face with her hands, put her head on the desk, and sobbed.

*

It was light outside by the time Rose lifted her head. Her arms were sore and her neck felt stiff because she'd cried with such rage and ferocity that she'd exhausted herself, and when she stopped, she'd fallen asleep, head on the desk. She shook out her arms and stretched her neck, and although it was only 6am she decided to get to work. She opened one of her desk drawers, pulled out all the paperwork linked to her mum's estate, switched on the desk lamp and took a deep breath.

The cruise and the holiday she already knew about, and it didn't take her long to spot more withdrawals to holiday companies and hotel groups. She would have wagered that the dates would tie in with trips Richard had told her were for work, or weekends away playing golf with clients or the guys from the tennis club. She could also see that over the years he'd moved money from Violet's savings accounts into her current account and even cashed in an investment. Then she spotted how he'd managed to pay the rent for Sally's flat.

She dug out all the paperwork linked to the rental of her parents' house. Rose had never known what fees had been agreed with the letting agent or rent with the tenants. Richard had always seemed offended when Rose asked any questions, so she backed off. He was a trained accountant, after all, a professional. Anyway, he wouldn't do anything bad involving Mum, would he? They adored each other, didn't they? Now she realised he'd done a great deal of bad.

From the rental agreement she could see that the letting agency was supposed to deduct their fee from the rent every month and pay the rest of the money into Violet's account. Only the 'rest' was a fraction of what her house should have fetched. Rose worked out that Richard must have used the same letting agent for Sally's flat and agreed with them that after taking their management fee they should also deduct the rent for Sally's place before depositing what remained into Violet's account.

How could he do this to her, and to Violet? Rose squeezed her fists tight, looked up to heaven and keeping all the sound inside so as not to wake her mum, she screamed and screamed and screamed.

*

By the time Violet got up a couple of hours later, Rose felt completely wrung out. She moved to the kitchen when she heard her mum but was exhausted from having had very little sleep and so emotionally drained she hardly knew what she was feeling. Violet appeared to notice nothing, she just went about the business of making tea for them both, toasting some bread, and setting the table for breakfast. Rose sat still and watched her mother pottering around the kitchen, turning towards her every now and then and giving a wary smile.

'Tea?' Violet asked.

'Yes please Mum,' Rose replied.

At the word Mum, Violet paused and flicked her eyes over in Rose's direction, a confused look on her face. Then she carried on filling the teapot with boiling water. They drank the tea and ate the toast in companionable silence. Then Rose said, wearily, 'Mum, if it's okay with you I'll go to my room to lie down for a little while.'

'Do what you like,' said Violet. 'But you'd better be gone before my Vernon comes back from work. We're having a tea party for our daughter tonight. It's her birthday. I'm baking her a cake that's going to have a little ballerina on top, and Vernon's bringing her present in with him. A bike. Just what she wanted. And we don't want your type hanging around us while we're celebrating.'

Rose stopped and stared. She had no idea what her mother was talking about and no energy to find out. She needed to lie down, recoup her strength. Slowly she climbed the stairs to her bedroom and just before she got to the door her eye was caught by the framed photograph of her and Richard

226

standing on that beach on their honeymoon, arms around each other, heads back, laughing. She picked it up, looked at it with a smile as though recalling a happy memory, then threw it at the wall with all her might. Glass shattered everywhere, the frame broke into pieces, and the photograph, when it landed on the carpet, was ripped to shreds. Like her heart.

TWENTY-FOUR

A week later

The following Friday Kate skipped yoga but was waiting anxiously for Pascalle in the library cafe.

'Thank goodness you're here,' she said the moment her friend arrived at the table.

'Where's Rose?' asked Pascalle, confused.

Kate shook her head. 'Not here. It's a very long story and I'm really worried about her.'

'Oh no, what's happened?'

Kate motioned her friend to sit down. 'I can't go into any detail Pascalle because it's not my story to tell and I don't know how much Rose will want people to know. What I can say is that Rose has had some terrible news and I'm really worried about her.'

'Not her mum?' asked Pascalle.

'No, no, her mum's fine. It's to do with Richard. I last saw her on Tuesday night and although she was very upset, she said she was okay but I could see that she wasn't. Next day I tried phoning her but she didn't answer, so I texted her and she did reply that she was fine, but it was a brusque message. I've been texting every day and she keeps saying she's okay. I'm just not sure I believe her.'

'Should we go round to her house?'

'Pascalle, I really don't know. I don't think I'm her favourite person at the moment – that's part of the long story – and also what if we turn up like the cavalry and she answers the door all smiles? We'll look pretty silly.'

'Kate this sounds very serious, and if you're as worried as you sound, it might be worth looking silly,' said Pascalle. 'Why didn't you tell me about this earlier? You could have phoned me rather than worry on your own.'

'I know. I should have.' Kate sighed. 'But I can't decide if there really is a problem or my guilt making me have an overactive imagination. Plus you have your own worries at the moment. I don't want to add to them. What's happened with you since last week?'

Pascalle's shoulders slumped. 'Nothing new. I've spent the whole week worrying about what to do. I've been trying to picture life in Yorkshire. In my own space, smaller than the house I have now, but maybe that's a good thing - less to clean and look after. Stefan and Justine just a few seconds walk away so I'd see them every day and be able to do lots of things with them. Then there's the beautiful Yorkshire countryside to explore. I'd still have my car and could go for outings, take Steffie with me when he wasn't at nursery or school. Yes, I can see from the look on your face that you think it all sounds lovely!'

Kate smiled. 'I think it does. But you obviously don't.'

'It's a new life. Starting over.'

'But you've started over before,' said Kate. 'When you came to Britain and after Trevor died. You know you can do it.'

Pascalle shrugged. 'You're right of course. But that was different. When I came to England it was at a time and to a place of my choosing. This wouldn't be. And when Trevor died, I had no choice but to start again, and let's face it, I didn't do too well at it until I met you and Rose.

'Just having you two as friends has changed my life. I have new hope. I feel the old Pascalle rising to the surface again and I'm so thrilled about that. I'm terrified that moving to Yorkshire, to a place and at a time *not* of my choosing will feel like I'm being forced onto another path I don't want to be on, and it will set me back.'

Kate could see that her friend was really struggling with her dilemma and she wished she could do or say something helpful. 'I'm so sorry Pascalle that you are having to deal with this. It's such a difficult decision to make, especially as if you stay, you'll see so much less of your grandson.'

'And that, Kate, is at the root of my dilemma. I love having them nearby and now that I've started being more like a mother and grandmother again I definitely don't want to upset Justine or push her away, especially after all she's done for me. And particularly as Evie lives so far away.'

'Did she move to be close to your family?' Kate asked.

'Yes, she did. I have two brothers who are married with children. One brother lives in our old family house, while Evie has a flat on her own in the next village to them.'

'Even so, isn't it a bit lonely for her being far away from her parents and sister?'

'She doesn't seem to think so. When the girls were little we used to spend the long summer holidays with my mother. Evie absolutely loved it and when she was old enough she announced that she was moving there permanently. It broke Trevor's heart. But I could see a lot of me in her and I knew it would be futile to try to stop her.

I didn't want to repeat the mistakes my mother made with me, so I persuaded Trevor to let her go.'

'Mistakes, Pascalle?' asked Kate. 'You know I always imagine you having a carefree childhood, turning cartwheels in a French wheatfield, collecting stray cats, painting, climbing trees and running a bit wild. Then at the end of the day, you'd sit down to an evening meal with your lovely family around a scrubbed wooden table in an idyllic French farmhouse kitchen. Does any of this match up to your real life?'

Pascalle laughed and nodded her head. 'Well, yes, you're right about the cats and the cartwheels, and even the painting. Not so much about the running wild through a wheatfield. We lived in the village of Arras in the north of France. Our home wasn't a farmhouse, but I definitely did have a lovely family, and it was wonderful while my papa was alive. But when he died, it all went wrong. Not many people know.'

Her friend looked so sorrowful as she spoke that Kate regretted asking her. 'I'm sorry Pascalle, I shouldn't have been so nosy. I've obviously brought back memories that are difficult for you.'

'Oh Kate, please don't think that,' Pascalle begged. 'We all of us have sad memories, don't we. Perhaps I've kept mine locked up for too long. Perhaps that's why letting go of Trevor was so hard for me, because I hadn't really dealt with the grief and the emotional upset from my past. Trevor knew everything, the girls know a little, but that's all. One day I'll tell you, but today we have to worry about Rose. What shall we do?'

Kate shook her head. 'I'm not sure. Maybe I'll text her again on my way home and ask if it would be okay for us to visit her tomorrow. Say we're missing her.'

'Sounds like a plan,' agreed Pascalle. 'Unless I hear otherwise I'll come round to your house first thing tomorrow to pick you up and we'll go over in my car.' Just then her phone pinged and when she checked the message she looked surprised.

'I'm sorry Kate but I have to go. Evie has turned up at my front door and she's wondering where I am.'

'Ooh how exciting,' said Kate. 'What a lovely surprise. Or is it…?'

'Truly Kate, I'm not sure. But one thing I am certain about is that Evie doesn't just pop over from France on a whim – she has something thorny on her mind.'

TWENTY-FIVE

Late morning that same day

When Pascalle drew up outside her house, Evie was sitting on the doorstep, a small carry-on sized suitcase beside her, and looking outraged. She had inherited her mother's long black hair and olive skin, and the richly embroidered coat she was wearing suggested she also shared her love of brightly coloured clothes. She also had her mother's directness.

'Why weren't you in?' she demanded.

'Perhaps because I didn't know you were coming,' Pascalle replied airily, locking her car and walking up the path.

'How could you not know? I texted you last night.'

'I didn't receive any text. Didn't you wonder why I didn't reply?'

'No Maman, I just assumed you were in some kind of sad place and didn't want to be disturbed.'

'Well I wasn't, my darling. Now can you please move so that I can open the door and let you in before the neighbours start to wonder what all this noise is about.'

Once they were both inside the house and the door was closed, Pascalle turned to her youngest daughter. 'Now come here, let me look at you, let me hug you, let me kiss you. I can't believe you're actually here. You look amazing ma chérie.'

Evie put down her case and walked into her mother's arms.

'And you too Maman, you look so good. Way better than the last time I saw you. You have colour back in your cheeks, and you're smiling. It's lovely to see.'

'Merci ma chérie, now come into the kitchen and I'll put on the coffee and you can tell me why you've decided to surprise me with a visit.'

Evie took off her coat, threw it over the end of the banister revealing a figure hugging fuschia pink dress, and tottered into the kitchen on a pair of hot pink six-inch stilletto heels.

'I've come to talk some sense into you about going to Yorkshire,' she stated flopping down on a chair at the kitchen table. 'I can't believe you're even considering staying here.'

'And you came all the way to London to say this? Wouldn't a phone call have sufficed?'

'Not when one is dealing with a person as stubborn as you Maman. It has to be said face to face.'

Pascalle laughed and looked at her daughter. Trevor would have called her a chip off the old block, and there was no doubt she was the image of Pascalle as a young woman. Her daughters knew only a little about her past life because she'd never felt the need to tell them her whole story. But her feelings about this move to Yorkshire were so entangled in the events of her past, that perhaps now was the time to speak. Evie, who was so like her, was probably the only member of her family who might understand. Pascalle made a decision.

'Evie, I'm going to trust you with a story, a real story, and I know in the course of hearing that story you will judge me, but I hope that at the end of it you will also understand why I am so reluctant to leave my life here.'

'Maman, you sound so mysterious,' Evie laughed. 'Before you begin, can we have some bread and cheese, please? It's lunchtime already and I haven't eaten for hours and I can't concentrate while I'm hungry.'

From her shopping bag, Pascalle pulled out a baguette she'd bought fresh that morning, gathered a few cheeses, some beef tomatoes and grapes from the fridge and set them all on a wooden platter on the table. Evie grabbed a knife to dig into the cheese. 'I'm ready Maman,' she said.

Pascalle took a deep breath and began.

*

'You know that your grandpapa, my father, died when I was young.'

Evie nodded.

'What you don't know is that after his death I went a bit wild.'

'What kind of wild?'

'More mad really. I ran away to Paris.'

Evie looked shocked. 'Wow Maman. I had no idea.'

'But that's not the worst of it. While I was there I met a man and fell madly in love.'

'Love?' asked Evie, surprised. 'How hard did you fall?'

'Very, very hard, ma chérie. Enough to marry him.'

Evie looked perplexed. 'So you knew Dad when you were really young? I thought you'd met him later in life and in England.'

Pascalle nodded. 'I did meet and marry him later on. No, this man was called Noah.'

'Noah? So Dad was your second husband?'

'Not my second husband, ma chérie' answered Pascalle. 'My third.'

'Third!' exclaimed Evie. 'Maman what on earth are you talking about?'

A weary half smile passed across Pascalle's face. 'I'm talking about two terrible mistakes I made in order to please other people, and how I don't ever want to find myself in that situation again.'

*

Pascalle told her daughter about Noah, a young artist who used to come into the café in Paris where she worked. He was handsome and free spirited and unlike anyone she'd ever met before. He'd arrive splattered in paint and tell her about what he'd been working on that day, then they'd go out to gigs in little clubs down Paris's backstreets and she fell in love with this way of life as much as with him. One day on a complete whim he asked her to marry him. The

238

word yes was barely out of her mouth when she was running down the road, hand in hand with Noah, to the registry office to book their wedding.

'It was so exciting,' Pascalle recalled. 'After all the darkness of your grandpapa dying, I'd found someone who was full of light and fun and I wanted to spend the rest of my life with him.'

'So what went wrong?' asked Evie.

'Your grandmaman. I was so happy I decided to go home and share my happiness with her and with my brothers. By this time I'd been away from home for about a year, and I wrote to my mother to ask if I could visit. In her reply she sounded so thrilled I imagined everything would be fine, that she'd be excited to see me, she'd realise that I'd done so well, and be pleased that I'd found love. But I was wrong. Very wrong.'

Pascalle told Evie about the day she arrived at her mother's door, with Noah walking up the path behind her. Her mother had thrown her arms around her daughter, crying and exclaiming how happy she was to see her. Then Pascalle remembered Noah, who was standing shyly behind her, and introduced him as her husband. Her mother's face changed within seconds.

'She looked at me as though I was dirt. "Are you pregnant?" she demanded. "Is that why you have married?" When I told her I wasn't pregnant and that I'd married Noah because I loved him her face softened and she invited us into the house. She made coffee, cut some cake, and ushered us into the best room to sit on the elegant furniture used only for guests.

'It was as though she didn't quite know what to do with me. Then suddenly she started crying and asking me why I had done this terrible thing to her. Why had I run off, leaving my poor widowed mother distraught? Why had I kept silent for a year, only to return with this "husband"?

'She spat the word out as though he was some kind of devil. I tried to explain how lost I'd felt after Papa died, how angry. That I had all these emotions I didn't know how to deal with. But she wouldn't stop crying. My two brothers stood behind her in silence, looking shocked. Afterwards they told me it was as though all the emotion she'd felt at Papa's death and all the months and months of worrying about where I was, not knowing if I was still alive, had come flooding out that afternoon. Noah sat there, not knowing what to say or do.

'We ate dinner in the kitchen in virtual silence, and immediately after, Maman took to her bed and stayed there.

I pleaded with her to let me in to speak to her, try to explain some more, but she said nothing. Through the door, all I could hear was her crying. Noah was completely stunned. I'd painted this picture of my wonderful welcoming family and they'd been the complete opposite. He was offended at the way they'd treated him and although I tried to persuade him that things would calm down and he'd see how nice they really were, he begged me to return to Paris, so three days after we arrived I packed our bag and we went back to our flat.'

Pascalle paused and glanced towards her daughter. Evie looked shellshocked.

'You know I always sensed a strain between you and Grandmaman, but I had no idea if it was real or I imagined it,' said Evie. 'Now I'm beginning to understand.'

'No, you're not even half-way to understanding ma chérie There's plenty more to tell. Look it's almost dinner time, let's open a bottle of wine and heat the stew that's in the pan in the fridge. This story is going to take a while.'

The two women worked together in companionable silence, getting the food ready, pouring the wine, each one processing what had been said and what was to come, and then once they were settled with their food and their glasses of red wine, Pascalle continued her story.

241

'With all the time that's passed I admit I can now understand my mother's reaction,' agreed Pascalle. 'But back then I could only think about myself and what I wanted. As it turned out, Noah was feeling pretty much the same about himself. I don't know whether he thought we were a very strange family, or whether my mother's rantings struck a chord with him, but when we returned to Paris things were never quite the same between us.

'One evening, a couple of weeks later, I came home to discover the flat was empty and he was gone. I looked for him everywhere, at his studio, at our friends' houses, but no-one had seen him or ever saw him again. Then after about six months, a letter arrived from a solicitor. Noah wanted a divorce. I can't say I blamed him.

'While he was missing, I had time to think about Maman and how difficult it must have been for her not knowing where I was, whether I was safe, alive or dead. I began to feel so guilty, and about three weeks after the solicitor's letter arrived, I decided I wanted to be back with my family for good.

'I wasn't without fear. My mother and I had parted on difficult terms and I didn't know what kind of reception I'd get this time. But I knew going home was the right thing to do and it was a relief when Maman seemed pleased to see me, especially when she realised that I was no longer married to Noah. Even so, our relationship was strained. I think she felt I'd crossed one line too many, caused too much hurt.

'Of course, the divorce wasn't entirely welcomed. It brought shame on us. We are a Catholic family and Catholics only get divorces under very specific circumstances. Making a mistake in your choice of husband isn't one of them. I felt that Maman did want to forgive me, I truly believe that, but it was as though there were too many barriers in the way - Papa dying, me disappearing, returning with a husband, divorcing - that she could only go so far, and not far enough to accept me completely back into the family. I knew she still loved me, but I felt held at arm's length.'

Pascalle told Evie that despite her mother's coolness she'd stayed in the village and trained as a primary teacher, getting a job in her local school. She still had friends in the area and one of them introduced Pascalle to her brother, Martin, and they began a romance.

'He was so kind, and my mother loved him which of course made me happy. Before I knew what was happening, he'd proposed! While he was down on bended knee, my mother was practically holding out my hand to receive the ring.'

'She was there?' asked Evie, astonished.

'He was so sure I'd say yes that he proposed in front of the whole family!' Pascalle described. 'Maman was thrilled because it meant I'd stay nearby. So were my poor brothers who were worn out trying to keep the peace between these two volatile women, and they knew our mother would be happy with this choice of husband. As I looked down at Martin gazing up at me with the ring in his hand, a massive, confident smile on his face, and then at my family's eager faces, I knew I had no choice. I had to say yes.'

'But did you love him?' asked Evie.

'In a way, but not really and not enough. We were married at a register office in the village where I was born and had a blessing in the church where I was christened, by the priest I'd known my whole life. Because I'd been married before, I couldn't have the full mass or wear a big white dress, but Maman seemed prepared to overlook that, and during the blessing she sat in the front row, between my brothers, her eyes shining with happiness. This marriage meant I'd be home, nearby her, the past forgotten, the family's reputation in the village saved. She could be happy.'

'But you weren't, I take it?' Evie asked.

'No, Evie, I wasn't,' Pascalle said shaking her head, sadly. 'Don't get me wrong I tried to make it work, for my mother but also for Martin. He was a good man and didn't deserve an unhappy life. I tried very hard for three years, but in the end I had to accept that the only person happy with this arrangement was my mother. She kept going on at me about having children, but I wasn't in love with Martin and I was never going to have children with him. I couldn't tell him that, so he couldn't understand my reluctance. It was so unfair. *I* was being unfair.'

'Maman, what a tangle to be in. I really can't believe all of this happened to you and that for all these years I've had no idea. What did you do?'

'One day I sat Martin down and told him, kindly, that our relationship was never going to work and I thought we should split. He took the news surprisingly well. He was very calm, said he'd always known his feelings for me were stronger than mine for him. He told me he loved me, but he wanted to be with someone who loved him back. So next day we contacted a solicitor to start divorce proceedings.'

'And your mother?' asked Evie. 'How did she take that?'

'With silent fury. I went to the house, made her a cup of coffee, told her as calmly as I could as we sat at the kitchen table. She listened, nodded her head, stood up, walked out of the kitchen, went to her bedroom and didn't speak to me again.'

Evie was wide eyed. 'But she did, she always spoke when we were there?'

'Yes my darling, but that was after I met your dad. Before that, she didn't speak to me for 10 years. It was Trevor who brought us back together. But it was a hard road.'

*

As she told her story, Pascalle was growing in confidence that her reluctance to say an immediate yes to Yorkshire had been the correct thing to do. This warm and peaceful day sitting at a table in London chatting with her daughter seemed a million miles from her life in France, and yet the repercussions of that time had shaped her future, the woman she'd become, and would be influencing her decisions about what she would do next.

She recalled how hostile her mother had been to her when Pascalle, divorcing for the second time, moved back into the family home. It had been a terrible, agonising time, and after tolerating this for a couple of months Pascalle realised life there was never going to improve. She had followed her own heart and caused misery, and then she'd put another's happiness before hers and caused yet more despair. She felt she couldn't win. She had to get out, go somewhere completely different, where she could be herself and not the person her family thought she should be.

'What made you chose London?' asked Evie. 'You always just said that you sorted of ended up here.'

'And I did, via Brighton. A friend had told me years before about a holiday she'd had there. I loved the sound of the sea front with its long promenade, the antiques shops in The Lanes and the young artists who were working and exhibiting there. It all sounded very trendy and cool and just the kind of very different place I would flourish in. I figured schools there would be interested in a native French speaker who also spoke a little English, so I applied to a secondary school for a job as a French assistant.'

'How did Grandmaman take the news that you were leaving?' asked Evie.

'Badly,' said Pascalle, shaking her head. 'Very badly indeed. But whatever choice I made was going to be wrong for someone. If I left, I'd devastate my mother, but if I stayed I'd destroy myself.'

'You obviously chose to save yourself.'

'I did and the day I left was one of the saddest days of my life. I went to see my mother one last time, to hug her and to say goodbye. Tears were flooding down my cheeks as I took her in my arms. But she stood there, rigid like a statue, face frozen and saying nothing. I know her heart was broken, but mine broke too.

'I cried all the way from Arras to Brighton. My fellow passengers on the train, boat and bus must have thought I was mad. By the time I got to the hotel I was staying in temporarily, I was completely exhausted, wrung out, and I felt so guilty. But there was also something deep inside me, a spark of excitement about the adventure that I hoped lay ahead, and as the days and weeks went on, that spark grew and soon I was loving Brighton and my work. That was when I knew I'd made the right decision.'

Speaking about that time had brought a smile to Pascalle's face and her eyes were shining.

'Then I met your dad, and I knew for definite that I'd made the correct choice.'

'Where did you meet? Was it love at first sight?' asked Evie, obviously warming to the romance of this story.

'Mmmm, for him apparently yes! But for me, no. He was 10 years older than me, a maths teacher, very conservative in his dress and his views, and definitely not my type. Our eyes met across a very smoky staffroom.'

'So how come you ended up marrying him,' asked Evie.

'He wore me down,' Pascalle laughed. 'Seriously, the reality is that he was persistent and kind, and it became clear to me that he absolutely adored me. But what made me fall completely in love with him was that he loved me so much he was happy to let me be me, even when it drove him mad. Which as you know it often did.'

'Yes, I remember very well how frustrated he used to get at what he called your madness,' Evie laughed.

'We were the exact opposites, him quiet, me loud. Him a bit of a boring dresser, me bright and colourful. But I think secretly he enjoyed my energy and my quirkiness. And I loved him for that. So, when he was offered a job at a school in this part of London there was no question that I would go with him and we were married quickly in a simple register office ceremony with just a few friends as witnesses.'

At that, Evie jumped up went over to the dresser and returned with a framed photograph.

'Ah, that explains this picture of the two of you on your wedding day,' she said. 'I often wondered why someone who loved to dress up as much as you do Maman wore such a plain gown. Now I know. Gosh this is a lot to take in. I had no idea that Grandmaman could be so unforgiving. She always seemed so thrilled to see us. Did Dad know about your other husbands? It feels so wrong to be asking my mother about her "other husbands".'

Pascalle laughed. 'Yes of course he did, I didn't keep anything from him. I told him why I'd come to England and about my mother. Even though he hadn't met her at that point, it made him sad to think of how poor our relationship was. His mother had died when he was 14, and he felt the loss of her love so badly that he didn't want that to happen to me. When Justine was born, he persuaded me to write and tell her and ask if we could bring the baby to see her. It was my brother Michel who replied with an emphatic yes! So we went, all three of us.'

'Did you get a good welcome?'

'At first Maman was cool towards me and that made me feel very nervous but having your dad by my side gave me courage. When I showed her Justine she completely fell in love with her, and with your dad too, much to my surprise. One day she told me: "He has a kind spirit, which I like. Hold him close, Pascalle. Never let this one go."'

'So, she forgave you?' asked Evie, pouring the last of the wine for them both.

'I'm not sure she did entirely. I think there was something still there holding back her complete forgiveness. Maybe because I left her when she needed me, maybe because I hurt her more than I realised. I don't know. But over the years we learned to be mother and daughter again and when you came along and we named you after her, she loved you just as much as Justine, and she was thrilled when you chose to move to France to be near her.

'Every time I visited you there I saw you blossom and thrive and become the wonderful, happy, fulfilled woman you are today and I knew that you'd made the right decision for you. But I also began to really understand how my mother had felt about me moving away and never returning. I understood the yearning you have inside for your children. It's almost animalistic, as though your body is calling out for them.

'I think in her final years we grew to understand each other so much more. This is why I have such a dilemma about moving to Yorkshire. I can't upset Justine, I can't have her think of me the way Maman thought of me for all those years, but like you Evie, I need to be free. In Yorkshire I'd be living Justine's life, and I know that living the way other people want me to doesn't work for me.'

Pascalle sipped her wine and saw that her daughter was deep in thought.

'I understand now Maman, better than I did,' Evie finally said. 'I must confess I'm a little shocked. I had no idea my mother had had such a colourful past, and I'm grateful that you've told me about it. But I also know that your staying here will break Justine's heart. She's totally set on you going with them.'

'Oh Evie, it's such a difficult decision. Will you help me talk to her?'

'Maman I'll do my best but I have one thing to ask of you. Don't make your final decision until you've been up there and seen what it's really like for yourself, where you'd be living, and what your life there could be. Then if you still feel staying here is what you want to do, I'll support you.'

'That's good advice,' said Pascalle, getting up from her chair and starting to clear up the kitchen. 'Now I must get to bed. All this talking has made this a tiring day and I have to be up early tomorrow to go and rescue a friend. You sleep in your old bedroom, Evie. The bed is always made up ready for you.'

As her daughter hugged her goodnight, Pascalle said, 'Thank you for listening, Evie. It was a long story, and some of it I'm not proud of, but in telling you I think I'm clearer in my mind about some things.'

'I'm glad Maman, I really am, and I do understand better than I did why this is such a dilemma for you. I can't help hoping though, that the decision you make will be one that pleases Justine too.'

As she watched her daughter climb the stairs to bed, Pascalle pondered to herself, why can't life be simple? Why is it always full of tough decisions? And why do I end up always breaking someone's heart?

TWENTY-SIX

The next day

The next morning, Kate's doorbell went at 9am and she opened the door to find Pascalle standing there looking very bright and breezy.

'Good morning!' exclaimed Pascalle holding up a paper bag. 'I bring croissants, pain au raisin, and pain au chocolat. I wasn't sure which one you'd like so I brought all three. I hope you haven't eaten breakfast yet.' Then she noticed that Kate was still in her dressing gown and looking rather bleary eyed. 'I'm sorry Kate. I hope I'm not too early. I'm always a bit of an early bird, but usually I go back to bed with a hot drink and the newspapers. But this morning I thought I'd best get going.'

Kate mustered a smile and stood aside to let her friend head down to the kitchen where she plonked the bag on the breakfast bar.

'Now coffee,' said Pascalle. 'Where do you keep it?'

Kate pointed to a cafetiere sitting on the worktop and opened a cupboard to find a bag of ground coffee.

'Perfect,' said Pascalle. 'I'll make it.' Then she stopped, having realised that Kate hadn't spoken yet. 'Are you okay ma chérie? You're very quiet.'

Kate pulled herself onto one of the bar stools, put her elbows on the work top and rested her head in her hands.

'Sorry, Pascalle. I'm fine,' she said. 'I was just up half the night worrying about Luke and then worrying about Rose, so I slept in. The doorbell woke me.'

Pascalle was mortified. 'Goodness me. It's just that I'm keen to get on with things these days. It's just as well Evie was there and needed breakfast or I might have been even earlier. Never mind, help yourself to one of the croissants and hopefully that and some coffee will make you feel a bit more awake. I get them from a little French bakery near my house and they're delicious. The coffee won't be long.'

While Pascalle busied herself around the kitchen, looking in cupboards and drawers for cups, plates and cutlery, she saw Kate surveying the room.

'This kitchen is a bit higglty pigglty,' she mused out loud. 'Bits of it are falling apart. Some of the cupboards don't have handles and the drawers are broken. We talked a few years ago about getting a new one but didn't have the money at the time. Then once the children had left home and it looked as though we were getting into a better place financially, Jason died. I really want to get a new kitchen and I have lots of ideas about what I'd like and how I'd design it, but with Luke having such a bad reaction to what I've done in the living room, I'm nervous.'

Pascalle poured out two mugs of coffee and added milk to Kate's. 'I can understand why you'd be nervous. You don't want to push him away further. But equally, this is your home and only your home. It has to be right for you to live in. It has to be what you want.'

'I know that Pascalle, and already with just the things I've done I'm feeling more peaceful here. I can't use the word happy because I'm not sure I'm ready to be happy yet, but I do feel an inner calm now that I'm not surrounded by things that spark bad memories. But surely all of that shouldn't come at the expense of my relationship with my son?'

Pascalle sipped her coffee before answering. 'Grief, bereavement, loss throw up complicated and complex emotions that we somehow have to navigate our way through with no map. Trying to find that path can send us temporarily insane. I feel sure that's what happened to me after my dad died.'

Kate's eyebrows shot up in surprise. 'What do you mean?'

'Only that I went a bit mad after my papa died. I didn't understand what had happened, I was too young to process it all, I turned my back on the help my family could have given me because I didn't know that was what I needed, and it badly affected my relationship with my mother. But I learned many things from that time. Over the years I've reflected on everything that happened and whether I could or should have done things differently. For me there's no doubt I haven't come to terms with my dad's death, even now. That's maybe why it's taken me so long to face up to Trevor's death.

'Thanks to you and Rose I'm starting to move on, but I still have a long way to go. All of this takes time, more time for some people than others. The most important thing I've learned is that you have to talk. You have to keep open the channels of communication. Both of you sitting silently trying to work out what the other is thinking will get you nowhere. Talk to your son, even if it's difficult to get him to talk to you. As the adult and his mother, it's up to you to keep trying. You have to fight for him Kate, and if you keep trying, one day you *will* succeed.'

Pascalle saw a smile return to Kate's face. 'You're right,' she said. 'You're so right.'

'Of course I am,' said her friend, standing up from her bar stool. 'Now, wipe those crumbs from around your mouth and go and get dressed. We have a friend to rescue. I do hope she's okay, I'm feeling nervous about what we'll find when we get to her house, but hopefully between us we can help.'

*

They drove round to Rose's house in Pascalle's car. Kate texted to say they were on their way and hoped that was okay. Rose replied with a thumbs up emoji.

'Well at least we know she's still alive,' said Kate. 'Yesterday when I texted to ask if we could visit she replied with a bald 'okay'. By the way, you haven't said why Evie paid you a surprise visit yesterday. Is everything okay with her?'

'Oh yes, all is fine with her. She just came to persuade me that I *had* to go to Yorkshire with Justine.'

'And has she?'

'I think I may have persuaded her that it's the last thing I should do,' said Pascalle laughing. 'But I've agreed to visit and then decide. She's gone to Justine's today to see if she can put in a good word for me, but Justine's so set on my going that I don't think she'll get very far. She's heading back to France tonight, so I will have some peace to reflect on things on my own. Now which one is Rose's house?'

They'd no sooner rung the doorbell than the door was opened. Rose had obviously been waiting for them, and it was clear from her puffy eyes, grubby sweatshirt with drip stains down the front, and unbrushed hair that she was in a state, and had been for a few days.

'Oh Rose,' exclaimed Kate, moving forward to hug her friend.

'I wouldn't,' warned Rose. 'I expect I'm a bit smelly.'

'A bit of body odour won't put me off,' Kate laughed and put her arms round Rose who immediately burst into tears.

'I'm so glad you've come,' she sobbed. 'I didn't know what to do.'

As Kate guided Rose towards the sofa in the living room, Pascalle spotted the kitchen and went to put on the kettle. She was stunned by the mess two people had accumulated in just a few days. The worktops were covered in crumbs and tea stains, the bin was full of plastic containers from microwaveable meals, and there were dirty cups everywhere. Pascalle opened the dishwasher and the smell from the stale food on the dishes inside was pungent. She didn't bother to open the door of the washing machine because she could see there was a load of wet washing still in there and guessed it had been there for a while.

Just as she was surveying the chaos and wondering where to start clearing it all up, she heard footsteps behind her and turned to see an elderly woman standing in the doorway. Her short, grey hair was dishevelled and she was wearing just a nightie, dressing gown and slippers. Pascalle assumed this was Rose's mum, Violet.

'Are you Rose?' asked woman looking towards Pascalle. 'Are you? Only there's a lady who usually makes me a cup of tea at this time and she says that her name is Rose. Trouble is I can't remember what she looks like and I'd really like a cup of tea. I'm also feeling a bit hungry. Please say that you're Rose.' And at that, Violet dissolved into tears.

'Oh my darling,' said Pascalle putting an arm around the old lady's shoulder and leading her to a chair at the table. 'Come and sit down and I'll make you some tea.'

Violet looked straight at her. 'But you're foreign. Rose isn't foreign. You can't be Rose.'

'Yes, you're right. I'm not Rose. My name is Pascalle. Rose is having a day off today, but I'm going to make you a lovely cup of tea.'

Pascalle reached into her tote bag and pulled out a small brown paper bag. 'I've brought some croissants for you. I'll warm them up and they'll be just delicious.'

At the sight of the golden croissants, Violet's eyes grew wide with delight, she stopped crying and a sunny smile appeared on her face. Just then Kate's head appeared round the kitchen door.

'Oh my goodness, what a mess,' she whispered so that Rose couldn't hear. 'And Violet? Ah I see she's here. Good. Rose wasn't quite sure where she was. Pascalle, any chance of some tea?'

'On its way. I just have to attend to Madame Violet first, and then I'll bring some right in.'

At the words 'Madame Violet', Rose's mum let out a little giggle. 'That cake was lovely. Are there any more?'

*

Pascalle found a tea tray and loaded it with mugs of tea and the rest of the croissants and took them into the living room. Rose looked distraught, defeated.

'This won't solve your problems,' said Pascalle, indicating the tray, 'but it will make you feel a bit better.'

'Where's Mum?' asked Rose.

'Sitting in the kitchen munching on her second pain au chocolat,' replied Pascalle. 'I'm not sure how well that will fit with her diabetes, but she said she was hungry and there wasn't much else.'

'Oh thank you so much, Pascalle,' said Rose with such gratitude in her voice. 'I *have* been feeding her. Nothing very nutritious I'm afraid, just ready meals. I couldn't face cooking or shopping so I ordered a delivery from Sainsbury's and when they arrived, she dived in! She's definitely had several each day. She sometimes forgets she's eaten.'

Pascalle sat down beside Rose, put her arm around her and said very gently, 'It looks as though there's a lot you haven't been bothered to do. Can you tell me what's happened? Kate and I would really like to help.'

Rose's eyes refilled with tears at her friend's kindness, and silently streamed down her cheeks.

'It's been so awful, Pascalle,' she said. 'So awful. I haven't been able to eat or sleep or do anything useful for thinking about what that man has done to me. All I ever did was love him and give him everything he ever wanted. All

262

the time he was cheating on me, betraying me, stealing my mother's money, and ruining my life.' At this, Rose broke into sobs.

'It's okay, you cry,' said Pascalle, squeezing Rose tightly. 'Let it all out.'

Just then, Violet began calling Pascalle from the kitchen so she looked up at Kate and said, 'Okay, here's what I think we should do. Kate will you please go to Violet and make her more tea. Tell her that I've had to pop out but I'll be back shortly - that should satisfy her for a while. I'll take Rose upstairs and help her to shower and change, and while she's doing that she can tell me all about what's happened. Then Rose can help Violet get cleaned up while I make us some food and Kate tackles the kitchen. Once everyone and everything is freshened up, we can all sit down and make a plan of what to do next. How does that sound?'

'Absolutely perfect,' said Kate, heading to the kitchen.

Pascalle drew Rose closer to her. 'It will be fine, ma chérie,' she told her. 'Somehow, it will be fine.'

TWENTY-SEVEN

That same day

While Rose showered, Pascalle changed her bed, and as Rose put on clean clothes and dried her hair, she explained about the meeting with Sally, that she'd been Richard's mistress and had been with him the night he was killed, about his stealing Violet's money to pay for Sally's flat and all their fancy holidays, and, worst of all, about the vasectomy.

'I feel so betrayed, Pascalle,' she finished. 'I just don't understand how he could do that to me, He loved me, or so he said. We were married for more than 30 years, we did almost everything together. I gave him the wedding he wanted, we went on the holidays he chose, I worked hard to earn enough money so he could have the career and lifestyle he wanted. I knew he didn't work nearly as hard as me, but I did what I did gladly because I loved him and thought he loved me. Now I see it was all a lie. Everything we had together was a lie. The one thing I wanted was a child, and he took that away from me, while lying to my face. More than 30 years of lying.'

Rose sank down on the bed, shaking, frustration and anger etched onto her face. 'I don't know what's real and what isn't. I'm so terribly confused and humiliated. For believing him, for enabling him. I just can't see how the man I married and spent all those years with could be capable of hurting me so much. What's more, I don't understand *why*! Why would he be so cruel? Why would anyone be so cruel to the person they're supposed to love most in this world?'

'That is indeed a very sad story, and one with questions I'm not sure you'll ever be able to answer,' said Pascalle, gently. 'I know exactly how it feels to give yourself, to go against your own wants and desires for someone else. I also know it seldom has a happy ending. But now, we need to think positive. Richard is not here to vent our anger on or to punish, so we can only look to the future and to the things we can do. And I suggest you start with your mother.'

265

Rose smiled weakly. 'Yes, she does look a little neglected. I'll help her get clean and then we can have that chat about the future. I'd love your help, if you have time of course.'

Pascalle gave her friend's hand a reassuring squeeze. 'All the time you need.'

A couple of hours later all four of them sat down to a lunch of homemade carrot and coriander soup with fresh crusty bread. While Kate cleaned the kitchen, Pascalle had zipped to the parade of shops round the corner and found a mini market selling carrots, potatoes, baguettes and even some fresh coriander. She also bought grapes and apples to eat later with cheese and biscuits.

'You're a wonder,' said Kate when she saw the bags full of fresh produce.

Pascalle hummed as she chopped, simmered and blended, Kate got to work in the rest of the house, and Rose patiently helped Violet to shower and dress. She even blow-dried her hair so that she looked clean, fresh and somewhere close to the mum she'd always known. It wasn't an easy task. Violet seemed especially unnerved by having all these strange women in the house, bustling about, making noise with the hoover and singing in a funny language in the kitchen. But when the delicious smell of the soup reached her, she turned to Rose with a smile on her face and said, 'Oooh carrot and coriander soup! My favourite, and your dad's too. Do you remember I used to make a big pot on a Sunday for our lunch? There was never any left by teatime.'

Rose smiled at the memory and with the joy of having her mother back with her, however briefly. 'I do Mum, I remember it well. It was always so creamy and tasty. Perfect on a winter's day. You were such a good cook.'

The two women held hands for a moment, sitting on the edge of Violet's bed, Violet stroking her daughter's hand, lost in the memories. Then suddenly she stopped and looked to Rose's face. Her expression changed from one softened by happy thoughts to one of confusion and fear.

'Who are you?' she asked sharply. She pulled her hand away. 'And why are you touching me? I don't like being touched.'

Just then, Pascalle called up, 'Lunch is ready!'

'Lunch! Great! I'm starving,' Violet proclaimed, getting to her feet. 'Sounds like that foreign lady shouting. She's new, you know. Pastel she's called, or something like that. Something funny and foreign. Well, I'm going down because that soup smells delicious. You can come if you like. Pastel might let you have some.'

With that, Violet bustled out of the room. Rose sat for a moment staring down at her hands. Her dad was gone.

Richard was gone. Now to all intents and purposes her mother was gone. What was there left? Just her, with no family, no future, a horrible mess to sort out and crippling feelings of betrayal.

'Come on Rose.' Kate was standing in the doorway of Violet's bedroom, gazing at her friend. 'Let's eat, all together, so it feels jolly. Then we'll start making lists of what to do. I'm good at those, good at prioritising. And the first priority is getting some nourishing food inside you.'

Rose nodded and stood up. 'I am rather hungry,' she admitted. 'That soup smells divine. There must be some magic French ingredient in it to make it smell so appetising.'

'Well Pascalle is turning out to be a woman of wonder,' replied Kate laughing. 'She seems able to produce delicious food from nowhere! Definitely soul food. Something we all of us need at the moment.'

As they walked downstairs they were met with gales of laughter coming from the kitchen where Violet and Pascalle seemed to be sharing a joke.

'That's a sound I haven't heard in this house for a long time,' said Rose. 'Mum hasn't laughed like that in years! There's definitely magic in that soup!'

'Told you,' said Kate. 'Pascalle is turning out to be rather wonderful.'

*

After they'd eaten, they sat Violet in front of her favourite TV programme while the three women gathered in the kitchen where Rose talked them tearfully through everything she'd discovered about her mum's finances and the rental payments on Sally's flat. They all agreed it sounded very complex and would take a bit of time and patience to unravel, but Pascalle was clear about one thing.

'You must decide now what to do about your mum,' she told Rose. 'Once she's settled, you can concentrate on yourself. You'd already looked at some homes, hadn't you? Was there one you liked? If so, now is the time to move forward.'

Rose took a deep breath and thought hard for a few moments. Pascalle was right, she did need to sort this out, and yes there had been a home that she'd preferred over the others, but something had stopped her from committing to it. She couldn't quite express what this something was. Was it guilt? Or fear of the loss she'd feel without her mother around all the time? Although to Violet, Rose was mostly a stranger now, and the toll that this terrible condition had taken on Violet meant that Rose mainly didn't recognise the mother she once knew, she still felt a deep sense of loyalty to keep her mum with her as long as possible.

After all she was the woman who'd given birth to her, loved her and supported her, and had, to the best of her ability, comforted Rose when Richard was killed. Some days, Rose saw shades of that mum and wasn't ready to lose that as well as everything else.

'I know that what you're saying is correct Pascalle, but I don't think I have the emotional strength to deal with putting Mum into a home at the moment.'

'I understand that Rose but having her here is also taking a toll on you,' said Kate. 'You need a break, Rose. What about something less permanent for your mum? Perhaps you could find respite care for her for a short time which would give you some breathing space.'

Rose's eyes lit up. 'Of course,' she said. 'One of the homes I looked at offered respite care. It would be a good way to see how Mum gets on in there without making a permanent commitment and give me some time to process everything. I'll give them a ring on Monday and see if we can sort something out. Oh Kate, thank you. I feel so relieved! Thank you both.'

'You know Rose, I can see that things feel bleak at the moment, but you will find a way out of this,' offered Pascalle. 'Things will get better. Not tomorrow or next week. It will take time. And Kate and I will do whatever we can to help.'

Pascalle stopped for a moment in thought.

'I do have one more question. Kate why were you feeling so guilty about Rose? I don't see how you could have been involved.'

At Pascalle's words, Kate looked across at Rose and then down to her hands.

'I feel guilty because I have also betrayed Rose. You see a few times when I was at the tennis club I heard people talking about a member called Richard who was having an affair with the barmaid. Then after he was killed, all people could talk about was how terrible it must be for his wife, all of them wondering if she knew or suspected anything. Then when I met Rose, I realised it was *her* Richard they were gossiping about. As time went on and I got to know her better, it was obvious that if the gossip was true, she *didn't* know about it but by then I didn't have the courage to tell her because I knew how devastated she'd be.'

Pascalle's look of surprise spoke volumes. 'Yes I can see that it would have been very difficult news to break. What a dilemma you faced Kate.'

While Kate was nodding her head sadly, Rose leaned over and patted her on the knee.

'Stop worrying about it Kate,' she said. 'You did nothing wrong. It was all Richard. His bad deeds. And you shouldn't be drawn into that. You have absolutely nothing to feel guilty about, so let's just put that behind us and as Pascalle has suggested, try to move on.'

Kate breathed out an obvious sigh of relief, while the smile on Rose's lips said she hoped against hope that Pascalle's optimistic words would prove correct.

TWENTY-EIGHT

July

Two Fridays later the three women were in the library cafe, fresh from their morning exercise. It was Rose's first class since her mother had gone into the home for respite care, and Kate and Pascalle were eager to find out how it was all going.

They were thrilled to see that Rose's skin had lost the grey pallor it had had the last time they had seen her, the dark shadows had gone from under her eyes, and she'd been to the hairdresser and had her hair highlighted and trimmed into a neat bob which swung as she moved and shone under the ceiling lights. Her cheeks were pink from the yoga class and she looked so pleased to be with them again.

Kate was the first to remark on her friend's healthier glow when they'd met that morning on the way into the class, and now Pascalle was saying how great it was to see a smile back on Rose's face.

'I just feel lighter,' she told them. 'I'm sleeping better because I don't have to keep an ear out incase Mum goes walkabout in the night and tumbles down the stairs. And I've made some decisions about my life which means I don't have so many things swirling around in my head all the time.

'I've also been thinking about all the things Richard did, and trying to see them less as a poor reflection on me and more as what they say about him. All those hours of bereavement meetings and counselling didn't go to waste after all,' she laughed.

Rose may have been making light of it now, but the last two weeks had been tough. The home had been open to the idea of offering Violet a temporary place as a trial to see if it was right for her, and fortunately they had had a room available. Rose had taken a deep breath and, in a calm moment over their morning tea sitting at the kitchen table with a plate of Violet's favourite biscuits for her to munch on, Rose had talked to her about going on a little holiday.

'I've found a lovely place for you to stay. It would be for a couple of weeks, so I've made sure you'll have a beautiful bedroom, a lounge with a big TV where you can watch your favourite shows, and a sun lounge where you can sit in the warmth, reading your paper and looking out over a lovely big garden.

'There will be other people there too, friends to talk to if you'd like to, and maybe play cards with, or have a singsong with. You used to like singing, Mum.'

Violet bit into a second biscuit with the relish of someone who's normally only allowed one biscuit, and seemed to be considering what was being said.

'A little holiday?' she mused to herself, then sat up straight and asked, 'Will there be a beach? When Vernon - that's my husband - and I go on holiday, we always go to the beach.'

Rose's heart broke into tiny pieces. She felt such emotion for this woman who used to be her mother, and who was taking this news way better than she'd imagined she would. In fact, Violet seemed quite excited at the prospect.

Rose mustered a smile and said evenly, 'No beach I'm afraid, Mum, but a beautiful garden, way bigger than ours here, with lots of flowers for you to enjoy and help look after. You and Dad always loved your garden.'

A cloud passed over Violet's face as though she was trying to remember her own garden. Then the sun broke through.

'Well, no point sitting about,' she said briskly. 'We need to get on and pack my case. I'll need a hat for the sun and a cardigan incase it gets chilly at night. What time's our train? I expect we'll meet Vernon there.'

When Rose told her friends about the unexpectedly jolly trip to the care home they could barely believe it.

'And she was okay when she got there?' asked Kate. 'Was she still as excited when she realised she wasn't at the seaside, and that your dad wasn't there?'

'She wasn't at all fazed about the lack of sand and sea, infact she could barely believe her eyes at the size of the TV. When she walked around the grounds she said that the flowers were even more beautiful than I described. As far as my dad goes, she's still waiting for him. She thinks his train must be late coming in.'

'Oh Rose, well done for tackling all of that. You must be so relieved,' said Pascalle.

'Enormously. I'm glad that it all went so well and I've visited a few times and she still seems to be enjoying her "holiday". But I know that a bigger decision is looming, and I'm fretting about that. The good thing is that I'm in a much better place than I was two weeks ago, thanks to the two of you, so hopefully if all continues to go well I'll be better able to make the right decision for Mum. If that decision is for her to stay permanently and she's still happy, then it'll be easy.'

'I'm so glad for you Rose,' said Kate.

Rose smiled the broadest smile her friends had ever seen from her and took a deep breath before announcing, 'And that's not all. I've also been making decisions about myself and what the future holds for me, and I've started putting things in place. I went to see the letting agents and explained the situation to them. They were shocked that the arrangements for Sally's flat had been made without our knowledge and, probably because they were very keen to keep our business, said they'd do all they could to help us.

'I asked them to give Sally three months' notice on her flat, which I thought was generous. In fact, Sally had obviously seen what was coming and had given notice herself, so in a month's time she'll be moving out. I know she's not my problem, and she did take up with a man she knew was married, but I feel Richard manipulated and humiliated her as well, and in a way I feel sorry for her. I hope things turn out okay for her.'

'You have way more compassion than I'd have,' said Kate. 'You're obviously a much nicer person than me!'

'But it's more complicated than that, isn't it Rose?' interjected Pascalle.

Rose nodded her head. 'No matter how bad he's made me feel, I can't hate Richard. He's paid the ultimate price for his lies, he's lost his life, and although he's left a lot of unhappiness in his wake, at least I have a chance at a new life. I have to look on the positive side. Otherwise, I'll end up a bitter and twisted old woman living a miserable life and if that happened it would feel as though Richard had had the last laugh. I can't live full of resentment and hatred. I truly do wish Sally well. She's as much a victim as I am. Now I must look forward, find new ambitions.'

'Hear, hear!' said Pascalle.

'I like what you're saying, but easier said than done,' added Kate.

'True,' said Pascalle, 'but we're all experiencing the same feelings and I know we can help each other. What kinds of things are you thinking about Rose?'

'Top of the list is going back to work part time, not because I need the money, I just need purpose and structure to my day. Anyway, I love being an accountant. I'm good at it. You know where you are with figures. And I'm thinking about becoming a volunteer, although I don't know yet in what field.'

'Sounds like you'll be busy,' said Kate. 'I hope you still have time for our Friday class and coffee. It's the only thing keeping me going at the moment.'

'Don't worry,' said Rose. 'I'll be here.'

Pascalle smiled at her friend. 'You sound so confident Rose. You've really thought most things through haven't you. And I know you've said you're still considering it, but how close are you to making a decision about your mum? With these new things, you could be out more.'

Rose knew this was something she had to get absolutely right.

'That's very true. At the moment, I'm thinking that if she continues to be as happy in the home as she currently is I'll talk to them about extending her stay another month, and if that goes well, I'll agree to her staying there permanently. She seems very content. When I visit she's always chatting to someone. She barely registers I'm there until I produce a packet of biscuits!'

'I don't think you'll get a more positive outcome than that,' said Pascalle laughing. 'I'm so proud of you Rose, I'm proud of all of us. But with Violet gone how are you getting on in the house on your own? This must be the first time you've lived alone, except for Richard's sneaky little holidays.'

'It certainly isn't easy,' said Rose.

'You'll soon be out there buying curtains and sofas like me,' Kate laughed. 'Anything to fill that gap where Jason used to me. Unfortunately, it doesn't work.'

'Have you ever had that sense that the air at your side, where your husband used to be, feels cold?' asked Rose.

'I did all the time just after Jason died,' said Kate, shivering despite the warmth of the cafe. 'It felt icy. Not so much now, though.'

'Oddly I find his absence now feels entirely different than when he used to go on his trips,' said Rose.

'I guess it's because you know he's not coming back,' said Kate. 'The other day I was walking to the kitchen when I thought 'Jason, where are you?' It was as though my brain was still looking for him.'

'I had that too in the early days,' agreed Pascalle. 'It's a horrible feeling. Talking about horrible feelings....' she hesitated, then went on, 'I have one, that I'm going to have to decide sooner than I'd hoped about moving to Yorkshire. Justine and Peter are going up there this weekend to look at houses. They've seen two online that they think would be perfect for us, and they want me to go with them to see them. If we think one of them will work for all of us, they want to move as soon as possible.'

'Eeek Pascalle, how are you feeling about this?' asked Kate. 'This all seems very real now.'

'I know. I'm terrified if I'm being honest. I've told Justine several times that I'm not sure, but she just keeps on brushing my fears aside and saying, "Of course it will be a big change for all of us Mum, but I know when you get up there you'll love it." Then she always adds, "And don't you want to be able to spend more time with little Steffie?", and of course I melt! He's so adorable, and I absolutely love the time we're together now. Where he's concerned I have as much backbone and resolve as a chocolate souffle.'

They all dissolved into giggles at the image of a chocolate Pascalle deflating at the sight of her grandson. Then Rose's face turned very serious.

'It's an important consideration of course,' she said, 'but don't allow yourself to make this massive change for the benefit of someone else. I've discovered the hard way what can happen when you give up your own needs, desires, ambitions to please another person. I'm sure that Steffie will not turn out to be the cheat and liar that Richard was, but the fact is he will go to school and be out all day, then he'll grow into a teenager who spends all his time with his friends and won't want to know his parents or his grandmother, and he *will* leave home eventually. Where will that leave you?'

Pascalle's eyes began filling with tears. 'You know, you two women are quite remarkable. I'm so blessed to have met you and to have you in my life. You are each prepared to share your innermost thoughts and feelings, things you aren't even telling your own families, because you know each of us will understand. That's meant more to me than anything.

'Having two women who know exactly what I'm feeling without my saying a word is a gift. You pulled me out of the dark and suffocating place I'd been in for years into a much lighter and more hopeful present, and I am sure that whatever lies in each of our futures, your friendship will help me through. Your question is a good one Rose, but don't worry I won't be making any rash decisions. In a way I'm looking forward to getting out into the countryside for a weekend, and I love poking around other people's houses. But I will try to keep an open mind about everything, because I know I have to be sure. I have to make the best decision for me, even if it costs me a piece of my heart.'

TWENTY-NINE

July

At 9am sharp the next morning Justine had rung Pascalle's doorbell and hurried her out of the house and into the car so that they could beat the worst of the traffic on the way up to Yorkshire. By 1pm they were looking round the first of the two houses on their itinerary.

'This would make the perfect little flat for you Mum,' said Justine, opening a door which led from the main property.

On the other side of the door was a modern and reasonably spacious open plan kitchen and living room. The kitchen units were white gloss and looked new, and at sitting end of the room were French doors which opened out on a small patch of garden that had been fenced off from the main plot and looked out onto rolling hills beyond. Through a door on the other side of the room was a double sized bedroom with an ensuite bathroom. Everything had been painted white and it looked well maintained, so there was no doubt it would just be a question of Pascalle moving in.

'Yes I can see that it looks very nice,' she told her daughter, trying to sound enthusiastic. 'It has everything I would need, and what a glorious view from the window. I must admit to feeling quite overwhelmed by the scenery in this part of the country. The green seems to roll on and on into the horizon and be never ending.'

She paused turning back towards Justine. 'Do you think there would be room here for my kitchen table?'

Justine scanned the room.

'Perhaps not,' she said quietly. 'I guess you may not be able to bring everything with you. But the style here is so new and modern, it would give you the perfect chance to start afresh with furniture and curtains. After all, you're always saying it's ages since you bought anything new.'

Pascalle nodded as Justine rushed on giving her words a bright, positive spin.

'And Peter and Stefan and I would be just next door. It's a connecting door so it locks on both sides for privacy, but if you needed us we'd be right here.'

Pascalle continued nodding. 'I can see the attraction of that, indeed I can. And the little village we just drove through looks very pretty.'

'What did you think of the two craft shops? Once we've finished here we can go and look around the village and see inside the stores. I thought you'd like them.'

'You've put a lot of thought into finding the right place not just for you but also for me, Justine, and I so appreciate that,' said Pascalle linking arms with her daughter. 'Now let's look round the rest of this beautiful house and then take a walk down into the village. I'm itching to see everything.'

The main house was ideal for Justine, Peter and Stefan plus any future editions to the family, so for them it was a definite contender. Once they'd discussed where furniture would go and what adjustments they may have to make, they strolled down to explore the village, which was just a five minute walk away.

The two craft shops they'd spotted on the drive in were very well stocked and definitely met with Pascalle's approval. She especially loved the second one which had a whole wall of embroidery threads and knitting wools in all colours of the rainbow. It was a stunning arrangement. As Pascalle stood fingering a skein of embroidery thread from the display, Justine threaded her arm through her mother's and squeezed up tight.

'This is you Mum, this place. I can see you here buying thread and wool and knitting and sewing lovely cushions and hangings for your new home. Look they have an artist's corner over there – you could take up watercolour painting again. The countryside around here would provide amazing inspiration.'

Pascalle smiled at her daughter. 'Yes, it is absolutely beautiful. But no decisions yet – we still have one more house to look at.'

The second of Pascalle's prospective homes was a modern bungalow that had been built in the sprawling garden of the large family property, and it had its own living room, kitchen, bedroom and bathroom.

'You could definitely fit more of your current furniture in this house,' suggested Justine. 'I can see you here. Perhaps on reflection the other place was too small for you, Mum.'

Pascalle smiled in agreement. 'Justine you've selected very well, and I can imagine many happy times here, thank you.' Justine beamed at her mother's response.

That evening over dinner in a local pub, Justine, Peter and Pascalle excitedly discussed what they'd seen that day and decided to revisit both houses next morning. On the second viewing, Justine seemed to be favouring the larger of the two houses, the one with the bungalow in the garden, and after a late lunch, during which Justine and Peter talked about how they couldn't wait to start their new life and Pascalle tried to sound enthusiastic without committing to anything, they all piled back into the car and headed back to London. Thankfully Steffie fell asleep almost immediately which meant that Pascalle, sitting in the back seat beside him, could also have a little snooze, although her brain was much too active to allow her to drop off. Instead she pretended to sleep while trying to untangle her thoughts.

It was 10pm on Sunday night before she walked through her front door again, having agreed to talk to Justine in a couple of days' time and give her decision. It had been a busy, full-on weekend and Pascalle felt very tired.

She put down her bag, boiled the kettle while she took off her coat and hung it up, made herself a cup of camomile tea, and sank into the cuddler armchair that sat at the end of her kitchen. It was a favourite spot of her and Steffie's, partly because it was big enough for them both to snuggle up on while she read him a book, but also because of its view of the garden that Trevor had tended for all those years with love. Tonight, it was too dark to see the weeds that had sprung up since he'd gone and Pascalle, who was more a potterer than a gardener, was grateful for that.

She thought back over the previous two days. There was so much she'd loved about the trip – spending time with her family, poking into every nook and cranny of the houses with Justine, and discussing how her daughter and son-in-law could make them their own. As she sipped the soothing tea, she looked around her kitchen. In this home that she and Trevor had made together, this room was her favourite. It was large enough for a traditional French farmhouse scrubbed pine dining table, and she loved the French windows in the bay at the end of the room. Everywhere she looked she saw reminders of happy times here.

She'd cooked in this kitchen, nourished her family, sat with her daughters while they did their homework at the table, enjoyed coffee and chat with friends before Trevor's illness, and she'd decorated it using her skills. She'd embroidered the covers for the kitchen chair cushions with motifs of flowers and birds, she'd spent hours sewing a picture of the countryside around Arras, where she'd grown up, onto a huge wall-hanging which took up most of one wall, and she'd even painted each of their initials onto four little tiles which gathered in a cluster on the wall beside the dresser, itself stacked with hand painted plates and bowls she'd brought back from trips to France.

Now this room was a sort of sanctuary, a place of happy, comforting memories where she could see so many echoes of the old Pascalle. Was this the room, the home, where she would best find herself again and restart her life? Or was that with Justine and Stefan, in one of those new properties, living among the young, embarking on a new adventure, where no-one knew her and where she could be whatever and whoever she wanted to be? Not Pascalle the widow, but Pascalle the hippy…albeit an aging one!

'What would you advise me to do, Trevor?' she asked into the silence.

She smiled at the thought, drank the last of her tea and stood up, ready to go to bed. It had been a long, confusing couple of days, but she knew that she'd sleep tonight. Her decision had been made.

*

A few miles away, Kate was also pondering the future whilst lounging on her new pink velvet chaise longue, legs tucked up under her, snuggling into a soft lambswool throw pulled around her. She'd not long come off the phone with

Lila, during which they'd discussed Luke. She had barely heard from him since the disastrous birthday dinner, and she was missing him.

'I send him some jolly 'How are you doing?' type of messages, but I get very little in return,' she'd told Lila. 'If I'm lucky I'll get a 'Yeah all fine, just off to the football". Most of the times his reply is just a thumbs up emoji. What does he say when you see him?'

'He's fine Mum, honestly he is. But we don't talk much about you, because any time I mention you his face goes all dark and I don't like to see him like that so I usually change the subject.'

'That's so depressing, Lila. How has it come to this that my lovely son can't bear the thought of me? I keep thinking about what Pascalle told me about how she reacted to her dad's death and how it ruined her relationship with her mother, and I can't allow us to go down that same road.

'I'm sorry to burden you with this Lila. I'm sure you have plenty going on in your life without listening to me. I'll work it out somehow.'

'I really hope you do,' replied Lila, exasperation in her voice. 'I'm tired of being the middleman.'

As Kate pondered the call she recalled Pascalle's words, 'You have to fight for him. You're the adult, you must be the one to keep trying.'

Kate knew that Pascalle was right. It was up to her to mend this rift with her son. She let out a great long sigh. Sometimes she missed Jason so much she felt the weight of it might overwhelm her and this was one of those times. But she also knew she had to set aside her own grief and help her son through his. She picked up her phone. This time she wasn't going to let him get away with a bland response.

THIRTY

July

On Tuesday morning Justine arrived on Pascalle's doorstep. As she marched down the hallway into Pascalle's kitchen, with her mother following behind, she couldn't contain her excitement.

'Mum, Peter and I can't stop talking about that second house we saw and we really want to go for it. And that sweet bungalow would be just right for you. I could see from your face that you loved it too, and we really want to put in an offer before it gets snapped up. Please say you agree, Mum, please say you'll come to Yorkshire with us.'

Pascalle stood in the kitchen doorway looking at her lovely eldest daughter chattering on, her face bright, her eyes shining at the prospect of what lay ahead for her family, and her desperation that her mother be part of it, and she knew she was about to destroy everything.

'Sit down my darling,' she said kindly. 'I'll get us some coffee, and then we can talk.'

Justine's face fell. 'No Maman, no, please don't say that you won't come, please!'

Pascalle didn't reply, instead she busied herself making coffee and setting out the cups, all the while trying to formulate in her head the words that she hoped would make her daughter understand.

Finally when the coffee was ready, Pascalle sat at the table and poured it into two cups, placing one in front of Justine who had sagged into one of the chairs.

'Maman, I know even the bungalow was smaller than this house,' Justine tried again, desperation in her voice. 'I understand that leaving here and having to part with a lot of your furniture will be a sacrifice, but I hoped you'd see that it was a chance for you to start again. I've missed you so much these last four years, and I feel as though I've just got you back and I don't want to lose you again. Please come with us.'

Pascalle smiled a gentle smile. 'I too feel as though I've come back to life, my darling, back to you and to Stefan, and I have felt so happy being involved in your life again. I loved Yorkshire, it's a beautiful county, and the house you'd like is perfect for you. I can see all three of you, and perhaps a new little one, all living there and enjoying the fresh country air and all that space. But ma chérie I'm sorry, I won't be coming with you.'

At Pascalle's words, Justine's face turned stormy. 'I can't believe this Maman. I truly can't. How can you not come with us? Who's looked after you all this while, who's going to look after you when we're gone? Because like it or not Maman, whether you come or not, *we* are going.'

'Darling I'm only 66. I'm not ready for the knackers yard yet.'

'This is Evie's doing isn't it!' Justine fumed. 'That's why she came here. I thought it was to support me, but instead it was to support you. She told me this mad story about you having lots of husbands and running away from home and needing to find yourself, and how you couldn't live in Yorkshire because you'd be living someone else's life. But I didn't believe a word of it because I knew you'd come for me and you'd come for Stefan, but now I see I was completely wrong. Evie said I was being selfish. I think it's you who's being selfish Maman.'

'Justine, please try to listen to me. This has nothing to do with Evie. This is about me and my needing to live my life on my own terms. I grant you, the story does sound a bit mad, but my darling it's true.'

Visibly shaking, Justine snapped: 'If it's true then aren't you pushing me away just as Grandmaman pushed you away?'

Pascalle tried to remain calm. 'I can see why you'd think that. But I'm not pushing you away my gorgeous girl. I'm letting you go. This is what *you* want to do. This is *your* adventure. Yours, Peter's, Stefan's. I will always be grateful to you for standing by me these last four years, looking after me, not letting me drop right down to rock bottom. Justine, you kept me buoyant, you helped to save me, and you did that so that I could start living again. Now I must get on with that life, here in this house that I love, that's filled with memories that I can finally bear to recall and feel happy about.

'This is where *my* new life starts, *my* adventure. And you must get on with yours, in Yorkshire with your husband and son. You must live as you want, just as Evie does, and I must live as I want. I love you and your sister more than anything and part of that is letting you both go. Evie has her life in France, now yours will be in Yorkshire, and I will visit so often you'll wish you'd moved somewhere much, much further away.'

Justine dropped her head into her hands and sat still for a few moments. When she finally spoke her voice was choked with emotion.

'I just can't take this in, Mum. You've ruined everything. Everything. I think you're being incredibly selfish. I need to go now, talk to Peter. We need to think about this again.'

Justine grabbed her bag and coat and rushed out of the kitchen and down the hall. When she got to the front door she turned to Pascalle, her face a mask of absolute fury. 'Maybe Grandmaman was right to shut you out,' she spat. 'I certainly don't want you anywhere near us for a very long time.'

With that she slammed the door shut, leaving Pascalle standing alone in the hallway. She let out a long sigh and looked skywards. Trevor, please tell me I've done the right thing, because if I haven't there will be no coming back from this.

*

On Friday it was a subdued Pascalle who told Rose and Kate about her conversation with Justine.

'So what did she say when you told her?' asked Kate.

'She was devastated,' described Pascalle wearily. 'Furious. Told me I've ruined everything and was being selfish. Then she stormed out saying she didn't want to see me again for a long time. I don't feel good about it.'

'Have you heard from her since?' asked Rose.

'Not a word. Evie's phoned several times to tell me off. Apparently, Justine's been on the phone to her every evening, crying and saying how my pulling out has ruined all their plans. You see they needed me to sell my house here to be able to afford a place for us both. Now they can't buy the house they loved, and on top of that she's worried that once they go and I'm on my own I'll sink back into my depression and there will be no-one to get me out again.'

'You have us now,' quipped Kate. 'We'll haul you back up out of the gloom…if there is any more gloom.'

'Oh I'm sure there will be some gloom,' laughed Pascalle, 'especially when Justine does go, and she will because of Peter's job, but yes I do have you too lovely ladies to help me. And I'm honestly not worried about being in London on my own. Yorkshire and France aren't that far away – I can visit and they can visit. In some ways, I'm actually quite excited about it. I feel a sense of freedom. I only wish I knew what to do with that freedom.'

'Don't worry,' said Rose, 'you'll soon think of something. Just to be clear, you're staying and we're stuck with you?'

Pascalle nodded.

'Thank goodness for that!' Rose exclaimed. 'We need you.'

'I second that,' said Kate. 'I need more of your help on the Luke situation. I took your advice about keeping open the channels of communication and I basically bombarded him with texts asking to meet for a coffee and finally, after three days, he relented.

'We met yesterday morning at a coffee shop near his work, neutral ground I thought, and while he was quite frosty at first, I just chatted away, keeping things light, not mentioning anything to do with the house, and by the end he seemed a bit warmer towards me. We only had half an hour because he was on his morning break, but I asked if I could come again next week and he said yes. He hesitated at first, but he did agree.'

'I'm impressed,' exclaimed Pascalle. 'Well done you. Just bear in mind that you need to take baby steps. Stay patient. You've done a brilliant thing by contacting him, making the first move and being persistent. Now let him mellow a little and hopefully gradually he'll start coming towards you.'

Then Pascalle laughed, struck by the irony of what she'd just said. 'Listen to me, giving family advice. Me who's prepared to see her daughter and only grandchild move 200 miles away without her.'

The three women sat for a moment, contemplating the morning's discussion. Then Rose grabbed her coffee cup, held it up and said, 'Let's do a cheers to us…and to new beginnings. Whatever they may be.'

THIRTY-ONE

Still July, two weeks later

Kate and Rose were pulling on their shoes after their Friday yoga class when Kate asked how Violet was getting on in the home.

'Honestly, she's so happy there,' said Rose, rolling up her yoga mat. 'When I went in yesterday she was sitting in a circle with some other ladies, singing her heart out. Her eyes were shining with joy. I haven't seen her look so contented in years.'

'That must be such a relief for you, Rose.'

'In a way yes, it's a relief but it's also sad because I feel I've lost her entirely now. She barely looks at me when I visit. She has no idea who I am and when I sit down beside her she ignores me until I produce a packet of biscuits.

Funnily enough she always remembers that they're her favourite.' Rose laughed. 'But seriously, knowing she's so happy does lessen the guilt.'

'Have you decided whether to accept a permanent place for her there?'

'Definitely. I asked yesterday and they said from Monday she can be permanent. So now I can get on with focussing on me. I've started working again. My friend Nicky, who owns a café and is also my longest serving client, has come back to me and brought her brother who's a builder. Two clients aren't quite enough to keep me busy, but I don't have a mortgage and I have a good pension so I'm not really doing it for the money.'

'Sounds like you're pretty sorted,' said Kate, rolling up her yoga mat. 'I wish my finances were in as good order as yours. Maybe you could help me with them. I could be client number three.'

'I'd love to help you,' smiled Rose. 'And I'd only charge you mates rates! The one thing I haven't dealt with yet is the money from Richard's life insurance, but I can't bring herself to touch anything to do with him yet.'

As they walked into the cafe, they heard Pascalle come bustling up behind them. She'd stayed behind in the class to ask the teacher about one of the exercises she was finding difficult, and was now cheerily calling out, 'Wait for me, dippy hippy French woman coming through!' She was moving so fast that she accidentally bumped into Rose and knocked the bag and jacket she was carrying to the ground.

'Oh no, I'm so sorry,' she apologised. 'Let me help you pick all this up. My goodness Rose, this jacket is beautiful. Where did you get it from?'

Pascalle was holding up a black slimline jacket with a dramatic red and pink rambling rose applique which started just above the buttonhole and trailed up over the right shoulder, diagonally across the back of the jacket, finally curling round to the front and ending just below the button.

'I made it,' said Rose proudly. 'Do you like it?'

'Like it? I love it,' cried Pascalle. 'The tailoring on the jacket is exquisite and the applique is beautifully sewn on. It looks professional. I had no idea you could sew so well.'

'I've always loved sewing,' Rose said as they sat down at their table. 'In fact before I married Richard I used to make most of my own clothes. I particularly love making a plain garment and then decorating it to make it unique. But Richard hated handmade clothes and he was so discouraging about what I produced that I stopped sewing shortly after our wedding.'

'What made you start again?' asked Kate.

'I was sorting out a cupboard a couple of weeks ago and I found a pattern for the jacket and decided to give it a go. I wanted to see if I still had the talent,' she smiled.

Pascalle was quick to respond. 'If this jacket is anything to go by, you certainly do!'

'I did enjoy making it. It was quite cathartic because when you're focussing on getting something precisely right, you can't think about all the other things going on in your life. It's like you give your brain a break!'

'I know exactly what you mean,' said Pascalle. 'I used to make all my own clothes, and for the girls. I'd even dye some fabrics to get the right colour for a garment. Sewing is very good for the nerves. When Trevor was ill I'd have benefitted from escaping for an hour to a craft group or an artist's studio to just remind herself of who I was. Do something different. But there weren't any of those around.'

'Once I got started I really enjoyed it,' said Rose. 'I altered the pattern quite a bit and enjoyed making it my own. The more I sewed, the more confident I seemed to get.'

As Rose talked her eyes shone and her cheeks pinked up.

'It certainly looks as though it's done you good,' remarked Kate. 'I don't think I've seen you looking this animated and well about anything. It's done for you want those bereavement groups couldn't.'

'You know Kate, you're absolutely right,' said Rose. 'I can see now that I went to those groups looking for answers to two questions: Why had Richard been killed? And how was I meant to go on? No-one will ever be able to answer the first question, but because of the help you've both given me I have answers to the second one. The sewing has allowed me to rediscover a part of myself that I'd thought was dead and buried. While I was working out the pattern I felt the old me emerging again, and there was something really interesting about being the person I was before I met Richard. I liked her! I'm keen to be her again. I'd be happy to go on with life as her.

'I mean the bereavement groups did serve a purpose and they helped to some extent. Now if it had been a bereavement group that offered sewing - that would have been perfect!'

Pascalle's eyes lit up. 'Ladies,' she said, 'I think you've just given me the best idea ever! I'm not going to say what it is yet. I need to ponder it a bit more.'

'What idea? What did I say?' asked Rose. 'Go on, tell us.'

'No, I'm saying nothing. I need to think. I'm going to go now before you put me on a rack and torture my idea out of

me! All I'll say is if it comes off, it could be the start of
something new for us all.'

THIRTY-TWO

August

The café was busy when Kate arrived and she was pleased to see that she was first and that their usual table was free. She'd been meeting Luke here every Thursday for the last four weeks and she felt that this table was definitely the best. It was tucked in a corner so it felt private and it had a clear view of the door which meant she could see Luke's face as he arrived and before he saw her. She felt that gave her a clue to how he was really feeling about meeting her, and she was pleased to see he usually looked pretty neutral - neither happy not anxious - although she couldn't help feeling a little disappointed when his face creased into a lacklustre smile at the sight of her. Still, she tried to reassure herself, at least he was still coming to meet her.

Although this was their fourth coffee, conversation was still a little strained. They stuck to safe topics like work, what he'd done at the weekend, how Cyn was doing, family news from Scotland. It wasn't at all the usual free flowing chat and banter that she'd usually have with Luke, but it was keeping open the lines of communication and Kate was happy to settle for that.

She checked the time on her phone. He'd be here any minute. She nervously played with the sugar sachets that had been tucked into a little container at one end of the table, as always feeling on edge before he arrived, half worried that he wouldn't turn up, and then where would that leave her?

The sound of the door opening drew Kate's attention away from the packets of sugar. Here he was, thank goodness. But this time he had a frown on his face, and a second later Kate realised why. Right behind him was Cyn.

Kate hadn't seen her since that terrible birthday dinner, hadn't heard from her, and frankly hadn't wanted to. Kate felt strongly that Cyn was fuelling a lot of Luke's anger towards his mother although she couldn't really understand why. She'd always got along pretty well with her daughter-in-law, who was usually pleasant when they were together at family gatherings. Kate knew she'd never have the same kind of relationship with Cyn as she had with Lila, but she was delighted that Cyn had seemed so keen to join in the Latimer family events, and things between them had been amicable. Now while Cyn appeared friendly on the surface, Kate felt her digging a knife into her back.

'Hi darling,' said Kate as Luke approached the table. 'And Cyn, lovely to see you too. Sit down both of you and I'll go and order us some drinks. Cappuccinos alright?'

Kate knew that this was Luke's favourite coffee and he'd had it every week they'd met, so she felt on safe ground.

'Yes fine,' said Luke, flatly.

'I'll have a latte if that's okay Kate,' said Cyn with a supercilious look on her face.

Kate smiled. 'Of course, whatever you want.' As she walked away from the table she was aware that the atmosphere between Luke and Cyn was strained. She couldn't hear what they were saying but standing at the counter placing her order she saw them whispering to each other, Cyn smiling, Luke appearing cross.

'They're bringing the drinks over,' said Kate, returning to the table. 'How are you both? You look well, Cyn.'

Kate kept a smile on her face and her voice light. She couldn't understand why Cyn had come today but she didn't want to question her because time with her son was precious and she didn't want it spoiled.

Cyn was wreathed in smiles as she told Kate about the lovely weekend away she'd just had with her sister in Brighton where they'd stayed in a posh beachfront hotel, did a bit of sunbathing, explored the antique shops in The Lanes, admired the work of the artists displayed along the promenade, and went to a couple of clubs in the evenings.

'It was such fun, Kate,' she simpered. 'We ate fish and chips and ice cream and just had a great time!'

Kate tried to sound interested. 'Your sister?' she asked. 'I always thought that you and Donna didn't see eye to eye.'

'That's all in the past, Kate. We're best friends now,' Cyn smiled.

'I'm glad to hear that you're getting along better. It's good to hear of family being close. Luke, what did you do while Cyn was away?'

The drinks had arrived and Luke was looking at his so intently that Kate thought it might explode at any moment. The tension in his voice was palpable as he answered, 'The usual, Mum.'

Kate felt on the back foot. She'd come for a quiet coffee with her son and now she was the referee in a battle between him and his wife, with no idea what the fight was about.

'What about you, Kate?' asked Cyn, with a butter-wouldn't-melt look on her face. 'What lovely things did you buy for your house this weekend?'

Luke's face froze and Kate felt as though she'd been slapped. She couldn't believe her daughter-in-law, someone she'd shown only warmth and kindness to, was taunting her like this and ruining this precious time with her son. She'd resolved to stay polite and civilised, but that resolve was weakening in the face of Cyn's hurtful sarcasm. If only she knew what this was all about.

Kate took a deep breath to clear the emotion from her voice but just as she was about to respond, Luke stood up. Clearly furious, he said very quietly with obvious great restraint, 'We're going Cyn.'

'But I haven't finished my latte…'

'We're going,' he ordered. Then he turned to Kate and said, 'Sorry Mum.'

Kate didn't know what to do or say as Cyn reached under the table for her bag, then smiled sweetly at Kate saying, 'Bye, lovely to see you. Thanks for the coffee.'

She strolled away, Luke charging behind her, practically pushing her out of the door.

Kate sat there stunned, feeling a mixture of devastation and confusion. Her hard-fought meeting with her son had been taken over and ruined and she didn't know why. What had she, Kate, done to deserve such viciousness?

All the way home on the train she went over and over the events of the morning, trying to understand them. She managed to hold off the tears until she got to her front door, and once inside her house they fell.

Frustration overwhelmed her. How could she fix this if she didn't know what it was all about? Losing Jason had been bad enough, now she was sure she'd also lost her son

THIRTY-THREE

August

The next day a text arrived on the YogaBunnies group chat from Pascalle.

Come to my house on Saturday at 2. There's something I want to discuss with you. Tea, wine and cake will be provided

*

On Friday when they met for yoga, all Rose and Kate could talk about was Pascalle's mysterious message and what she could be up to. Their curiosity was all the more piqued when she didn't show up for the class.

'Do you think she's ill and wants to tell us the bad news at her home?' speculated Rose.

'I don't think she'd be offering tea, wine and cake if she was sick,' countered Kate. 'Whatever it is I wish she'd come here to tell us. I so wanted to tell her about my awful meeting with Luke this week and see if she could help me make sense of it.'

Kate was still fretting about the encounter with Cyn on the Saturday when she heard Rose's car horn sound outside. They'd decided to travel together and Kate was pleased to be distracted by yet more speculation about what was behind Pascalle's text.

'One thing's for sure,' said Kate. 'The cake will be good!'

When they arrived, Pascalle's face was pink with excitement and as she ushered them to the kitchen table it was obvious that she was bursting to tell them her news. The table was set: a huge carrot cake covered in a thick layer of sticky frosting was on a stand ready to be sliced, the tea was brewing in a big blue and white Burleigh teapot, and a bottle of red wine was open and ready to be poured into the waiting large glasses.

Pascalle filled one of the glasses almost to the brim and then looked over at Rose.

'No wine for me,' said Rose. 'I'm driving.'

Pascalle laughed and said, 'No, no this is for me, to calm my nerves! You two get started on the tea!'

As Kate and Rose poured the tea and served themselves cake, they were becoming increasingly concerned. What could be making Pascalle so agitated? Kate spoke up first.

'Okay Pascalle, we're stocked up with tea and cake,' she said. 'Now put us out of our misery. What's behind your mysterious text?'

Pascalle took a deep breath in and began to explain. 'It all started,' she said, 'with Rose's beautiful jacket...'

*

Kate and Rose heard Pascalle out and then sat in silence, nodding.

'Well...?' asked Pascalle expectantly. 'Don't you love it?'

Kate and Rose looked at each other, and then smiled. Pascalle, who was by now sitting bolt upright and clasping her hands in anticipation, let out a long sigh of relief.

'Yes, I certainly do love it,' said Rose. 'But I want to make sure I'm absolutely clear, so go over it one more time.'

Pascalle swallowed hard and outlined her idea once again.

'I want to set up a bereavement centre…sort of. Only it wouldn't be a centre as such, more of a regular meeting place, and it wouldn't just be for the bereaved, it would be for people who'd lost or were losing someone or something important to them, and that someone could include themselves.'

Kate and Rose nodded. 'Ok got that, go on,' said Kate.

'As you know, when Trevor was ill I was so immersed in looking after him, trying to keep him alive, trying to make every one of his days special that I lost all my fire, my sense of humour and fun, I lost myself. Even when Justine came to sit with Trevor to give me a break, I had nowhere to go that felt right for me.

'In the early days of his illness, I'd go for coffee with my friends, but they didn't want to hear me talking about how ill he was, all the intimate and messy things that it broke my heart to do for him, or about the nights I lay awake beside him, listening to him breathe, wondering if each breath was going to be the last. They had their own things going on and they were looking for a jolly chat about all the places they were going with their husbands, the wonderful restaurants they'd been to, the laughs they'd had, and have their minds taken off their problems. They didn't want to hear about mine, only I had nothing else to talk about. I was ground down, tired, terrified.

'In the end, I stopped contacting them and they stopped contacting me. Instead I'd spend my couple of hours of freedom either wandering aimlessly around the nearest shopping centre or, if the weather was nice, sitting on a quiet bench in the park having a cry. Neither of which was helpful. What would have given be a boost would have been going somewhere that was bright and lively, where I could talk if I wanted to, to someone who was sensitive, who'd listen and who'd understand. And if I didn't want to talk, I could quietly read a magazine or a book, or knit or sew, and no-one would bother me.

'The key would have been that this was a safe space with the right atmosphere. Somewhere I could feel like me and where I could choose to wear a fuschia coloured sequin top if I felt like it and laugh a little and not feel judged for leaving my terminally ill husband on his sickbed. Somewhere that I could get expert help and advice if I wanted it. That's what I want to create. A place where people who are grieving or bereaved can go and just be.'

'This sounds like a pretty ambitious project, Pascalle,' said Kate.

'Yes, it is,' Pascalle agreed. 'But in other ways it's simple because it's come out of our experience. It's formed from what we each faced, and how the three of us together have helped each other to get through it.

'Rose, wouldn't you have loved a bereavement group where there was no pressure to speak, where you could sew and listen and think and grieve among people who understood your situation? Where you could quietly allow your mind to process what had happened or ask for help of a professional if you felt you needed it, so that you could finally answer all those questions you kept asking yourself? Wouldn't you have preferred to just drop in when you most needed it, to a place where the expectation was zero, but the benefit was knowing everyone was in a similar boat and you could feel safe.

'Kate, wouldn't you have gained so much from going somewhere that wasn't full of couples holding hands, gazing into each other's eyes and cooing into each other's ears? Where you could sit and stare into the distance, away from reminders of Jason, work and people constantly asking you if you're okay and but not wanting to hear that you're not?'

Pascalle sat back in her chair and waited. There was silence in the kitchen as Kate and Rose processed what their friend had just outlined. Finally Rose spoke and when she did she had the most enormous smile on her face.

'Pascalle, you know I think you're amazing and wonderful, but now I'm adding brilliant to that list. What a great idea. But...I still have questions.'

'Fire away.'

'Ok, here goes! Where would it be held? How would it be financed? Who'd run it? Would it be a permanent space, open all the time? Who exactly would it be for? Surely bereavement means that someone has died, and yet you said you'd have gone there while Trevor was still alive?'

Pascalle calmly took the questions one at a time.

'I'm thinking it could be held in my local church hall. That's where I was yesterday. I went to have a meeting with the vicar, Pauline. I got to know her well when Trevor died. She said she could see merit in the idea and knew many members of her congregation who'd benefit from it, but she needed to know more before saying a definite yes. But she agreed in principle.

'In terms of who'd run the centre, I imagined that I'd run it with the help of a volunteer bereavement counsellor, and I really hope that both of you would get involved too. The financial side is yet to be sorted out, and whether it's a permanent place or just open a few hours every few days would depend on money and what the vicar will let us have.

'As for your final question, would it only be for those whose loved one has already died? That's a definitive "No". While Trevor was alive, I was grieving. I was bereaved. I'd lost the man he once was and the happy life we'd had together. When he died, the loss of the person was as huge as if he'd dropped dead just like your poor Jason, Kate.

'Rose you are dealing with the loss of your mother. She's still alive, but she's no longer recognisable as the woman who was your mother, and I'm sure that's as difficult to bear as the loss of Richard. Bereavement doesn't always start at the end of life, grieving for what's been lost can start much earlier and for some people it never stops. This can be a place for people who are grieving for whatever reason to escape, breathe, reconnect with themselves and head back into the world a little refreshed.'

Silence fell around the table as the women reflected on their own losses. It wasn't yet a year since Jason had died and Kate still felt a sense of disbelief, had days when the sadness seemed to reach deep down into every part of her body and stay there like a ton weight, crushing her spirit, making her believe she'd never feel anything other than sad again. And yet she *had* laughed again, they all three had.

319

Over time, Kate could see that they could feel joy again. In being able to speak to someone who knew how they felt, they'd each had fewer days when the sadness made them feel like they were walking through treacle and more when the world seemed sunny and bright, when the heavy black clouds were replaced by a piercing blue clear sky, when they raised a smile at a memory rather than shedding a tear.

Rose picked up the bottle of wine and poured each of them a healthy glassful. She raised her own glass and said, 'I know I'm driving, but I think this calls for a celebration. Pascalle, I love your idea. I can see how it would work and I for one am definitely in. What about you Kate?'

Kate pondered for a moment longer, and when she spoke her voice was full of emotion.

'Pascalle, this place you want to create sounds truly wonderful, and I would be honoured to help you set it up and run it. And since it will be powered by the three of us, I don't see how it could be anything other than a huge success. I think this calls for a group cheers!'

They clinked their glasses together and took a long drink.

'This wine is delicious,' said Rose. 'I hope you have another bottle because we have a lot to discuss and we're bound to need more than one to oil those brain cells. Kate, I hope you don't mind but we're getting an Uber home.'

'I don't mind at all,' laughed Kate, 'and I do have one more question. What would it be called?'

'Well,' said Rose looking round the table, 'we three of us have one thing in common, so why don't we start there. I vote our working title is "The Dead Husbands Club"!'

With another round of cheers, the women got down to the serious business of setting up Pascalle's centre for those who'd lost but wanted to find.

THIRTY-FOUR

August

Kate sat on her pink chaise longue surveying her living room. There was no doubt it had changed in the 11 months since Jason had died. She didn't really understand how she'd found the energy to do all of this in the midst of her bewilderment about what had happened to Jason, but she'd felt an irresistible drive to change the look of her home and now after a bit of trial and error over colours and patterns, she felt she'd got it right. For her.

Some of Jason's books were still there, tamed into a few shelves. The hated black velvet corner sofa unit and the matching saggy armchair that had been his favourite place to sit had gone to the tip. His games console and games were packed into a box now in the loft incase Luke wanted them one day.

The living room was now a symphony in blush pink and grey, Kate had to agree. Never in a million years would she have had those colours while Jason was still alive, but she loved them. The scheme made her feel happy inside, secure. She could look round at this room and see warm, comfortable spots not flash points.

The pink had followed her upstairs and she'd swapped the blue and teal ikat for long pink linen curtains at her bedroom windows, held back with pretty soft chiffon tie backs that Rose had helped her make. She'd splashed out on a matching linen duvet set and added cushions and throws to the bed, plus a raspberry pink velvet chair in one corner. Much as she missed Jason in this, their private sanctuary, missed his warmth beside her on chilly nights, missed chatting and planning the day, weeks, months ahead, missed laughing with him - and she did miss all those things - she no longer felt lost and alone in this room, because it felt like her.

Lila had laughed at how pink the house was becoming when she came to help Kate repaint the hall and giggled as she was applying the first coat.

'Mum, what colour did you say this was?' she asked.

'Oriental Jasmine,' said Kate. 'Why?'

'And what colour did you think that was going to be?'

'I was expecting a soft and pale yellow. Something very mellow.'

'Well, this looks remarkably like pink to me!'

'I don't understand,' said Kate confused. 'It didn't look pink when I painted a sample square.' Then she burst out laughing because she couldn't disagree, there was a definite pink tinge to this paint! 'Oh my God! Everything's pink! No wonder Luke hates it,' she exclaimed. 'Maybe I'm subconsciously trying to create a womb-like environment.'

'Well, you're succeeding,' said Lila. 'Mind you, it does look quite pretty and happy, like looking at everything through rose tinted glasses.'

Lila's words struck a chord in Kate because it was something she'd been worrying about. Maybe she was only focussing on the positive these days, not letting her mind gradually deal with the grief. Thinking about Jason was still so painful that she couldn't often do it. Most times when he came into her mind, she felt a door slam on the thought. Was she in denial, closing her mind to the reality that he was dead? And was this fake 'I'm fine' front that she put up actually doing her emotional harm? All her friends

324

seemed to think that because she wasn't a continual sobbing wreck, that she must be 'fixed'.

'You're doing so well,' they'd exclaim. 'You look *so* well.'

Inside she'd be saying, yes that's because I'm standing here in front of you with a smile on my face looking chipper. You don't see me on a Saturday morning sobbing my eyes out at the prospect of yet another weekend ahead on my own while you're out having a great time with your partners. Nor do you see me sitting on my own at every single dinner time, picking away at some ready meal because there's no fun in cooking for one and even less in eating alone. But she didn't say any of this out loud because Kate had been brought up to get on with things and that was what she was doing. She wasn't getting it right all the time - her pink palace was an illustration of that - but she was doing her best. She so wished that Luke could begin to understand that.

Kate sighed, looked at the book on the little marble topped table that sat beside her chaise - 'this is my reading nook,' she'd informed Lila - and was about to pick it up when the doorbell rang.

Surprised, Kate checked the image on the Ring doorbell. It was Luke. Initially her heart soared at the sight of her son making an unexpected visit, even thought it was quite late, then it sank - she really wasn't in the mood for another argument. Still, she couldn't turn him away. At the door she took a couple of deep breaths, all the time counselling herself to stay calm regardless of what was going to happen next, and opened the door. Luke stood there, head bowed with tears were streaming down his face.

'Oh Mum,' he sobbed, and fell into her arms.

Stunned, Kate wrapped her arms around him and held him close, all the while reassuring him, 'It's okay Luke, I've got you. Come in so I can close the door. Now tell me what's happened.'

She spoke with a confidence that masked her feelings of utter terror. Her heart was racing as fast as her thoughts. Had something terrible happened to Lila or Cyn? Or even Luke himself? He seemed intact, but utterly inconsolable.

After a few moments she managed to manoeuvre both of them along the hall and into the living room. When she went back to close the front door, she checked the street for police cars. None. So, a family member hadn't been in an accident or been murdered.

Back in the living room, she sat beside Luke on the sofa, arms cradling him again and begged, 'Luke tell me what's wrong. You're scaring me. Please tell me.'

Finally he found enough breath to whisper, 'I'm sorry Mum. I've been an absolute pig to you and I'm so sorry.'

Kate held him ever more tightly. 'Don't worry love, don't worry,' she soothed. 'We've all had a terrible time since your dad died. But it's okay, it will all be okay.'

They sat together on the sofa in each other's arms for a full 10 minutes while Luke's sobs subsided, his breathing became normal again and he gradually calmed down. Kate was reminded of all the times when he was a little boy that she'd soothed him like this after he'd fallen over or had a fight with a friend. There was the time toddler Lila had broken his favourite Buzz Lightyear toy, and Luke had sobbed for a full day. Or the day he was too ill to go to school and was devastated because he had the starring role of Joseph in the nativity play. 'But Mum I'll be fine,' he'd pleaded, despite being white as a sheet with black circles under his eyes from being up half the night vomiting.

'No Luke you won't be,' she'd told him. 'You have norovirus and what if you're sick into the crib - where will baby Jesus lay his little head then?'

In those moments, when her child needed her, Kate had felt most like a mother and even though he'd hurt her over these past months, caused her to cry many tears of her own, and stirred up feelings of fear that she'd lost him and would never get him back, she knew she would forgive him. He was her son and she loved him, and her arms would always be open and ready to welcome him back.

Finally, he seemed calm enough for her to loosen her grasp. 'Cup of tea, darling? Or something stronger?'

'Do you have any brandy?' he asked.

Kate went to fetch it with a smile on her face. Her son was back. The question was, was he back for good?

THIRTY-FIVE

That same evening

While Kate was holding close to her heart the warm hope that she and Luke could work things out, a couple of miles away, Pascalle's heart was heavy with sadness. Justine, Peter and Stefan were leaving for Yorkshire in two days' time, and they wouldn't be returning. Although she had stood by her reasons for not going with them, Pascalle had nevertheless been dreading this day.

Justine had sounded frosty on the phone when she'd called yesterday to tell Pascalle that they'd decided to rent a house in Yorkshire for a few months and buy when Peter was settled in his job and they'd had a chance to properly get to know the area. They were renting out their London house through a management company so they wouldn't have to worry about it, and nor would Pascalle.

Then Justine's voice had softened as she whispered, 'There's still time for you to change your mind, Maman.'

Pascalle's heart had lurched and tears sprang to her eyes. It would be so easy to say yes. To go with her wonderful little family to the glorious green countryside of Yorkshire. To start everything afresh there - her life, her centre, her mind and her emotions. But no, she thought, no. It has to be here, in my life on my terms. She held fast to her decision, even though it broke her heart.

'My darling girl, I love you so very much,' she'd said gently, for she knew that what she had to say would in turn damage her daughter's heart even more. 'I love all of you very much, but I'm not coming with you. This is your adventure, yours and Peter's and Steffie's, and whoever else may join your wonderful family. My adventure is here, so this is where I shall stay. But I send you on your way with all the love I have in my heart.'

There was quiet on the other end of the phone, just the sound of breathing. Finally, a little voice said, 'I love you too, Maman.' And the line went dead.

Pascalle cried for a full hour and then resolved to put on a cheerier face and go to see Justine tomorrow before they

330

left and bid them all a safe journey. But first she had to find something.

She knelt down in front of the chest of drawers in her bedroom, opened the bottom drawer and lifted out a small wooden chest that she kept there. She called it her box of treasures and it contained all those precious things she'd collected throughout her life, things that had no monetary value but were priceless in terms of memories. She opened the lid and sorted through locks of hair from the girls' first haircut, a pretty Brussels lace handkerchief her grandmother had given her, a silver bangle that had been a gift from her other grandparents when she was a baby, and various other keepsakes until finally she saw, sitting at the back of the box, the corner of a small parcel wrapped in purple tissue paper. This was what she was looking for.

She lifted out the parcel, opened the delicate paper and once again was overwhelmed by the beauty of what lay inside. It was a heart shaped cushion, no bigger than the palm of her hand, made of the softest blood red satin. Exquisitely embroidered across the front of the cushion in a fine silk gold thread were the words, 'Mon Coeur'.

Just weeks after she'd met Mattieu, and knowing that he was the man for her, Pascalle's mother Evangeline had made the cushion and given it to him as a sign of her love.

'I can give you nothing else but my heart,' she'd whispered to him. With tears in his eyes, he'd told her that he would never ask for more.

When Pascalle turned 18, her father had gifted the cushion to her with the words, 'What greater gift can a father give his daughter than his heart.'

Pascalle had treasured her father's gift, carrying it with her to Paris, to Brighton and to London. Two husbands knew nothing of this precious object, but when Pascalle was sure she wanted to spend the rest of her life with Trevor, she gifted it to him. Just as Mattieu had done, Trevor wept and held Pascalle to him, and told her he'd never ask for more. Now he was gone, but her heart was still full of love, and it was time for it to have another home.

She rewrapped the little satin heart in the tissue paper, found a pretty gift bag and put it inside. On a label she wrote:

'Ma chérie Justine, believe that however far away from me you travel, wherever your adventures take you, you will always have my heart.'

With that, she tied the label to the bag and set it beside her handbag for the morning.

THIRTY-SIX

Still that same evening

Back at Kate's, the double measure of brandy she'd served up seemed to have worked its magic and within a few minutes of drinking it, Luke was still shaky but calm. Kate suggested they have a hot drink and Luke followed her to the kitchen. They worked companionably around each other making tea for Kate and coffee for Luke, while cutting slices of the lemon drizzle cake Kate had baked that afternoon.

'I felt like doing something homey and traditional, so I baked a cake,' Kate explained. 'It's as well you came round because if I'd had to eat it all myself I'd be the size of a house by the end of the weekend.'

'Don't worry Mum,' said Luke. 'It's my favourite so I'm more than happy to take some off your hands.'

They chatted as they worked and then sat down at the breakfast bar as they'd done every afternoon when Luke and Lila were children and couldn't wait to tell her about their day at school. As they'd grown older, the conversation had turned to jobs and relationships. Now they were making general small talk about work and who they'd seen recently and how were Lila and Cyn.

Realising that Luke's state wasn't caused by an emergency, Kate decided to keep things light in the hope that he'd eventually feel secure enough to tell her what was wrong, and it was obvious that he was doing his best to be sociable. Suddenly he became a bit more anxious and started fiddling with his coffee cup and capturing the last crumbs of cake with his finger as he spoke.

'The thing is Mum, I just miss him,' he said, his voice thick with emotion. 'I miss Dad *so* much.'

Kate let the words hang in the air for a few moments, then said in a soothing voice, 'Of course you do, Luke. It's less than a year since he died. You're bound to still miss him.'

'You know Mum, there isn't a single happy memory that I have that he's not in,' Luke went on. 'I've tried to use those to make me feel better. People say, don't they, that their happy memories of the dead person bring them comfort. But I don't feel that at all. They make me worse. Sometimes I think that without Dad I'll never be truly happy again. Not ever. How can anyone live feeling like that?'

Kate tried to summon some words to comfort him, but Luke carried on speaking. It was as though he was releasing feelings and thoughts that had been bottled up for way too long.

'Then I come here to see you Mum, because I do want to see you, to help you, to support you, I really do. But every time I come there's something of Dad's gone, replaced by something new that he'd never have had in the house. The curtains, the sofa, that pink chair! They're all lovely Mum, don't get me wrong, and I accept that they make you feel better, but this doesn't look like the home I grew up in and that makes me feel even more sad. It's as though you've pushed Dad out, and I've lost my childhood as well as my dad. And that makes me feel angry towards you, and I don't want to feel angry towards you because you're my mum, and the only parent I have left.'

Kate opened her mouth to try again, but Luke had worked up a head of steam and there was no stopping him.

'And something else, Mum. Something else I really can't understand. When we were growing up you were always saying we couldn't afford this and couldn't afford that. If Dad took me or me and Lila out somewhere fun, you'd always complain to him when we came home about how much it had cost. Usually, you'd have a fight about it. I remember you standing at the breakfast bar in here, fists clenched, obviously seething about something he'd said, while Dad sat feet up watching TV in the living room, completely ignoring the fact that you were upset.

'Now you're spending money like water. How come? Where's it coming from? Why now when you only have one income can you afford to spend all this money on things that used to be out of the question? I don't understand it, Mum.'

Kate was startled. Some of this she'd been expecting, but not all, and she didn't quite know where to start. She thought for a few moments, debating with herself about how much to tell him. Then she thought about the pain she'd seen in Rose's face when she realised that Kate hadn't told her about the rumours about Richard's affair. Even though Rose had forgiven her, Kate still felt guilty about keeping Rose in the dark, as though her decision to hide what she knew had added to Rose's sense of betrayal. At that moment, Kate knew that telling the truth, no matter how painful it was to hear at the time, was the right thing to do. So, she took all her courage in both her hands, stood up and said gently, 'I'm going to make us another drink and then I'll tell you everything. It's not going to be easy, and some of it you won't like, but you're a grown man and you deserve, no *need* to know the truth.'

Luke's expression changed to one of panic. Then he nodded his head and appeared to brace himself as Kate, having refilled the drinks, sat down again at the breakfast bar and began to tell her story.

*

When Kate had first met Jason he was a final year student at Strathmore University near Glasgow, and she was already in her first job on a local paper in her home town, just a few miles away from the city. She was earning and Jason only had his university grant, most of which went on his digs and the student union bar. Or so Kate thought.

Even though she didn't earn much, since she was in paid employment it seemed natural for her to pay for most things. Jason was almost always skint, but on the odd occasion when he had money, he'd treat her to a fancy meal, or they'd slip away for a romantic night in a lovely hotel. When he had money he was flash with it.

After they married, they both moved to London because Kate got a job on a magazine and Jason trained as a secondary school teacher. Once he qualified he easily got a job, so they were both working. Initially, paying rent on a flat and then a mortgage on a house, even at London prices, should have left them enough from two salaries to have some fun, only Jason still always seemed skint.

'At first I thought he was just useless with money and blamed his mother for not teaching him how to budget,' Kate explained to Luke. 'I tried to educate him in the art of eeking out his salary to last a month. I even put the electricity bill in his name and set up a direct debit on his account to force him to leave some in it to pay the bill, in the hope that would teach him how to manage money. When we were almost cut off for three months of non-payment, I began to realise there was a problem.

'Basically, he'd spent every penny of his salary without a thought for the bill. Fortunately, we hadn't gone down the route of having a joint bank account or we'd have been in real trouble. I had enough savings to pay the arrears and we kept our electricity.'

Until that point, Jason had always been dismissive when she had tried to talk to him about money, but this time she made him sit him down and insisted they discuss it. She

338

asked him straight out what he spent all his money on. After about an hour of arguing, with Jason initially brushing off Kate's concerns as 'just her imagination' and then being downright insulting to her, he finally revealed that most of his money went to the bookie.

'The bookie?' broke in Luke. 'What, you mean he bet his money on racehorses?'

'And the dogs, and the football results, and if by some miracle he won something, he'd take his winnings off to one of the casinos in town and lose it all there. Every single penny.'

Luke looked completely stunned and sat shaking his head. 'Dad was a gambler? I had no idea.'

'Yes he was. Totally addicted. And it didn't end there.'

In admitting everything to Kate and seeing how distraught his wife was, Jason agreed to get help and promised to stop gambling. Kate took over the responsibility for the bills with Jason paying a set monthly sum from his salary into her account to cover his share of the household bills, and for a while everything seemed okay. Luke and Lila arrived, and Jason absolutely adored his children. He and Kate progressed in their careers and earned more, which should have meant more being contributed to the household pot as expenses for a family increased, but every time Kate suggested to Jason that he up his contribution, he got angry. His eyes would blaze and his face grew hard, and he'd change into someone she didn't recognise. She knew he'd never physically hurt her, but she hated to see him change from her fun-loving Jason to this raging stranger.

'The thing is Luke, I always avoid talking about money. With anyone, even my husband. I'd rather pay for things myself than ask others to contribute, so I never knew how much your dad really earned, and I hated the arguments that would follow me asking for an increase in his contribution, so I stopped asking. I'd just use more of my own money, but I should have been braver, because I knew there was a problem brewing. I just didn't want to face it.'

The first signs that the problem was mushrooming came when Jason started being flash with his cash again. He'd organise a day out at a paintball centre for him and Luke and a few of his friends, or he'd take him for a 'boys' weekend' to a racetrack for a driving experience complete with slap up dinner afterwards, and a night at a fancy hotel. Or he'd buy himself the latest gaming console and a whole collection of games. Sometimes he'd hand Lila £100 and tell her to buy herself a treat. But he never treated Kate.

'That's when I realised what was really going on,' said Kate. 'For an intelligent man, he could be really dumb. He thought I wouldn't notice how flash he was becoming with the two of you, and that if he didn't spend his winnings on me, I wouldn't suspect he was gambling again. How could I not notice all the fun and expensive things he was giving you both? By this time all my money was going towards keeping the house going, paying for childcare and food. Every year I'd try to save enough money for us to have a week's holiday on the Isle of Wight but affording that meant I had to go without fairly basic things, like new clothes. It was so frustrating, and he couldn't see the effect it was having on me.'

'Oh my God Mum, so did he owe thousands?' asked Luke.

'Well, he gambled thousands and thousands over the years, and with the advent of online gambling it was easier than ever to lose money, but no, he never got into huge debt, thank goodness. Once he'd paid his very small contribution to the household bills, he gambled the rest plus almost everything he won, but he didn't go beyond that.

'But that's why our furniture was decades years old, why the kitchen cupboards are falling apart, why the curtains were so offensive to me because they'd been washed into submission, and why I couldn't wait to get rid of the corner sofa. That was the only piece of furniture we bought in the last 15 years. Our old one was literally threadbare, and I desperately wanted a corner unit because I had this picture of us all snuggling up on it watching TV together on something really comfy. The one I wanted cost £3,000 and I saved for that sofa for two years. Even though it was me paying for it, Dad wasn't convinced we needed a new one and kept insisting we should spend the money on something more fun.

'But it was *my* savings, so I told him I was going ahead. He said it was his house too and he should have a say in how it was furnished, so he insisted on coming to the shop with me to help me choose. To appease him and try to make the shopping trip more pleasant, I told him he could choose whatever sofa he liked, the only restriction was that it had to be a corner unit and it couldn't cost more than £3,000. There were three in the shop that I liked and one that I hated. He chose the one I hated. I felt devastated, but couldn't go back on my word, so we got the one he selected, and I hated it every day for 15 years.'

Kate paused, realising that all those feelings of frustration and rage she'd experienced at the time were bubbling up inside her again. She couldn't let them overwhelm her now. She had to stay calm for Luke, but also because what was the point of staying angry at a man who'd lost the only thing that was really worth having…his life.

'So maybe now you can understand that every time I looked around the living room or the kitchen or the bedroom, I didn't see happy family memories, but fights, confrontations, arguments, resentment. I couldn't even begin to move on with my life if I kept the things that sparked the bad memories.'

'Mum, I'm so sorry, I didn't realise any of that,' Luke said, shaking his head, bewilderment written all over his face. 'Why did you never tell me before this?'

'And destroy your view of your dad?' Kate replied. 'I could see that you worshiped him. To you he was just fun Dad coming up with all those great ideas and exciting adventures for you both. I couldn't spoil that. But I was the one left worrying about how we'd be able to pay for it. And when he paid for things himself, I'd knew that he'd won big but that I'd never see a penny of it.'

'You must have felt so resentful, Mum.'

'Yes I did. And frustrated. He was having a great time while I was always the party-pooper. I miss your dad like mad, of course I do, but I don't miss the way he made me feel a lot of the time. So, I've been trying to make myself happier with his life insurance money. I've been spending it on me, on what I want. I'm sorry it's made you feel angry and sad. To be honest, I didn't put too much thought into how either you or Lila would feel about it. Naively perhaps I thought since neither of you live at home, you'd just be happy for me. I'm sorry that I've caused you pain. And now you know…'

Luke shook his head and looked as though he was trying very hard to come to terms with what he'd just heard.

'This is a lot to take in and I can understand why you'd feel like that,' he said finally, 'but I don't understand why you stayed with him.'

Kate rubbed her face with her hands and let out a long sigh. 'Because I loved him,' she said simply. 'Luke, the truth is that there were many times when I thought about divorcing him. On a couple of occasions, I even got as far as dialling the number of a lawyer. But I couldn't go through with it. I couldn't stand the idea of you and Lila being without your dad…and I didn't want to be alone. Ironic isn't it, when that's exactly what I am now.'

Kate paused for a few moments, deep in thought. Then she reached over and took her son's hand in hers.

'Luke, I want to you know that I did love him. I loved him with all my heart. I loved him from the moment I first saw him, and no matter how difficult and frustrating things became I couldn't forget that love. Plus, we had some great times together, just the two of us, and then all of us as a family. He was great fun. Now I want to get to a place where that's what I remember. I can't stay angry at him, Luke. He didn't want to be dead, and I can't be angry at someone who in the end had such enormous bad luck.'

'Oh Mum, I just hate all of this,' said Luke his voice heavy with emotion and frustration. 'I can't stand that he's dead. I can't do anything about that, but I can do better for you Mum. I'm so sorry.'

By now Kate felt completely spent. She'd said things tonight that she'd never spoken out loud, never confided in anyone. She'd kept Jason's gambling hidden, a terrible secret, for all these years and revealing it now had brought back so many difficult memories and exhausting emotions, but she was also glad that it was out in the open.

Luke leaned over and put his arm around Kate's shoulders. 'I feel stunned because it's such a different picture of our family life to the one I have in my head, and I guess it'll take me a while to digest it all, but at least now I understand.' Then he smiled. 'And now that I understand, I'll do my best to start liking pink!'

'That would be a welcome large step in the right direction,' laughed Kate.

'Does Lila know about any of this?'

'If she does, I've never told her, but she's a smart cookie and she was at home longer than you were, so I reckon she suspects. I'm not sure I can tell her, go through all this again, so up to you whether you tell her or not.'

Luke stood up, stretched, checked his watch and said it was time to get back to Cyn.

'Luke,' said Kate, 'while we're being honest with each other, I want to tell you how hurt I've been by the things she's been saying to me.'

'She's been pretty awful to me too,' Luke confessed. 'Really winding me up. I'm not sure what's at the root of it, but I will talk to her about it. All this honesty has made me hungry. Can I take some cake with me for the trip home?'

Kate laughed and cut him a huge slice. At the door she gave her son a hug. 'Thank you for coming and being so open with me love. I hope we've helped each other.'

Luke gave his mum one final squeeze and as he went to go out the door, Kate said, 'Please keep coming back, and we'll find a way to work it out. But I do have one request.'

'What's that?' asked Luke, his brow furrowing.

'Next time you come, please use your key!'

As they both laughed, Kate felt sure and so relieved that her darling son was back in her life to stay.

THIRTY-SEVEN

September

It had been two weeks since Justine and her family had left for Yorkshire, and Pascalle's heart still ached every time she thought of them. Given that she thought of them a lot, she was in a constant of state of sadness that they'd gone, and anxiety that she'd made the wrong decision not to go with them. In her more rational moments she could see that she had been right and she'd give herself a little pep talk which would sustain her for a few hours. Then she'd spot a photo of little Stefan or Justine would call, and she'd be back to square one.

At least, she told herself, Justine *is* calling. They spoke every day, taking it in turns to phone. At first Justine seemed a little cold, but then Stefan would come on to chatter away about his new nursery, the cows he'd seen or his new bedroom, and everything would feel more jolly.

Afterwards, Pascalle would have a little weep over what she'd lost, and then before she could sink into complete self pity, she'd tell herself to pull herself together, remember that they were just a phone call away, and that she still had a life to live, so she'd better get on with it.

It was after one of the phone calls, in a bid to perk up her mood, that she'd phoned Rose and invited her round to talk about the bereavement centre. Although she and Kate had both been very keen to get involved, Rose had texted to say she had some ideas to put to her, and Pascalle was intrigued. So, with a cup of coffee in front of both women as they sat at Pascalle's kitchen table, and a pile of newly baked chocolate chip cookies to sustain them, Rose excitedly outlined her ideas.

'Since the evening you told us about the centre, I haven't been able to stop thinking about it. It made me reflect on why I'd gone to all the groups after Richard was killed, what I'd been looking for, and why none of them had been able to help me. I've come to realise that the answers I was looking for were never going to come from a group of strangers talking about their own grief. That style of group is obviously hugely valuable for many people, but it wasn't the right environment for me. I did need to get out of the house, I did need to be in a safe space, but what I needed most of all was time out to process everything that had happened. Because the answers to my questions where inside of me all the time.'

Pascalle nodded and made as though to speak, but Rose carried on.

'Thanks to you and Kate I've found the courage to bear so many of the other terrible events from this year, and while I'm by no means through it all, I feel I'm on the right path. The more I think about it, the more I'm convinced the centre could play a big part in my future.

'You see it's the informality that appeals to me, that it goes at your pace, with the offer of support or friendship for when the time is right to take it up. I can also see huge benefits for those whose loved ones are still alive. You were right about how I feel about my mum. Why do I have to wait until she's dead to start grieving for all I've lost?

'So Pascalle, here's what I'd like to do. First of all, I'd love to help you in setting it up and running it. Whatever time needs to be spent on it to make it work, I'll spend. Secondly, I'd like to finance it.'

Pascalle had been smiling as she'd listened to her friend speak with such strength and determination and now she sat back, eyes wide open, obviously surprised at Rose's offer.

'Finance it?' she asked. 'What do you mean?'

Rose beamed with excitement. 'I'd like to finance the whole scheme. Pascalle, I see the opportunity to create more than just a centre here for people to meet. I think it could be like a café and a craft centre, which would give it a really informal air and make it so easy to pop into on your own. Creating a café atmosphere, buying crafting materials combined with paying rental for the space will cost a fair bit of money every week, and I want to fund that out of Richard's insurance money. I don't really need it and, more to the point, I don't want it because it's money that I have partly because he betrayed me.

'Maybe one day I'll be able to understand why Richard treated me the way he did, but for now I can't and I don't want anything to do with his money. But I do want it to do some good, and I can think of no better way to spend it than on this cafe. It'll more than cover all the start-up costs and keep it running for quite a while, so we wouldn't have to worry about sustaining it.'

Pascalle felt overwhelmed with emotion. 'But Rose, that's so generous. It's *too* generous.'

Rose shook her head and spoke with determination in her voice.

'No Pascalle, you're the one who's been generous. Giving me the opportunity to be involved in this. It will be my absolute pleasure to do this and maybe, way down the line, it will make me feel grateful that I met and married Richard, because for the moment, I wish I'd never set eyes on him.'

Pascalle sat up straight as though stung by the ferocity of her friend's words. Rose too was surprised by what she'd said even though she'd felt this way ever since Sally had told her about the affair. Truthfully, it wasn't so much the affair that hurt, maybe on its own it would have just wounded her, but it was the vasectomy that devastated her. Every time she thought about it, the pain took her breath away, but she hadn't been able to put her thoughts into words...until now.

'I'm sorry Pascalle,' she said. 'I shouldn't have said that.'

'You must have needed to get that out or it wouldn't have come. But Rose try not to dwell on those feelings, because the deeper they go, the harder it is to move on from them. Feelings of loathing and resentment have a habit of multiplying if we don't check them. You are a strong, intelligent, attractive woman with so much to offer the people around you. Keep your eyes on the positive - that's the way to get through this.'

'This cafe is my first positive step,' said Rose. 'I know I have work to do on myself, and I also know it will take time. I can't forgive Richard, I may never be able to, but I can take some comfort from the fact that I can put his money to good use.'

She stopped speaking, took a breath and then all her courage left her and she crumpled, tears streaming down her face.

'Oh Pascalle, I just feel so betrayed! I adored him, was devoted to him, and I thought he loved me back, and that everything we did in life was for us. I can't get over the fact that none of it was for me. It was all for him! It's absolutely devastating to discover that 30 years of marriage was a complete lie. Nothing was as I thought it was. How can I ever get over that?'

Pascalle moved round to the other side of the table so that she could sit side by side with her friend. Gently, she rubbed her arm as she told her, 'Frankly my darling Rose, that's the thing you may never get over. But you can do an enormous amount to replace those feelings of betrayal with a sense of purpose. Make the next 20 or 30 or 40 years be as *you* want them to be, on *your* terms. Live the life *you* want to live and don't let the hurt he's caused do you any more damage.'

Rose wiped her eyes, sniffed back her tears and said with more resolve than she felt, 'That's exactly what I will do.'

Pascalle looked thoughtful and then leaned further towards Rose and said in a gentle voice, 'Forgive me if you think I'm crossing a line with this question, but did you ever suspect he was having an affair?'

Rose looked down at her hands, considering her answer. 'Would it make me sound foolish if I said I never did?' she replied quietly.

Then she shrugged her shoulders and looked up at Pascalle. 'Or maybe I did, but just didn't want to admit it to myself. You see I never really understood why he chose me in the first place, why he always came home to me, or so I thought. I mean I'm not what you'd call beautiful or glamorous and Richard was both of those things. He was forever catching the eye of gorgeous women.

'We met at university while we were both training to be accountants. I was always top of the class and going to be successful– he wasn't. Now I see that I had something he prized above looks and charm. I was gullible, naïve, grateful and I could earn money. I was willing to do whatever he wanted, accept whatever terms he demanded in that charming way of his, because he was this dazzling creature and he wanted me. I couldn't believe my luck, and I was terrified of losing him. Maybe part of that fear was not even entertaining the idea that he could betray me with someone else. Until the night of the accident that is. Then I started to suspect.'

'He couldn't have stayed with you all those years just for the money,' Pascalle said softly. 'He must also have loved you.'

'I have no doubt that he loved the part of me that worked hard and made money for him to spend. He didn't love the Rose that wanted a marriage, wanted his children, wanted to build a family with him. That's who I am, and he didn't want that part of me. That's hard to live with.'

Both women fell silent for a few moments. Then Rose shook her head and spoke. 'We've become too sad. Right, Pascalle, help me out of this. Give me a job to do so that we can move forward with our cafe.'

Pascalle threw her arms in the air. 'Hurrah! We're all on our way to something new and fun in our future, and I can't wait to work with you and with Kate. So, let's get down to some real planning.'

As Rose was leaving later that evening, Pascalle hugged her goodnight and said: 'You know the way I see it is that we've been given a gift. Yes, we've lost our husbands, our soulmates, our life partners, and that's tragic. But we are still here. We have the chance to live and we should take that chance, because I believe that's the best way to honour those we have lost. I'll never forget my Trevor and everything I do now is in his name. My hope is that one day you'll feel the same way about Richard.'

Tears glistened in Rose's eyes as she returned Pascalle's hug.

'Thank you,' she said, 'for agreeing to join us for a drink that evening at the party, for sharing your wonderful sense of fun, joy and colour with us, for helping us with your wise advice, and most of all, thank you for bringing the idea of the cafe to us. It's going to be great, and because of it, we're going to be okay. Now I'm going to go before I cry so much I make your hall carpet soggy!'

As Rose walked down the path she called back, 'I'll be back on Tuesday to do a bit more planning work. Just make sure you have a good supply of tissues. I spent the first 63 years of my life refusing to cry but I certainly seem to be making up for that now!'

THIRTY-EIGHT

September, the first anniversary of Jason's death

Kate woke up with the sun peeping around the edges of her bedroom curtains. The pink fabric cast a cheery glow around the room. She stretched, enjoying the way her body felt, warm in the cocoon of the bedclothes. Her first thought was that she'd had a really good sleep. It felt like a victory after weeks of wakeful nights and fragmented dozing. Her second thought was 'It's today'. Those happy feelings vanished in an instant. Today was the first anniversary of the day that Jason had literally dropped dead on the garden patio, and Kate had been dreading it.

She lay there, trying to work out how she felt about this day now that it was here. She recalled the long chats she'd had with Pascalle and Rose about anniversaries, why we mark such sad days, and how to survive them. Rose said she used to find some comfort in the anniversaries of her dad's death because she felt it gave her permission to spend a day thinking only of him, the good times they'd had together, all his little quirks and foibles that she'd loved to indulge. She used to buy his favourite cakes and would have a little tea party, just her and Violet reminiscing about good times. She'd decided there would be no such day for Richard, not yet anyway.

'Since I can't think a good thought about him, I've decided not to think about him at all. I want the day of his anniversary to just slide by,' she decided.

Pascalle, the most religious of them, hoped that Rose wasn't banking emotional trouble for herself, and said she found it comforting to have her mum, dad and Trevor prayed for at church by the whole congregation.

'Even though none of them knew my parents or Trevor, as he wasn't much of a church goer, it makes me feel good that the community is praying only for them, and in doing that they're remembering me and my loss,' she explained. 'I hope that when it's my time, someone will remember to pray for me.'

Listening to them, Kate felt sorry for Rose and a little envious of Pascalle's beliefs. But she still couldn't understand why anyone would want to mark a day that was the worst day of their life.

Just then, Kate's alarm went off. 8am. She set it more out of habit than concern that she'd oversleep. It was midweek, but she wasn't going to work. Lila had insisted that Kate take the day off and plan some nice things to fill it, so they were going to have lunch at a new posh cafe round the corner from the house. Then Luke was coming over and they were all three going to the local cemetery together to visit the spot where Jason's ashes had been interred.

Even though Kate had ordered a small plaque to mark the place, they had yet to visit it. Luke thought maybe it was time they did, and Kate, not wanting to endanger their fragile relationship, had reluctantly agreed even though she wasn't sure what they'd do when they got there. Lay flowers? Spend time in silent contemplation? Pray? Kate had no idea. Jason was an atheist, he wasn't waiting at the pearly gates for enough prayers to boost him into heaven. Well, whatever they did when they got to the cemetery, they'd do it together, and for that Kate was grateful. She threw back the duvet, got out of bed and walked over to the window where she pulled back a curtain and looked out.

The sun had come up, the birds were singing, cars were driving along her road. It was a day like any other. And yet for Kate, this was a day like none other. 'I miss you Jason, I love you and I miss you, but the world hasn't stopped revolving since you left it,' she said into the silence. 'Somehow I have to revolve with it, so I'll go along with the children's wishes, and support them, but I can't give any more of myself to you this day than I've done every other day in the last year or will do for the rest of my life.'

She closed the curtain and went downstairs to get ready for Lila.

*

In the café, Kate noticed that Lila was quieter than usual. She tried to keep the chat light and amusing and usually her daughter would respond in kind, but today she was giving just one-word answers.

'Are you okay darling,' Kate asked.

'Yeah, fine. I just feel a little sad, that's all.'

'Of course you do.'

Just then Luke arrived and enveloped them both in a hug. 'Hey Mum, Lila. I'm feeling a bit edgy, do you mind if we skip coffee and head to the cemetery? Get it over with.'

Luke and Kate walked along the road chatting. She was aware of Luke's nerves so was trying to keep the conversation easy. Neither of them realised that Lila was falling behind.

This is exhausting Kate thought as she kept up chat about this and that. Trying not to be sad was hard work. When they reached the cemetery gates Luke suddenly stopped and turned to her. 'I don't think I can go in.'

Kate put her arm round his shoulder. 'I know it's hard, and I won't force you to go in if you absolutely don't want to, but if you don't it will be even harder next time. Today, we're all here together and can help each other.'

'I just feel that the moment I see the plaque with Dad's name on it I'll know it's real,' said Luke, starting to shake.

'Darling, it *is* real.'

Her words seemed to release something in Luke and he looked up into his mother's eyes and nodded. 'Yes, you're right. Let's go in. Facing it now will be easier.'

Kate was about to steer her son through the cemetery gates when she heard a loud keening sound. She looked around trying to work out where it was coming from, and after a few seconds realised it was behind her. She turned to see Lila standing about 100 yards down the road, stock still, tears pouring down her face, sobbing for all she was worth.

'Oh, my darling girl, my gorgeous girl, what's happened?' Kate called as she rushed back to her and took her in her arms. But Lila just stood there, crying, not speaking or moving. Almost paralysed. It was then that Kate realised how much her poor girl had been holding inside. All those months of helping Kate, supporting her, standing in the middle of the tension between her mum and her brother, always being happy, willing, and available, always giving of herself, with no-one noticing how much she was suffering.

She ushered Lila to a nearby bench and sat her down, all the while saying to her, 'That's it darling, just let it all out, don't hold back.'

Eventually Lila managed some words through her staccato breathing. '…strong for you Mum…not like Luke…can't stop…just miss Dad so much Mum.'

Gradually, Lila's sobs subsided. Kate sat quietly. After a few moments Lila said, 'I'm sorry Mum but as we got closer and closer to the cemetery gate the reason we are here hit me.'

'Darling, you have nothing to apologise for. It's me who should be saying sorry. I've leaned on you so much over this last year and that wasn't fair. I guess I've been so wrapped up in my own sadness I didn't give enough thought to how you were feeling and how this day might affect you.'

Luke came over and sat beside them and Lila gripped his and her mother's hands tight. Having found her voice, Lila kept talking. 'It's not just today, Mum. It's every day. I miss Dad so much, all the time. I just don't say when I'm with you because I don't want to make you sad, but when I go back to my flat I cry and cry.'

Kate's heart shattered at the thought of her brave daughter sobbing in her bedroom all on her own. Guilt overwhelmed her but she knew there was nothing she could do now for Lila but let her talk.

'It's been pretty hard for me too seeing how you've changed the house, even though I understand why you're doing it, and I agree with Luke it feels less like home now. But more than that I miss having my dad around. I know he wasn't perfect but I loved him because he was *my* dad, and now when I see other girls with their dads it makes me feel so bad.

'I passed a father and daughter in the street the other day and I heard him call her Princess. I'll never hear my dad say that to me. I'll never be able to pick up the phone and ask him to come round and fix my washing machine or put up a shelf like my friends can do. And what happens when I get married? Who's going to gaze at me with tears in his eyes and tell me how beautiful I look in my wedding dress? Or walk by my side down the aisle? These might all sound silly, but they're things I'll never have because I'm a daughter without a dad.'

At this Lila burst into fresh sobs and Kate drew her tightly to her, cuddling her for all she was worth. Her lovely daughter had stood strong beside her this last year, and Kate hadn't noticed what a toll it was taking on her.

'Lila I don't think I'll ever be able to tell you how sorry I am. You shouldn't have had to shoulder my burden but I've been so wrapped up in my own grief I haven't given enough thought to yours, in fact to either of you.'

Shaking his head, Luke spoke. 'Mum, I don't think there's a manual for dealing with the death of a husband or a dad so I guess we've been making it up as we go along, and we've all made mistakes. Lila I'm sorry you've had some of the fall-out from me, and Mum I promise to do better to support you. As the eldest child and the big brother I should have helped you both more.'

Kate felt in her pocket for more paper hankies and discovered that it was empty.

'It seems that we've run out of tissues so I suggest we agree to one massive group hug, say that we'll do better to look out for each other, make a quick trip over to see Dad's plaque and then go straight home. It's been a tough day for us all and the best Latimer remedy for that is chocolate and ice cream and I have loads in the house. What do you say?'

'You're on,' Luke and Lila answered weakly.

At Jason's grave, they stood close to each other, holding hands, saying nothing. Silently, Kate spoke to her husband.

'Darling Jason, it feels like only yesterday but also a million years since I last saw you or heard your voice. On this day a year ago, I didn't think I'd make it to the next morning, now here I am 12 months on still here, and still missing you like mad. Despite all the difficult times we had, you were my Jas and I miss you every second of every day. Just because I'm moving on doesn't mean I'm leaving you behind. I'll always carry you with me in my heart because I'll always love you. Wish me luck, darling Jason, and wherever you are, please take care of our beautiful children. They are the best of us and they need you. We need you.'

Kate linked arms with Lila and Luke and in silence they turned around and walked home.

*

By the time they got back to the house, Lila was feeling calmer and went off to wash her face while Kate made tea. When Lila reappeared, they sat around the breakfast bar and clinked mugs. Kate kept thinking about how she'd failed her daughter. 'I'm so sorry Lila,' she said. 'I should have seen how much you were suffering.'

Lila tried to brush off her mother's concern. 'No Mum, it's fine, don't worry, you had a lot on your plate.'

'It's not fine, Lila, just let me say this. I should have known because I know what it's like to lose a dad, especially so young. I know all about the precious moments you can only have with a dad that are lost when he dies. I hoped you were okay because you always seemed it, but I should have done more to find out. It's ironic because that is exactly what I have been accusing my friends of – accepting me at face value and not digging deeper to find out how I really feel. Forgive me.'

Then Luke reached across and put his arms all the way round Lila and squeezed her in a bear hug. 'And I'm sorry too, wee sis. I've been so wrapped up in my own misery that I didn't spare anything for you. I didn't even try to imagine what you were going through. I've been an awful brother and I'm so very sorry.'

His words started fresh tears from Lila, so Kate abandoned the tea, filled three wine glasses and opened two packets of chocolate biscuits.

'But they're the ones you save for guests,' Lila protested through her tears.

'They're also the perfect remedy for sadness, so dig in and let's see if they can bring a smile back to our faces!'

A little later, Kate told her children about Pascalle's idea for a bereavement café. 'It's not just for husbands or wives, it could be for anyone who's grieving. Lila is this something you might be interested in getting involved in?'

'Mum, that's an amazing idea. Well done Pascalle! Put me down to help out in any way I can.'

'Luke, I know it's a bit far for you to travel to but might you want to get involved?'

'I'm not sure Mum,' Luke shrugged. 'I feel I've got enough on my plate at the moment with work and with Cyn.'

'Ah yes, Cyn,' said Kate. 'How are things going with her?'

'Truthfully, I'm not sure. When I went home that night after seeing you, I confronted her, told her how hurtful she was being, and how I felt she was trying to take me away from my family. She broke down, claimed she was missing Dad too, that he'd been the kind of father she'd always wanted, and now he was gone she was finding it hard to manage her feelings.

'She wanted me to focus on her not on you or Lila, so she'd tried to make you look bad in my eyes so that I'd turn my attention to her. Now she's realised she's gone about it all the wrong way. I agreed that yes she had, but to be honest Mum, I'm not sure she was telling the truth. It all sounded very complicated. I still don't know what's going on with her, but I'm trying to put it behind us and see if we can get back to how we were. One loss in my life is enough for now.'

'One loss is enough for any one of us,' agreed Kate, feeling totally exhausted. 'It hasn't at all been the kind of day I expected, but tomorrow is another one and hopefully now we've all got our feelings out in the open, it'll be a lot better.'

*

Later in bed, Kate reflected on the events of the day. Despite the anniversary, despite the copious tears that had been shed, and the terrible guilt she was feeling, she decided that it had been a good day. The first year was behind her. There was more honesty between her and her daughter, and a resolution of sorts with her son. They could all three draw a veil over the last year and concentrate on looking ahead.

She knew she could never have the kind of future she'd foreseen with Jason, that any future now would have to be a short term one, and that she'd have to get used to walking into it alone, but there would be a future, she was sure of that. The first thing to look forward to would be the opening of the cafe next week, and she was so excited at the prospect.

Kate yawned and stretched, feeling warm again in bed. A year without Jason sharing it with her, snuggling down beside her, his toasty feet warming her freezing toes, his gentle breathing turning to snores as he fell asleep. Despite all his faults, she'd loved him and she missed him more than she could say, but she was proud that she'd got through this 12 months and had a glimmer of hope. And there was one other positive. No more snoring. She'd absolutely hated his snoring! Now, she was keen to see if she could have another night of straight sleep, because that was something she could definitely get used to.

THIRTY-NINE

September, and the opening of the bereavement craft cafe

'Well ladies, what do you think? Do you love it?'

Pascalle, Kate and Rose were standing in the middle of what had once been a naked and depressing church hall, but was now gloriously colourful, vibrant and welcoming. Cheerful African fabrics hung from the walls, low round tables were distributed randomly around the room, each one topped with a colourful tablecloth, and surrounded by comfy looking chairs.

A larger table was set against one wall strewn with magazines and books and in its centre sat an enormous wicker basket packed with wool, embroidery threads, knitting needles, samplers and sewing needles. A smaller table sat just beside it lined with a row of what looked like

Pina Coladas. It was the opening day of the bereavement cafe, whose name had been changed from 'The Dead Husbands Club' to the more appealing 'The Great Escape'.

Pascalle had dressed for the occasion in a calf length cotton floral print dress which was a riot of different colours, and some silver sandals. The two other women were also wearing their brightest clothes – Rose in a lilac skirt and purple top that she'd made herself, and Kate in a flowing blue silk dress.

Pascalle was desperately searching the faces of Rose and Kate, looking for signs of approval, and practically vibrating with excitement. All three of them had spent several hours in the church hall last night setting up, but she had returned early that morning to add some finishing touches - including the drinks, each one topped with a maraschino cherry.

'Don't worry, they're mocktails,' she explained to her friends. 'I'm calling them Pina Noladas. We don't want to encourage alcoholism, just provide a bit of a fun treat for our opening day.'

Two of the corners had been partitioned off for people who wanted to sit on their own and have a quiet read or just listen to the bustle around them. In another corner was a coffee machine, a stack of bright new mugs, and a pile of

French pastries. These had been donated by Rose's café owning client and friend Nicky who'd thought this enterprise a great idea and had been only too happy to help. In fact, she'd said that if the bereavement cafe got busy, she would volunteer one of her members of staff to help for a couple of hours every week.

'Anything that puts a smile back on your face, Rose, as this has done, has my utter support,' she'd said.

In the background music was playing, a rolling jazz-reggae beat that was fun and happy. It was loud enough to create a light atmosphere, but quiet enough not to interrupt thoughts and conversations.

Kate scanned the room, as though trying hard to take in every tiny detail. 'Pascalle, it's a triumph. An absolute triumph! Can you believe that we've actually done this? Who'd have thought when we were first pushed together at that drinks party, Rose, and then you spotted Pascalle, that we'd be here, less than a year later, doing this together?'

Rose smiled with joy. 'What an amazing place. I know we've done it, but I do have to keep pinching myself that it's for real. It's a great achievement, ladies. What a trio we are. But I think a special thanks needs to go to Pascalle for coming up with the idea, *and* for persuading the vicar to let us open two days midweek and one at the weekend *and* keep all the wall hangings in place when we're not here.'

Pascalle laughed. 'I think it was less my powers of persuasion and more the generous rent we were able to offer her, thanks to you Rose. Plus, it looks so good, I'm sure more groups will want to hire it on the other days.'

She slotted her arms through theirs and guided them towards the Pina Noladas. 'Let's have an exotic drink to toast our success. I'm so proud of us three. We've each opened a new chapter in our lives, and while the pages might look a bit blank now, I feel sure there are some exciting times ahead - with hopefully not too many twists and turns.'

Just as she raised her glass to take a second sip, Rose noticed a figure at the door.

'Our first customer, I think,' she said, motioning towards the doorway.

A woman was standing there, her skin pale and her eyes dark ringed with tiredness, but she was wearing a brilliant fuschia pink cardigan over a white blouse and brown skirt. Pascalle walked across to her and as she got closer, she recognised the mix of anxiety, bewilderment and hope in this woman's eyes.

'Welcome,' she said, softly. 'I'm Pascalle.'

'Hello,' said the woman, holding out a quivering hand for her to shake. 'I'm Sylvia. I hope I'm in the right place. I saw a poster on the church noticeboard advertising The Great Escape and I thought it sounded interesting. I must say, I didn't really know what to expect.'

As she was speaking, Sylvia was taking in the room, the music, the brilliantly patterned wall-hangings, the pastries and the drinks table.

'Ooh, those drinks look very inviting,' she said, nervously, spotting the sign by the Pina Nolada glasses. 'In fact everything looks welcoming and great fun. It said on the poster that this was where people could be themselves and that anything would go, and it's so long since I wore something colourful that I decided to dig out my brightest cardigan. I thought it might give me courage.'

Tears sprang to Pascalle's eyes as she recognised how much it had taken for this shy woman, her spirit bashed by some trauma, to come here today. She swallowed the lump of emotion that had come into her throat and said, 'I'm extremely glad the cardigan's powers were strong enough to bring you to us. Now would you like to come over here and sample one of these drinks? There's no rum in them I'm afraid, but there's still plenty of sunshine in every sip.'

As she led Sylvia to the drinks table, Kate and Rose smiled at each other. A customer already. If any confirmation were needed that this café was a good idea, they had it now.

Sylvia laughed at something Pascalle said and her face lit up. Then the door opened again and in walked a short elderly man, well dressed, wearing a shirt and tie and nervously fiddling with a hat grasped in his hands. He looked around uncertainly. Rose walked over to greet him.

'Welcome to The Great Escape,' she said. 'Thank you for coming.'

'Thank *you*,' he said quietly. 'Is it okay if I come in? I wasn't sure if it was just for women.'

'It's for everyone,' smiled Rose, as she steered him over to the drinks table. 'Everyone who needs it.'

Just as Kate was wondering what she should do, she heard a knock at the door. She walked over to answer it and as she approached a woman opened it and came inside. Behind her trailed a little boy, about seven or eight years old, carrying a small cardboard box and he was sobbing.

'Sorry, sorry I wasn't sure if we had to make an appointment or anything,' said the woman. 'Can we come in? I saw your notice outside. It's my son. His guinea pig was put to sleep this morning. We've just come back from the vets. He won't stop crying and I can't send him to school like that. Can we sit in here for a while?'

Kate smiled at the woman. 'Of course you both can.' Then she looked down at the little boy. 'I'm sorry to hear about your pet. What was his name?'

'Geronimo,' spluttered the boy.

'Great name,' said Kate. 'And yours?'

'Simon.'

'Well Simon, while your mum has a coffee – which I'm sure she's in great need of - would you like to have a seat over here with me and you can tell me all about Geronimo? Maybe even draw me a picture of him?'

Simon nodded and his mother smiled her thanks as Kate lead him to the craft table. 'Let's see if we can find some paper and coloured pencils here.'

While Kate settled down with Simon, Pascalle looked up from Sylvia and scanned the room. She felt so proud. Proud of herself, proud of Kate, proud of Rose. Each of them was on their own path to a new future. And what a future it promised to be.

MORE FROM LIZ MURPHY

We hope you enjoyed reading *Friends for Life*. If you did, please leave a review.

If you'd like to gift a copy, this book is also available as an ebook.

Follow Liz Murphy on Instagram at lizmurphybooks or on her blog Selfish At Sixty at selfishatsixty.com

Printed in Great Britain
by Amazon